TORRID ZONE

A Mystery Novel
by ReBecca Béguin

New Victoria Publishers

Published by New Victoria Publishers Inc., a feminist, literary, and cultural
organization, PO Box 27, Norwich, VT 05055-0027.

Printed and Bound in Canada
1 2 3 4 5   2001   2000 1999 1998 1997

Thank you to Elaine Smith, Madeline Larsen, Linda Lane, Beth Dingman,
Claudia Lamperti, Ruth Sylvester, Lee McDavid and especially, Holly Wolff
for her steady, loving support of time, space and opportunity to write.

Cover Design Claudia McKay

Library of Congress Cataloging-in-Publication Data

Béguin, ReBecca.
    Torrid zone : a mystery / by ReBecca Béguin.
        p.   cm.
    ISBN 0-934678-81-2
    I. Title.
    PS3552.E374T67   1997
    813' . 54--dc21   96-45121
                                                                CIP

To Krystyna Bobrowski

Other books by ReBecca Béguin
Her Voice in the Drum
Runway at Eland Springs
In Unlikely Places
Hers Was the Sky

One

On one of those suspiciously perfect mornings you get in early May with the trees just leafing out and the pastures lush enough for grazing at last, I was in the barn mucking out horse stalls. After one bitterly slow spring, the five horses were as delighted as I was to be out in the sunshine.

After flipping horse apples into a bucket from two stalls, I stripped down to my tank top, and leaned on the manure fork contemplating my stained jeans, my barn boots and my hair newly shorn for spring. At last, I affirmed boldly, surely I have released the past which has so long had its icy thorn in me.

If Gem had been around she would have teased me saying, "Yeah, yeah, Ida, like hell you want sun, you just want to flaunt your muscles—and you, flirting with middle-age!" I'd have chuckled, "Heh, heh, baby and don't you love every inch of my farmer's tan?" I'd be able to accept the tease because I felt of a piece, whole in a way I hadn't for years, or so I thought.

Lorraine who owns this Vermont farm which I manage for her, was up for a long weekend. We were expecting the vet to come and give shots to the horses, Lorraine's dog and the four barn cats.

As I cut open a fresh bale of shavings to put down for bedding, I heard Lorraine's voice, high notes, low notes: "Ida! Pho-hone!" Couldn't think who it might be. Certainly not my neighbor because if she ever wants me she careens into the dooryard in her pickup, leaning on her horn. And certainly not Gem because she writes to me; prefers writing, thinks it's a forgotten art and that we really lost it as a civilization when we got on the phone. Fine by me since most of the time I don't have a phone or am not near one. So we have this game of writing to each other, notes on recycled material, declaring our passion in cryptic messages. In fact we do have kind of a coded language. That's the other thing she's big on—she claims traditional dyke language, no, traditional sapphic language, is coded. She says, for instance, that thanks to Gertrude Stein, a cow by any other name might just be an orgasm.

So, anyway, the phone call.

"Gem...what a surprise!" I said cradling Lorraine's cordless phone in my shoulder as I sat on the back doorstep and tugged off my boots. Ah, Gem, what a sucker I am for Gem with her sweep of silky hair, those sparkling eyes, that lithe, fully curved body, those sinewy hands with rings on exactly the right fingers. "This isn't in character!" Already I had a small shiver down my neck. Something had to be amiss.

"I know I know I know. I gotta talk to you. I need you to do me a favor." She was breathless as usual, sure sign of stress.

Gem and I have an 'academic marriage'—she's the academic, a real career woman—is gone most of the time and in another state. Obviously she has to go where the work is—not Vermont. She follows opportunities, usually semi-permanent positions, always in search of that elusive tenure track. Someday, she says, someday. Meanwhile she comes 'home' to me every so often in the country for the relatively fresh air and the chance to see stars on a clear night. Once in a while I go cityside when she gets tickets to something she says I can't possibly miss. I stay with her in her cramped apartment, go out to eat at chic restaurants.

"Yeah, where?" I teased because Lorraine had conveniently vanished. 'Favor' was one of Gem's code words.

"Uh…not now, babe. I want you to listen for a minute—"

I drawled languidly, "So when are you coming up?"

"Look, I have a serious problem I want to talk to you about!"

I sighed, remembering that for her, phone was what you used in the office, a necessary evil in a career. So, she was at work. "One of my girls is in some very hot water—"

One of my girls! By that she meant one of the students from the Honor McKee Institute. Listen, even I didn't know about the place till a year ago when Gem got her job there. The McKee Institute of History and Political Studies, now a university college but still with independent endowment—so the recruiting brochure goes—enrolls students, (read: both male and female) with goals of majoring in those areas. Included under the umbrella is, hurrah, Women's Studies—and a job for Gem, uncertain as it may be.

"Well?" I prodded.

"Well, indeed. Budding reporter that she is, she took on the task of talking to women students about date rape. As these things usually go, it all started on a very personal level when she found out a friend was raped at one of the supposedly friendly university fraternity parties across the way. The student was so traumatized she left school. Enraged, my student wrote a heated and very pointed exposé that the official student paper wouldn't run. So she ran it through one of the student 'zines."

"Uh-huh…"

"Yeah, and even though she writes under the guise of 'Maid in the Shades' apparently her identity isn't that big a secret, especially since she is big into visibility and walks around campus in a lavender cap with the word Dyke emblazoned on it, along with about a dozen or so other girls wearing sunglasses whenever they plan an action—which seems to be often enough to irritate the Dean. So, first she received threatening, anonymous notes like 'we know you're a dyke etc…' the usual obscene stuff—"

"Thank you for not spelling it out." And I meant it.

"Then she began being stalked. The first time she noticed it was in the library stacks, then she was followed at night. One time she came back to her room and found it completely trashed—luckily she was carrying her laptop with her—everything else totally smashed, ripped up…everything. Then she woke up yesterday morning to find her car, which is a beat-up old thing held together by political bumper stickers, had a bullet hole through the windshield. The slug lodged in the back of the driver's seat. So finally, she reported it to the police, feeling pretty sure by that point that she could identify one boy in particular—her friend's assailant. The police are investigating. That move has put the fraternity in question on the defensive to say the least; they say they're being victimized by her, falsely accused in her articles. No brother of theirs would be sending out death threats or shooting into a car—or raping anybody."

"So, the long and short of it is, she needs some place away from here—for things to settle a bit. As the college dean has put it very plainly, 'allow time for the rape victim to come forward with charges…if they are real.'" The fervor of her personal outrage made her stop to catch her breath.

I didn't like where this was leading. "But aren't finals coming up?"

"Exactly. All her professors, thanks to yours truly, are letting her write essays, except for one course in which she can't seem to get by without an exam, and so that will be an incomplete. But that's not what I need to talk to you about."

"Uh…"

"She needs a safe place to go, not family, not friends, not anywhere she can be easily tracked down—"

"…oh."

"And that's why I need to send her to you."

"Me?"

"Ida, I have to. Don't you see? She's a nineteen-year-old freshman who saw her friend get really hurt, and went out to help her. It has turned nasty down here. I think she needs a place where she can get some perspective, clear her head. A safe place. Even if she was able to get a restraining order on the one boy, school would be out by the time it came through. She's angry and confused right now, not to mention afraid—things got out of hand. Believe me I have tried to think of other places but—"

"You want me to take care of some babydyke here on the farm, and keep her safe?" The very idea made me sweat.

"Maybe she just might take care of you! Look, I know we don't ask things of each other, we really don't. I keep my life with you very separate and special. It's my safe place, my haven." She started to sound like a prof. on a committee; I could see her pen tapping the table as she spoke slowly and clearly, "She's a solid A student, promises to keep a low profile—"

I grunted. "Low profile, my ass! You just said she was big into visibility…why that lavender—"

She talked right on through me. "—I need to know she is somewhere safe until things cool down here. Besides, I thought you might be able to help her with a women's history project."

Nonplused, I stuttered, "What?"

"She has an incomplete, right? She has an independent study to do and she wants to do it on some aspect of dyke history and culture, self-sufficient 'wimmin's land' stuff…I thought maybe you could tell her about the Blue Corn collective, you know, how it worked and all."

I sat back down on the doorstep, blind-sided. The farm seemed to spin around me, my vision blurred by a sun too dazzling. I grabbed the doorpost for support waiting for the edge of nausea which I knew would come.

"Ida? Ida, you there? "

My voice cracked, "Yeah. Yeah, I'm here…"

"You okay? You're not having one of your anxiety attacks over this?"

I gulped, "I just can't believe you'd ask that of me, knowing what I went through then. Knowing how it still makes me feel. I can't. No way. You're really going too far. I'm not dredging up old stuff that happens to be very personal for some student term paper."

"Ida, what does herstory mean? Herstory means—"

"Herstory means it's over." We finished in tandem, but I wasn't buying that line of hers this time. "I'll…I'll offer a safe-house but that's it. "

"Come on, Ida. I'm sending a kid to talk to you who's been through some trouble herself. I thought you of all people would relate! I'm not sending some kind of tabloid vulture." She sighed in exasperation. "It's a paper for me. Twenty or so double-spaced pages. Cut and dry. No big deal. I'm the only one who's going to read it."

"You?" I relaxed just a bit. "That's even worse."

She laughed and I have to say I love that low, husky laugh washing over me like a warm wave of seduction. "Maybe she'll reveal an angle on you I don't know. Look, I have plenty of students researching urban collectives and co-ops present and past. I need some papers on rural dykes, wimmin's land, all that—"

I snapped out of her warmth that had coddled me. "Cut and dry, huh? I don't know how to make something cut and dry. Nothing about it was cut and dry. I mean, I only told you anything at all because you're an intimate. How am I supposed to even begin? I'll never get past the end... That's where everyone wants to start and it's a giant hurdle."

"Don't you think I know that?" More gently now, she said, "Ida, forget that part. Think—think back. You learned a lot about land— weren't you all urban girls at first? Look how it affected you— you're still in the country farming, and the aspects that made it unique are always great to compare with other experiments—"

I spat, "Experiments! It was my life. I don't want to...it just brings back all the pain—"

Her voice went into that no-nonsense tone that always set me back on my heels. "Honestly, stop being so self-absorbed. How many years has it been now, huh, huh? Six, seven? Seems to me it's time to let go once and for all. Let go of it. This will be great opportunity for you to think about some of the good stuff from...before...you know—" Sparing me, she didn't finish. She must have heard my gasp.

Her approach became more cautious. "Look, I know that nothing, but nothing can diminish the pain—Rune's death and all. But before that there were nine solid years put into the collective—into Blue Corn...Before...

Nightmarish memories hit me like shards of light—a deserted and wind-rattled house, an oak veneer casket burying the body of a woman with a name she had long discarded, a hard bench in a stark police station—all became a blinding bolt of unresolved pain. Grief, disbelief, anger and dread—all became a knot behind my eyes. Cradling my head, I put the phone down beside me on the step.

When I managed to pick up the phone again, it was to Gem's coaxing, "Ida, you want our dyke history to live on, don't you? Remember, I must publish to make it in my career, and she's essentially a research opportunity..."

I rubbed my temples to numb the ache. "Wait a minute, you said this paper was just for you—"

"Yeah, but if she does a good job, I can use elements in my comparative studies. She'd be a much better source than I would because of our—"

I swallowed hard, swallowed my old pain and fear. I wanted to scream that Gem wasn't being fair, that once again she was much too demanding. Doesn't ask things, my ass. All I wanted was my little scrap of relative peace. But I knew Gem had me in a double-vise.

She could do that to me, what can I say? I only look like the butch in this relationship.

I found myself saying, "So how and when is she coming?"

"She's on her way now."

"Before even asking me?" I burst in outrage.

"Look, Ida, I did try earlier but the machine was picking up," she pleaded, a desperate edge to her voice she had kept under control until now. "Everything's happened so fast. I had to get to the bank for some cash—"

"You mean you weren't going to take no for an answer."

There was a long silence before she said, "I couldn't afford that. Look this has been very hard for me too. You think I'd do this if I could think of something else? And I knew you'd understand. I even gave her my car, let's see, that was fifteen minutes ago. She should be there in two or three hours. She does have your number in case she gets lost."

Suddenly the May morning was less bright. Had to be those high clouds coming over. I sat with my chin in my hands gazing out at the horses in the pasture, telephone still wedged in my shoulder, fingers still pressed against my temples. I had spent a long hard winter imagining quite a different kind of spring and summer for myself. Resigned I said, "So, what's her name?"

"Vivian. She goes by Viv." Now that Gem had her way with me, her voice was quiet, almost apologetic.

"Do I call you later, or will you check back?"

"No need unless she doesn't show up. Otherwise I'll let you be."

"And I'm supposed to feed and clothe her?"

"Oh right, glad you mentioned. Food, hm—beans and rice in her case. Absolute vegetarian, pure as your Blue Corn days. I sent my camping gear along with her, and she was instructed to buy what she needs. I know she doesn't have much money—I gave her some cash—and in a phone conference her parents said they agreed to the plan, and of course will help out. But she knows she's supposed to pitch in, work the way she did here for her student job—"

"And when are you coming? You haven't been here since mid-March."

"Look, I told you…I'm up to my ears in work; it's the end of the school year and I have to make a good impression—"

"I would have come down, you know. You didn't come in April because of work. I could've come down. Guess not now, huh?"

"Hang in there, babe. I'll see you soon. For the whole summer!"

This arrangement with Gem—sometimes I wonder who strings who along. Since it's been about seven years, you might think I shouldn't worry. Except that lately she's been sending me all the latest poop on non-monogamy she's been reading. Purely academic interest, of course. Triangular and circular relationships. Could make a girl wonder.

"I'll have to talk to Lorraine, you know."

"Oops. About Viv, yeah." Then she squeaked, "You'll just say she's up for research?"

"Gem, I always talk to Lorraine about everything. I can't hide this. It would come out anyway and I'd be worse for wear in the meantime. What if something happened?"

"You talk to Lorraine about everything?" Suddenly it was as though Gem had forgotten the whole scheme and could only think about herself. Pff, talk about self-absorbed.

"Take it easy." I sighed. "I think I do love you though. Anyway—I'll let you know in a few weeks for certain."

I could almost hear her smile, and I love her smile...the deep dimple in her left cheek. "Thanks, Ida. And nothing's going to happen so don't be an alarmist. Oh, and I didn't explain about us. I did not even think of it. But it's just as well. It's not because I'm not Out here...it's a privacy issue."

"Yeah?—Come on, be realistic. I'll say something without thinking. You're sending her smack into your bit of privacy."

A pause. "Yeah, I know. That's exactly why...would you take that photo down of me? Okay? You know I wouldn't just ask any of this—"

"Sure, sure, no big deal. A couple of weeks. Let's hang up. Write me: Is a bird in the hand worth two in a bush?"

And she laughed. "Is the bush thorny?"

Trouble with portable phones is you can't slam them down on the receiver. Punching a tiny button, Talk-Don't-Talk, just doesn't cut it. But damn it, she was due to come home soon and now this instead. I needed to be with her, well, badly. Ever since March when she said to me after what I thought was a particularly languid session of love-making, "We don't come like we used to."

And I thought, well maybe not this time. It was slower, not dramatic. Not over the edge this time. I just thought we were different, that's all. Tired. It was March, the dregs of winter. But the difference had to do with anticipating touch rather than being surprised. I just thought that now we knew what pleased each other. Her hand, one more finger at a time, sliding inside me, finding the place that just simply threw me. She knew where, yes. And I knew she liked me to knead her thighs and ass before going on to more.

I was aching for her. I wanted her to come up here and let me surprise her. I've been saving up for that rainy day, as it were. New configurations. As she likes to say, "Always innovate."

Hm, could make a girl wonder whether she shouldn't just take her hot One Act on the road; find a new leading lady here and there.

I remember saying to my Gem, "But why can't we just, you know, keep doing what works?"

"What? And head straight into the throes of bed death? Surely, you wouldn't eat the same sandwich every day just because it was your favorite, would you?"

I guess I'd been told.

Let me tell you, long term relationships do have their challenges. A constant test of the limits to one's imagination. Kinda like being a successful serial writer but without relying on the same old formula too much. Gotta change the tease and the timing. Either a girl's going to wear out or else rally and become, well... a best kept secret?

Two

With the phone still in my hand and still barefoot, I walked into the kitchen. It was one of those days where the house was cooler than outside, and Lorraine hadn't made a fire in the kitchen cookstove. Like me, she has a thing for cookstoves and this one was an old Glenwood in mint condition, but stone cold.

With reading glasses slung halfway down her nose, she was sitting at the large kitchen table going over her farm records. I slumped heavily into a chair opposite her, gently laying the phone next to her papers. She just looked at me over her rims with those big brown eyes.

Funny—Lorraine and I go a long way back already; she knew she didn't have to ask any questions, put out any openers. Early sixties with salt and pepper hair which swept back from her forehead, a handsome face and graceful build, she has one more year till early retirement when she can pursue her passion full time—her passion in life is her Morgans. While I help as gofer, groom and companion rider, she's the one who likes to dress up in her elegant black riding jacket, white breeches and silk shirt, real leather boots, and go eventing. I have to say I get a tremendous kick out of her when she dresses up like that. Quite a turn-on. I know Taylor, her husband, likes her that way, how he grins ear to ear, crinkles at the eyes as he leans on the railings of the dressage ring to watch her. That slight, amazed shake to his head, saying, "Looks good in drag, doesn't she?"

Odd as it may seem, Lorraine and I didn't meet over horses at all. We met at a market-garden coop years ago when I still worked with my separatist lesbo commune, leasing that land and house, yeah, when I was still young, and thought the project I was involved in would be a life time. Well, it was a life time, a life time ago...

Lorraine. To say that she saved my life is not entirely exaggeration. Back then she surely didn't know whether or not I was capable of working my butt off. She knew I was a gardener like she was, both of us part of projects to sell our vegetables at a time when outlets were still low-key, not like the organic, super-specialized summer markets these days. And at the time, she probably smoked about as much home grown hemp as I did, lying out nude in the summer sun.

Maybe I saved her life too, I don't know. All I know is when my

13

commune crumbled about me, she offered me work on her farm which had been in her family a few generations though sadly smaller now. Still there, still viable, she wanted it to work, and said, as long as she could stay on it, I could if I wanted.

How did she put it at the time?—I remember I was packing up baskets at the end of the cold October day with unsold pumpkins and root crops. My prospects for the winter were bleak, and my heart was already cold. Five members of the farm collective were gone—that left three of us, but I had a gut feeling I'd be alone in the big, ramshackle old farmhouse for the winter because the other two were moving into a trailer on their new land while they built their house—and I hadn't been invited. I didn't have enough wood for the winter, and the day's haul of cash wasn't going to help solve my problems. So I was definitely supposed to find a place to move on to.

I had never really talked to Lorraine, sure, crop stuff, weather, a bit of ecological politics, but she was a straight girl and we, the collective, had always stuck to our own, walking around with single earrings and inch long hair. It was a 'tribal thang'. She must have noticed that my tribe had vanished, and that I was looking more morose by the week.

I remember her leaning against my battered truck and saying, "I'm not going to garden anymore. It isn't working. I have one Morgan mare which I have had for pleasure, but I'm going into Morgans as a business venture, the reason to keep farming. What do you know about horses?"

I looked up at her dumbly, maybe even suspiciously, from the tailgate which I had slammed shut. "Nothing."

"Fine…You interested? There's haying, fencing projects. I have to reorganize the barn—I'll teach you how to groom the horses, how to handle them when I can't be there."

I just nodded. We didn't shake on it; she smiled broadly and gave me a hug, a real hug. Wow. And that's how I became a groom and gofer for Morgans on Curley's Ledge Farm.

Taylor, well, I'm never quite sure what he does in his world of high finance. He likes to be cityside most of the time, but switches his base to the farm during the summers because he likes to get out of business suits and walk around in cut-offs, leaving the phone to his answering machine. Don't think I don't know where a lot of the money comes down from, and the good wine.

"That was Gem," I said pointing to the phone but Lorraine knew. "Apparently, she has sent a student of hers up to…uh, for me to help on some research paper she's doing. For a few weeks." I thought that was the best point to begin with. "I'll put her up, but she…uh, well, she'll lend a hand, of course… Well, to get to the nitty-gritty—" I went on to explain the situation.

Lorraine took off her glasses and set them aside. "Gem was right to call you… Well, you know—as long as she has some spunk and good humor, she's an asset, right? Good attitude towards work?"

I shrugged. "Don't know! But I'm afraid I'm going to be stuck with her for awhile. I mean, Gem sprang it on me!" I paced the kitchen floor in agitation which I hadn't wanted to be so obvious about, but I can never hide from Lorraine, nor do I need to. "And I can't just get rid of her if I don't like it—" I was thinking especially of the careful balance between me, Lorraine and Taylor. And that while I had a life on the farm, ultimately it wasn't my place to do just as I pleased. Well, I never had. We always conferred, and obviously the big money questions weren't mine, and while they didn't have to include me in those matters, they often did. All in all we went about our separate tasks.

Lorraine roused me out of my worries. "If she can put in enough time to count towards meals, I think that would be fair. Can she cook?"

"Yes," I said too brightly. "Rice and beans?"

"We'll try it out then. If it doesn't work, we'll talk. Will Gem be coming up at all before June?"

"She gave Viv her car, so I guess not. Not till after finals and she has graded papers. Then she likes to cool out a little, and I don't know when she sublets her apartment. Certainly by haying." Gem had always been a great volunteer, the kind we counted on. And that's why Lorraine was being flexible—she considered Gem a friend.

"What's her research about?"

"Not sure. Wimmin's land stuff." I shrugged. "Life as a rural dyke."

"I see…" Lorraine put her reading glasses back on. "Don't get all down in the mouth now. You don't have to rehash stuff if you don't want to."

She knew me only too well. I just shook my head slowly and stumbled out of the kitchen and back to my interrupted job.

Now, you might think mucking out stalls isn't much fun. But it is. It doesn't take five minutes or ten minutes; the job takes as long as it takes—and that is farming in a nutshell. You begin by removing the obvious pile of horse apples with the fork, then you seek out any more that have been moved about by horse hooves, then you turn all the shavings over, shaking them out, removing the wet spots. Horses reveal their personalities; for instance, Mosey and Cloud are always fairly tidy. You know where wet spots are but Fortissima, well I guess she's a girl who likes her bed wet. Next, maybe you put some new shavings in, then smooth the bed over so that a horse would just want to lie down there.

Usually while doing chores I think about a particular job relating to my trade. As my business card says, I build, maintain, or repair stone walls without mortar. Mostly that means rocks I can lift and move myself with a bit of oomph or with a little help from a crowbar. Sometimes I bring in the big machinery. I'm not above doing that though I do have my pride—and it means contracting out for help and a bigger budget.

And while I usually find peace in the combination of thinking as I work, my chores now did nothing to ease my nervousness about meeting up with some pale young woman dressed in black and white, Doc Martins on her feet and studs in her nostrils. That's what I thought a Maid in the Shades would look like. I realized as I rehashed my conversation with Gem that I hadn't thought to ask what this Viv person looked like. But then she probably didn't quite know what to expect of me either; Gem was not the type to sport a framed photo of me on her desk.

And why hadn't she explained about us? After all, unlike her, I do display a photo I particularly love. It gets away with being art. A portrait of her on a wild, windy beach. Gem's robed in indigo, her hair flying. The sea sparkles with its white caps, and she's pointing. Her outstretched arm matches the line of the horizon. I find it terribly sexy.

I simply didn't get it. Why did she want her privacy so much she wanted me to take it down? What the hell did it matter? And I was supposed to reveal *my* life to this student? I couldn't figure it, but Gem always sounds so damn reasonable that I end up agreeing. This too would make make sense in time.

Calming myself with that thought, I jogged down to my barn of a cabin. While I keep the big house going during the worst of winter, enjoying all the modern amenities (especially hot baths), during the warmer months I live in a small, converted barn next to a spring-fed pond. A place of my very own, the very first such thing of 'my own,' come to think of it, also a hideaway when Lorraine and Taylor come up from New York on weekends and holidays.

My own barn, hey—and all the while I'm dreaming how someday I'll take the money I'm slowly saving and go traveling to Orkney or Glastonbury Tor or Delphi or Machu Picchu or say, Easter Island!

But when I went to take the picture down I couldn't stand to hide it away. So what if it was of Gem? She was supposed to be a friend of mine, so I wouldn't hide her picture, would I? I left it on the wall.

And it wasn't just the invasion of my peace I resented. I was having an odd possessive feeling—that I didn't like the idea of this Viv person looking around, touching my stuff. It's not like I have anything much. Just some rocks I gathered in my travels. Big deal.

I hadn't even really moved back into my place for the summer yet—none of my clothes, my current books. My library on rocks, ruins, small houses and found spaces sat collecting dust on the shelf along with my organic farm and garden magazines. The dishes were dusty too. Everything needed dusting, as much as you can dust rough-lumber shelving. The rocks needed dusting. I was feeling awfully possessive about those rocks.

I mean, hadn't I chosen to live in collective situations, low impact living all these years, very much because I didn't want to be possessive? Wasn't I in the relationship with Gem for similar reasons?—keeping free, keeping clear. Yeah, yeah. And now I was suddenly clinging to…stuff? Who had I been kidding all this time?

I glanced at my watch. Putting on a long-sleeved denim work shirt I had left hanging on a hook since early spring, I made my way back up the track, adjusting the cuffs. It wouldn't do to be absent when Viv arrived.

A car pulled into the yard just as I got to the barn. I was relieved when I saw it was the vet. She had already opened the back of her station wagon, pulling out her necessary serums and needles. Always dressed in a one-piece, blue denim barn suit, she was small and sharp, like a ferret, talking in a clipped manner, laughing nervously. But give her an emergency and she was in her element.

I went with Lorraine to bring in the horses with a whistle or two and grain. Hepp, the yearling, the green one—that is, untrained—was already in her box-stall, kicking. We'd never have gotten her in; she'd have been at the other end of the pasture in a flash, mane and tail flying. You'd think she'd have this terrific bond with Dr. Bender who'd helped deliver her in a particularly hard birth.

So there I was bringing in the gelding, Mosey, and Hepp's mother, Juniper, a lead in each hand when Lorraine who had just put Cloud and Fortissima in their respective stalls, nodded at me, "I think someone just got here, I'll take those two. Don't worry, I can manage."

For a few minutes I had blithely forgotten. Slapping my hands against my thighs, I made my way out of the barn and saw Gem's blue Honda in the yard, the driver's door opening next to Dr. Bender.

"No, I'm the vet," she was saying, holding up her kit as she turned towards the barn. Smiling she turned towards me. "Someone looking for you."

"Yeah," I acknowledged, passing her as I scooped up my favorite barn cat, Hecate, come to meow at me. I closed her in the grain room along with the others Lorraine had already gathered up with saucers of milk.

Three

A young woman was coming towards me tentatively, but also curiously.

Stunning. Gem didn't tell me she was stunning. I can't say I would have provoked such an adjective at her age. I was still fighting acne. And I can avoid that adjective easily enough now.

She was about my height and size with brown hair pulled back and kept down with a lavender cap, visor to the back. Heavy, dark eyebrows overshadowed a set of piercing eyes, the sharpness in the gaze eclipsing the color. Straight bridge to her nose, a mouth with full lips smiling slightly—uneasily.

She was as nervous as I was. Round cheeks, she had a definite roundness to her, roundness completely of youth. I could see her chiseled, even gaunt in middle-age. She carried herself as though she had taken many dance or gymnastic lessons as a child. Yeah, you could tell she might just take a leap if she felt like it. And she wasn't in black as I had imagined, but in a large T-shirt, tie-dye design in green, yellow and purple, hanging loosely over her regulation, baggy blue jeans—holes at the knees. On her feet she wore classic canvas basketball sneakers. Purple sneakers with holes at the toes and no socks. I was transfixed—someone else I knew once had worn her sneakers just like that. 'My toes gotta breathe,' she used to say wiggling them.

"Hi,"she began with a dip of the head. "Sure is nice up here—"

"Uh…Viv, I'm Ida," I unglued my gaze from her feet, offering her my hand for a quick, firm shake. Her hand was strong. "Glad you noticed." Indeed she couldn't have given a better opener. The farm was beautiful. The shad was blossoming and the black flies hadn't arrived. "Paradise. What we pay dearly for all winter."

"Professor Cooper did get hold of you then." She sighed with visible relief, a slow blink to those eyes which seemed to soften. "I was really nervous I'd have to explain from scratch."

"Nope, that's taken care of, but there is one thing I think we should clear up. Could I see your cap, please?"

"What?" But she took it off, her hair falling around her face, almost down to her shoulders. Nice.

"Thanks," I said, taking it from her gently, and turning it. "Yep, this is your high visibility cap all right. DYKE."

She nodded.

I thumped it against my knee as if that action would make the letters shake off. "Well, you can't wear it here."

"You aren't out?" She looked at me, a side of her face screwed up.

"Yeah, I'm out," I said, fidgeting with the cap. "But I don't advertise, if that's what you mean. Not in-your-face."

She looked peeved, even disgusted. "If you're a person of color or physically challenged, that's in-your-face. Can't hide that. I won't hide being Queer."

"Hm...good argument. Don't you think I'm obvious enough with a butchy haircut and my wallet in my jeans?" Then I shook my head decidedly. "No. Not here. You're low-profile, remember? Now my neighbor over the hill there, Pepper, she traps animals for fur. Perhaps that bothers me, but it's part of the way she lives, and I have—"

"But I wear it all the time, everywhere." She protested.

She wasn't into listening, and what was I doing trying to give her advice? I said hastily, "A brave thing to do. Makes a great target too. Here, it would get in the way."

"Then that's not my problem. People have to get used to us. We're here to stay. Guys wear all kinds of stuff on their baseball caps—" Color rose to those round cheeks. "And what if I was wearing a Dyke T-shirt, would you rip it off me?"

I thought about that a tic too long.

"Great, really great."

"I certainly wouldn't." I said hastily. "This isn't a music festival so you can't go shirtless either."

"Any more *rules* I might as well know about?"

I was annoyed. "I hadn't thought about any rules. But you're coming into my space, my world which you don't know about. You may think you do, or maybe you don't care—most invaders do one or the other, even peaceful ones."

She shot me a look that put me on the defensive effectively. I don't think she knew the power of it. Withering. Must have been something she had learned a long time ago when she wasn't free to speak her mind. Why hadn't I ever thought of it as a kid?

"Also, I'm basically a squatter here."

"A squatter?" Her lip went up in a twist.

"Yeah, a lifestyle enjoyed by millions worldwide. And as squats go, this ain't bad. I'm free to take care of the land which is what I like to do—without that illusion of ownership. But it also means I can't do just any old thing. And when I go to the Feed Store I just want to buy grain."

"Horses?" She tilted her head in the direction of the barn just as one of them whinnied loudly and kicked its stall boards.

"Uh-huh. Now that's Fortissima without a doubt—" Before I could finish, sure enough, the mare went streaking down the nearest pasture.

"Oh, she's beautiful!" Viv loped slowly towards the fence line.

"You don't want to do that!" I hurried after her. "She's very territorial—!"

Viv paid me no attention but ducked under the electrical tape and stood there. Fortissima wheeled around and came trotting back slowly as Viv talked to her admiringly. Just at that moment Lorraine came around the corner of the barn, lead in hand and laughing, directing her words at me, "I didn't latch her stall door properly! One whiff of Dr. Bender and she swung it open and was outta there. And Hepp's being good as gold."

Meanwhile Viv sauntered up to Fortissima and crooned to her as she took her by the halter. Mouth agape, I watched like some old ranch hand in a B Western saying, 'Wahl, I'll be gosh-durned.' A mare that invariably puts her ears back to bite me and this kid goes up to her like a virgin to a unicorn. Galling.

"Lorraine, meet Viv," I gulped with nod of the head.

"You're hired, kid," Lorraine said as she clipped on the lead, all smiles. "How well do you ride?"

Viv shrugged. "Some. Before I went to college."

I could see Lorraine planning Viv's future then and there as she led Fortissima back to her stall.

"Looks like you're a natural," I said.

"My riding teacher used to say that. She said girls would die for what I had and that I didn't care. Can I have my hat back now? I won't wear the damn thing." She held out her hand after ducking under the fence again.

"I'll put it this way," I said, now twirling the cap on my forefinger, not willing to be charmed quite as easily as Fortissima had just allowed herself to be, "we can do a trade. I'll find you something else." I put the cap on, visor forward and grinned. It fit perfectly. "Come on, probably what you need is something to eat or drink." I led the way. "Come in and see the house. It's where I stay some of the year—during the coldest part. Lorraine is with the vet right now. We can meet her after awhile. In fact we'll have dinner together tonight. And the bathroom for our use is through there on the left, down that little hallway. You'll see you can enter the house through a side door there from the patio. We can always come in that way for the bathroom. I'm still staying in the room next to it."

I chatted our way into the kitchen, and when she came back from the bathroom I handed her a glass of lime seltzer. While she was gone I had hidden the hat in the broom closet. "How about some bread?—home-made every other day, or so. Some cheese?"

"Yeah, I guess I am kinda hungry," she said when she finally bit into a hunk of fresh bread and cheese, "though I did stop at a store, the one with the BP gas. Just down the road there, just before your turn-off. Had to get gas, Professor Cooper's tank was about empty. Good bread, by the way."

"You mean Hatch's?"

"Yeah, there." Then she gave me a look somewhere between impish and malicious. "I was wearing the hat."

* * *

We made it down to my place there along the track—a bit of left-over carriage road. I walked and let her do the driving. After all, Gem had entrusted her car to Viv, why should I get belatedly possessive? Opening and closing gates, I directed her through the last left-over bit of mud-season in the track where run-off from the pasture had only really begun to dry out in the last week.

We arrived at an open, sunny spot surrounded by an ancient apple orchard. Foundation stones still marked the spot where the old house-hole and barn stood on the western side, my converted living space being an add-on much later, and which remained standing when the old barn caved in.

"Wow," She said as I showed the interior of my barn with one broad sweep of my arm. "*Too* cool."

"Thank you," I said tersely, rather proud.

"Found space, right? The ultimate dyke cabin just like Cooper said."

"Oh?"

"Yeah, you know. Rustic, self-sufficient, bare-bones, even make shift. That's what back-to-the-land dykes make for themselves."

"She said that?" Thanks a bunch, Cooper. From the sound of it my humble abode must be Exhibit A in class. I mean, what others had she ever seen?

"Yeah, this was a barn, right?"

"Right. Part of a barn. Actually it was a tool and grain room."

What did she make of my place? I looked around at the twenty-by-fifteen foot space, the windows placed high on each half-gable end, the rough wood, the steep stairs going up to my bedroom loft, the white, painted plywood walls which hid the insulation, the white canvas panels I put in to soften the place up and where I hang my posters; lastly, my beloved cookstove in the center of it all. Kitchen to one side, living area with futon couch on the other. I suppose it did look like a barn, especially because of the sliding, plank door with a smaller hinged one set in. Ultimate dyke cabin, yeah, with no electricity, no bathroom. Bathroom—you have to be kid-

21

ding. I dig a deep, but very civilized latrine in the woods for myself every summer—deodorized effectively with stove ash.

"I *like* it." She was looking up at the loft above, then swirled to take in the downstairs again. "It reminds me of a ship, a big old wooden ship."

"Better be in dry dock then."

"Wow, and look at all these rocks."

"Ballast. Start heaving them if we spring a leak."

"Oh, look at this," she exclaimed, noticing the photograph of Gem. "Well I guess this place is *okay*—my own patron saint right on the wall."

"Glad you like it…" The moment stretched as she scrutinized the picture, enough so that I felt an inner nudge to interrupt. "You can put anything here on these shelves that you can't keep in your tent." I pointed to shelves I had not yet taken up for the summer, under the stairs. "You can use the sink here—only cold water. No faucet—it's gravity feed from out back, simply runs all the time, drains out into the trough outside through that tangle of copper piping for the horses."

"Can you drink it?" Ah, at last I had her attention again.

I turned sharply. "Drink? You bet. It's from a spring. In fact I should bottle it. Don't think I haven't thought about that. Feel it."

She did. "Cold!"

"If you want to heat water for washing or drinking, let me show you how this camp stove works."

"I brought one too—Professor Cooper's."

"Yeah, but that's a back-packing stove. You may just want to use this since it's all set up. It's kerosene from these refillable canisters. If you empty one, make sure you let me know. We have a can up at the barn and we can also get it at Hatch's.

"This yours?" She removed a stained green cap from a nail in the center beam. "*Beacon*." She screwed up her face. "Sound like some Christian Teen group, a cut above, say, 'I'll be a sunbeam for Jesus.'"

"It's a feed company. Out of business now. I wear that for haying."

She tried it on. "Well, I guess you won't now. I should send a picture of myself in this to my parents. I'm a p.k. Know what that means? I always say it means politically *korrect*, but for you!—it means preacher's kid. My parents wouldn't doubt for a minute I was at some church camp. Maybe that's what I should write and tell them!"

"Are they expecting you to come home this summer?" I took to sitting on three-legged stool on the kitchen side.

"Yeah, sure. They run a day camp out of the church during the summer, you know, for 'underprivileged' kids. I'm lined up to drive the van, pick up kids, do the field trips. I already got the license. They don't like my hat either, so maybe we could do a trade." She then went and slumped on the futon couch with a groan. "They are really upset and all. It's not the danger of frat boys out for revenge that I'm escaping from so much as not being where my parents can reach me. I mean, they don't yell or have a fit. It's all so damn serious and heavy. Something to pray about. Do you know what I mean?"

I nodded noncommittally.

"They can deal with the fact that I took up a cause I feel strongly about. They just think things should get talked out. They don't like it that my car was shot at."

"I guess I can see why."

"Oh, but *I* wasn't being shot at, just my car sometime during the night when no one was around. Just done to scare me."

"Not to warn you?" I could feel my right eyebrow arch up.

"Oh no. No warnings. I think they could have attacked me if they had wanted to, though I was careful not to walk anywhere alone after I realized I was being stalked, and the whole women's center set up an escort for me and so did the 'alternative' fraternity—all the enviro-anti-war and gay boys. It was overdone I thought. Until my car got shot at. Then there was hardly any time to figure what was going on. My car was impounded by the police. Then, within hours I was asked to leave, huddled in Coop's, uh, Professor Cooper's office making quick plans—someone to pick up my car and then the windshield needs to be replaced...all my stuff into storage. That's the part I still find too weird."

"You don't think you're really under any threat?"

She snorted. "I can still see that guy—" She gave a shudder of— no it wasn't fear—fury.

"What guy?"

"The guy who raped Se—uh, my friend. On the night she was assaulted, God I hate that word, it's like a euphemism. She was raped. Thing is see, she's very small, dainty. And dark. They said racist things to her. Her parents are from Sri Lanka, came over as med. students and stayed. Very conventional, and Christian. She's very sweet, shy. I kinda felt protective of her all the time, immigrant kid, sheltered, so sheltered. And when she came home that night she was just sobbing, sobbing." Viv moaned, concealing her face in her hands so that I wanted to touch her in comfort, but froze as though looking at myself, seeing myself huddled on a bench like that once. I sat back and let her talk. She spoke huskily, "I wanted to take her to the clinic, you know, report it to the police. And I couldn't get her to. I couldn't convince her she needed to get a pelvic exam. It was

23

too awful. And then she seemed to get it together a bit. I thought maybe I could help her after a day or two. I didn't know what to do. And she begged me not to tell. Then when we were in the student center meeting for lunch, she dropped her tray, and I saw her staring—she was looking at her rapist. Big angel-face blond guy. And he was snickering to his buddy—the one who had held her down. And I went over and shoved his tray in his face, yelled 'Rapist!' so everyone around could hear, turned to get her outta there, but she was *gone*."

"Gem, uh, that's what I call Cooper—Gem didn't mention that part."

"Oh well, nothing really came of it, that's why. It was just another campus incident. I heard some people laughing as I left. And I just wanted to do something awful to him and all his buddies. Because of what they had done. And my friend really lost it after that. Within a week she took a bus home. I haven't heard from her since though I have written."

"What about her parents? Haven't they started a stink with the school?"

"Are you kidding? She was just going to pretend to be real sick. She wasn't going to tell them. We're talking extreme shame here."

"But aren't they doctors...what kind of real sick?"

She pointed to her head. "Migraines again. She gets them bad anyway."

"What if she finds she's pregnant?"

"I don't know!" Viv leapt up faster than I could imagine possible. She began to pace, banging her forehead with her fist. "I just hope that isn't the case. She thinks he stopped in time because someone barged out the back door of the fraternity where they had her against the wall and started puking all over them. The point was, she was a virgin, she was from a conservative background—she'd had American sex ed., knows as much as I do about anything—*information*. But emotionally that doesn't matter, and not when you come from her family. I wish I could get her to come up here. I can't even help her work it out."

"And so you did what you could."

She looked up at me, that direct, pointed look, head bobbing. "Yeah. And see, I don't care if I have to pay a price for it—having to come here." She banged that central beam with her fist.

I felt as though I had bolted to my feet in response although I hadn't moved. "It doesn't bother you that you've taken the fall for her—?"

She looked at me squarely, "No. Why should it? She's the real victim."

Mentally I slumped back into my seat, chastised by her fierce courage that put my own past weakness to shame if not confusion.

"But it hasn't solved anything!" Her hands flew up in frustration. "It never ends, does it? If smallpox can be eliminated, why can't rape? I expected better by my lifetime. But no. It's still never go out alone, always have a buddy. Watch what shortcuts you take. Stay in well-lit areas. Don't dress provocatively! Don't go to wild parties and let them spike your drink! The whole bit. All ass-backwards…That's what they did to her fruit punch, you know. And she was even invited! When she began feeling weird she started to leave, but she felt dizzy. They even asked her if she needed an escort…he and his buddy walked her out the back door. She suffers mega damage and he's still walking around to class."

"He take the pot shot at your car?"

She leaned against the beam, her feet crossed. "I think so. It's pretty personal. We looked each other right in the eye there in the student center."

I coughed at that one and said nothing, but hoped secretly that she had dealt him one of her real blows with those fierce eyes. And I had a feeling he did feel threatened. But he also had a gun—such an easy solution.

She went back to flop on the couch, a long groan. "Wow, I'm tired. I haven't really slept for days and days. Too hyped. Do you think I could rest here a bit? It's so nice here. Peaceful. And then I'll set up my tent, if you'll show me where."

"O—kay." I pushed myself up from the stool, hands to my knees. Walked to the door. "You can pitch anywhere this side of that orange hot-tape there that marks the horse pasture. It isn't on yet because I haven't finished. In fact, I need to go clear fence-line right now."

"What?" She spoke from her supine position, almost sleepily.

"I clip saplings and weeds that might interfere with the electrical fence which I string up with portable posts, called wands, this time of year. I won't be hard to find. By the way, you can use the couch for now, if you want—I haven't moved back in yet, you know—especially if it gets cold or wet. And I'll show you how to do the woodstove." I couldn't believe it—there I was offering her my space.

"Thanks, but I'll use the tent," she said, arm across her eyes. "I plan to stay really independent here."

That stopped me on my way out the door. "What?"

"You aren't living in a self-sufficient way at all! That's what. I thought I was going to meet a truly independent dyke. Meanwhile you really live in that house up there." And she pointed.

I could feel my ear's go back like Fortissima's when she's pissy. I wanted to say a lot of things like: I've adapted to my habitat. You'll

25

be looking for the convenient washing machine and phone pretty soon too. One major downpour on Coop's tent and you'll be happy to sleep on that very futon you're so grudgingly accepting right now. She *irritated* me.

I just said, "See you later."

Four

Slowly the sun shifted to the western side of the farm, beginning to set a few more degrees north of the standing stone I'd put up to mark the Equinox. Actually, it was setting almost halfway to the summer Solstice stone already. A natural outcropping in the sloping horse pasture had provided the center for my calendar on Curley's Ledge Farm. Over the first two years there I used fiberglass wands at sixty-six paces from the center in each direction to mark the most extreme sunrises and sunsets. Once I had that fixed I found stones to mark the six points. Lorraine was delighted. We called them scratching posts for the horses. After I had done that I started to feel almost as much at home as I had at Blue Corn—transplanted and the roots taking hold.

The change in light created a different mood to the day, almost sultry except the breeze still had that leftover spring nip and suggested that frosts weren't over yet. I was in the swing of sawing down poplar saplings along the fence-line, clipping all the shoots that came up like hydra heads from last year's pruning. Every so often I'd glance up and watch Lorraine in the first pasture working each horse in turn on the longe-line. At the moment she was working with Juniper the bay, her favorite, the one we'd be taking 'in hand' to the shows with her yearling, Hepp. Black mane and tail streaming, her body a burnished bronze in the sunlight, she cantered in a circle to Lorraine's voice commands.

I wiped the sweat from my forehead, then slapped my ear. Of all things, the black flies had just arrived. Honestly, you get a perfect day, you can just about believe that the tropics exist, and then the black flies arrive to remind you that having a Vermont rain forest has its price. My ear was going to look like a cabbage.

Oh yeah, black flies and Viv. I'd almost forgotten about her as I had concentrated on work, thinking about various stone wall jobs I had lined up. I saw Viv walking up the yet open pasture. She wore the same shirt but with baggy shorts. Ooh she was going to regret that. Already I could see her slapping her neck. The hatchback of Gem's car was open and camping gear had been deposited just outside the horse paddock behind the cabin.

"How's it going?" She said cheerfully, looking rested.

"Fine," I muttered.

"Uh, I was wondering if you could help me with Coop's tent. There aren't any instructions and I'm not quite sure—"

"Fine." I eyed the last ten yards I had to do. "I'm almost done here."

She turned to watch Lorraine while I went back to clipping. "Don't you help work the horses?"

"I do, but not till Lorraine gets them going, reminds them of their Ps and Qs. I only help her in the ring when she can direct me and then only on Mosey, the gelding, or on Cloud, an even-tempered mare used to novices. I'm sure she could use your help."

"How come you came here then—?" She threw her arm out.

"By surprise. Call it the art of surviving," I said too acidly. "Just like turning out to be a squatter—it wasn't any great ambition. In college I thought I was going to be a sculptor. But somehow I became some sort of throw-back into peasantry. Unfinished chores from a previous life? Destiny is not always grandiose, sometimes it's pretty ordinary—except farming isn't ordinary anymore."

"How long have you been here?"

I stopped in mid-clip to think. "Going on seven years now." I had almost said three.

"Seven years!" Those heavy brows went up. "That's a long time. Cooper said you used to be part of a collective...but, seven years ago?"

Sure, in herstory, I thought. 'Herstory means it's over.' Yeah. Faded with age. Was I allowing my previous life to grow foggy, at last? "I was a market gardener. I was part of a collective, yes. Separatist lesbo back-to-the-land collective." Why did I say this with so much venom? Pff, was I really going to open that can of worms for her? I waited to see what she'd do.

"Were you a squatter then too?" She grinned the question as she sat down in the grass hugging her knees.

She made me laugh. "You bet we were. We were leasing the land with intent to buy."

Intent to buy. Hardy-har.

"Around here?"

"Nah. North New Boston. About thirty miles."

"Great. Will you take me there?"

"Take you? Why? It's not there anymore," I said roughly. "The farm was divided up into ten acre lots for upscale housing. The old farmhouse was demolished. Huge houses there now. So much for wimmin's land."

"Why didn't you buy it?"

I changed the clippers for my small bow saw and attacked a spindly maple at its base. When I had sawed almost all the way through I pushed the tree over so that it would fall into the woods, but it got hung up so I had to saw from the other side of its base till the trunk came loose. Then I could heave it. I turned back to where she sat in the sunshine, her hands fanning around her head. I hung the bow saw on a nearby branch. "The black flies are out. If you need some bug dope, there is some on my kitchen shelf." I was really hinting that I needed it.

"Oh, they don't bite me," she said. "I thought they were gnats."

Back to the clippers. "We didn't even get serious about buying anything. We had had a hard enough time making the taxes and rent, so the landlord didn't consider us much more than a stand-by...and we were there almost ten years! The eighties did us in, prices were doubling on land. Our rent went up, mostly because town property taxes went up. We were just realizing that if we were going to make it at all, we really needed to build a state-of-the-art greenhouse, specialize in some produce like tomatoes or lettuce— and not dope. It couldn't be some hippie-come-lately venture any-more. What we needed was equipment and technical know-how!" I stopped because I realized I was ranting. I threw an armful of clippings onto the brush pile I had made. "Besides, the landlord wanted to sell the land for development. There was no way we could afford the price."

"And so the collective broke up?" She was standing near me now in the shade, hands in her shorts pockets so that her large shirt bunched up.

"Don't hurry me," I scowled, wiping my forehead. "Do you really want to know?"

"Well, yes." She looked at me, backing off a bit. "That's why I'm here, right?"

"I can't just blab it out!" I exclaimed, recoiling. "It begins in a lot of ways and ends in a lot of ways. I can tell you stories, patches of them, but you'll have to be patient."

She shrugged. "So you could start by telling me who was all in this collective."

I tackled one more sapling with the saw, hauled it out of the way, wiping the sweat out of my eyes, or was it the sting of memory? I had now reached the corner post of the pasture—a pine tree with a yellow plastic insulator in it. Turning back I surveyed my fence line along the edge of the woods which angled eastwards away from my house. All I had to do now was string the hot tape.

But as I clumsily fought a knot in the spool of tape, it was the past I thought I didn't want to remember which was coming undone, and I found myself saying, "...It was my college friend, Rune, who got me to come to Blue Corn—"

Then I froze, my finger so clumsy on the knot that she took the spool from me and with nimble fingers, found the end of the tape.

My head pounded. Surely the sun was going into eclipse. I could see the calendar stones tilting. Rune was forbidden territory like the shadows cast by cold rocks.

Then I saw Rune standing before me. That is, I saw her feet, her holey sneakers, but as my eyes looked up it was into Viv's inquisitive gaze. "So...? Blue Corn?"

I rallied with a laugh to cover for my nervousness. "Oh, it sounded so magical, that's all. I thought it was like saying white elephant or purple cow. The specialty crop was going to be, see, different kinds of corn. And we should go because we could grow our own dope discreetly in the center of the corn fields. Oh yeah, we would grow herbs and vegetables too. And I could sculpt to my heart's content—oh sure, sure, but the thing I didn't know is once you start farming when can you find time to do art?

"It was Kite who was the gardener—she had a lease on her great uncle's land. She'd teach us everything—she, in fact, was a native Vermonter—grew up on a working farm. She had a lover, Mel, who was learning massage. Another couple was already there when we arrived—Willa and Spence and they soon brought along Elsa, their art professor who wanted to paint huge canvases and Kristy of the long dark hair, her model—except she didn't have long dark hair anymore except in Elsa's paintings...but they were pretty much breaking up the whole time.

"I was much more fascinated by Willa and Spence. I thought everything they did was cool. Willa was savvy and Spence arrived with the first spiked hair I ever saw real and in person. She had all the right lines.

"Rune," I cleared my throat, "right off Rune didn't like her and pointed out to me that Spence was a rich girl who could bail herself out of everything any time. And she did, in fact, bail us out that time—oh... Anyway, Rune was my working class friend, and I did not know what that meant either. She was my college friend. I was just wide-eyed and took everyone literally. What did I know about anything? I relied on Rune as a guide. I believed her too—above all. It's all just like this spool of hot tape—a tangle. Except with many loose ends. Where do I begin unraveling? Let's leave it for now and go pitch your tent."

I wiped my hands on my jeans, stuck the clippers in my back pocket, took the saw up my arm to my shoulder, blade pointing back, and strode down the field to my house, my right ear swelling and burning hot.

"Then let me untangle it!"Viv pranced behind me, her arms like a windmill keeping those gnats away. "Start with Rune. Tell me about Rune."

"Rune...?" I sighed, squinting at Lorraine, now with Fortissima on the rise of the hill, backlit by the sun. Rune was the very last one I wanted to start with.

"Was she your lover?"

"No, no." My head gave a long, slow shake. "Not that."

"Do you have a lover? I mean now?"

I paused in mid-step, let her walk beside me. "Yeah." As in, but of course, glad for the change in subject. A mixed blessing.

"But she doesn't live with you?"

"No."

"Do you see her often?"

I smiled. "Depends on what you call often."

"How long have you been together?"

"I met her round about when I came here. The first summer."

"Oh, so she's part of your new life."

"Very nicely."

Right at that moment we came upon the wad of a tent that was my truly beloved's. It reeked of stale campfire smoke stuck in a bag for one long winter. I remembered our canoe trip in the only major rainstorm of last August. Had she ever aired it out after that? It did not seem so. I remembered how she had had to hustle back to her job, promising to tend to her damp gear. But how can you in an apartment? I should have kept it for her. I also remembered that we had busted one of the tent poles when we were taking it down in our haste. No wonder Viv couldn't figure it out.

"So then, are you monogamous?"

"Very nicely." I nodded.

"Six years! And you still have sex?"

I wasn't quick enough to say, "Very nicely," there too. My mouth opened but nothing came out. Odd. I actually sputtered. "That's, well, that's...well...I don't think anyone's asked me that before."

"So?" And she stood with her arms folded.

"Well, actually, yes. Because we see each other just a bit too infrequently. If we lived together all the time—who's to say? We'd probably have broken up by now. Do you think?" I wanted to say, yes, I have sex with Professor Cooper and what's it to you? What I did say was, "Now if you pick that flat area over there and spread out the ground cloth and the tent, I'll get a sapling to fill in for the tent pole you're missing."

"So it's still fun?" Woah, she was as relentless as the black flies.

I didn't hesitate. "Yeah, it's still fun."

"You don't want to...like...branch out? Have a fling with someone else just for a change, for variety?"

"No. I'm a goner on this woman. Our germs have made a commitment to each other."

31

She gave a flick of a limp wrist. "Ooh, aren't we living danger-ously. What about toys?"

Gem—I sucked in my breath as I walked back up to the tree-line—and you wanted privacy?

Looking over my shoulder I watched as Viv prepared the tent. What is it about her, I wondered. She's taking it seriously, coming here to ask questions. But she's been given permission to ask things she might not otherwise—if I was just putting her up, that is. It was hard to say whether she was naturally inquisitive or insensitively rude or both. I would have to see if she asked Lorraine anything. Oh yeah—Lorraine, is it still fun?

* * *

And no, I didn't want to talk about Rune even though she was the very start of the rest of my life. Why I am where I am in Vermont. So I took the easy way out. I still had her letter in the book she gave me on ancient goddess temples made of marble. Ren, as Rune was still called back then, first wrote me about Kite whom she'd met at an herbal retreat. I handed the book to Viv, letting her find the letter herself.

Wanna come live on some wimmin's land? This womyn, Kite, got a lease on one hundred acres of her great uncle's run-down place which used to be a dairy farm. In Vermont! Barn fell in sometime ago but the old farm-house is okay, she says, if you don't mind rustic. There's a tight couple here—used to go to art school together—Spence…well, I'll tell you more about her later, and Willa, cool Black woman. They say they have a ton of records. So hey—music, right? We can all do our art too, see! Work on the land—grow our own food and herbs. Herbs—you know what I mean? And Vermont has tons of marble just waiting for you to get your chiselly hands on. They want this art teacher of theirs to come up too…she's looking for a place in the country to paint. I guess she does landscapes or something. So, wanna? Oh, and by the way, I'm calling myself Rune now. I'm claiming a whole new Amazonian personality for myself, cutting away my past iden-tities like past lives. You could start all over too!

Rune, her flowing scrawl had found me at a low time, already a few years after college. I was working as a house painter while sculpting bits and pieces out of plaster when what I really wanted was to be a Michelangela with a huge chunk of marble.

So, wanna? But I just went as myself, Ida. Couldn't think of any-thing else.

Even now I can still be in a half-sleep some mornings and smell just the hint—just the edge of a hint—of a hauntingly familiar aroma wafting up to me in bed, stirring me.

What…?

What is it? I struggle, my body tossing, throwing covers aside. Then, my feet can already be on the floor when I remember…

My very first morning at Blue Corn I followed that smell which would intertwine with the smell of dope and be the very smell of home. I tiptoed down the narrow, creaky, farmhouse stairs to find my new collective of sisters. The sound of a hand-powered coffee-grinder stopped at my approach and then continued.

There was Willa, coal eyes full of tease—some secret only she knew. Hair covered with a yellow turban, her dark hands began grinding the coffee again. With long delicate fingers she picked up pieces of vanilla beans and threw them in too. "Want some coffee, Ida? It's my specialty, sweet and strong like me. It's sex in a cup. Oh yes—first you have that unmistakable hint of vanilla and then a whole lot of deep dark coffee beneath it."

I didn't know what the hell she was talking about.

But knowing laughter came from the two other women in the room. Spence for one, in her denim overalls and no shirt, the bib barely hiding her large nipples and upright breasts, dark hair shorn to half an inch from her scalp. The muscles of her tanned back fascinated me as she turned to the beat-up electric stove. She was pulling a tray of corn muffins out of the oven, still smirking at Willa's comment. The oven door slammed shut with a squeal which would punctuate our flow of days, much like the floorboards creaked.

Willa went on, laughing. "All you need for breakfast is coffee beans and corn bread. Complete protein."

All around the large kitchen table were sacks of potatoes, some spilling across the table itself, and my very best friend in the world, Ren—now Rune, stood there holding half a spud in the air. She, the very reason I found myself part of this wimmin's land, 1977.

A saucer with an ice cube held a simple sewing needle as well.

"Want your ear pierced?" she asked with that wicked glee she always got when offering me a way to live dangerously—something she was always doing, especially since I had once been a been mild-mannered suburban girl.

I just looked at her. That's what I always did when she made such offers. And by then she knew I was just looking into the depths of the water before plunging.

Rune pulled at her left ear lobe. "I just did Spence's. See? And she did mine."

Spence toppled out the corn muffins into a bowl as she tilted her left ear towards me, sporting a gold post too. "It's a tribal thang. We just made it up, heh heh heh."

I didn't know it then but Spence had her own form of speech, more often than not a direct quote from the obscure third verse of some rock and roll lyric—the way she said 'thang.' No, it wasn't revealing her accent. I found out before too long that if I wanted to go around quoting all the pretty sayings that Spence pronounced and which I thought were so slyly witty, I'd be owing royalties to record companies. Even I knew she'd hit paydirt when Laurie Anderson boomed in on the sound waves.

"Yeah, where do you think they got those gold post from?" Willa laughed again, tapping her ears which each sported about five gold rings or posts and two empty spots. "Now I'll have to give you one too?" She poured hot water through the coffee. It seemed as though her very words were laughter. Contagious. Made me laugh for no real reason. The unsullied laughter of new acquaintances.

"Say, Ida," Rune tossed a potato from hand to hand, then juggled three, "we were thinking we'd go to the demonstration down at Seabrook nuclear power plant. Wanna? We might get arrested."

"With you, Rune, I could do that.What's with all the potatoes?" I asked, still deferring my answer on whether I really wanted my ear pierced or not. Arrested, well okay. But earlobes pierced?

Rune waved the spud around in circles, beckoning me. "You ever planted potatoes?"

"No, guess I can't say I have. I can do beans!"

Indeed, I still had everything to learn about soil conditions and mulching, about drought, about potato beetles and fungus on corn.

"We have to cut each of these up, see, so that there's just one eye to a piece, see. That's what we get to plant today. Kite says. She's plowing right now."

Kite says—there was no debate or consensus. We didn't question Kite when it came to running the farm. Maybe on other issues, but not how to farm.

"Yeah—I heard the tractor. Couldn't see from my room." Not in the attic quarters I had which only boasted one tiny window angled under the eaves and facing west. I walked over to the window by the kitchen sink and gazed out back, my heart surging. Kite was driving up and down the field on an old Ford tractor with its patchwork of blue paint. Mel, her one and only, sat on the big rear fender next to her, hanging on with both hands as they watched the plow follow behind. Faces inclined just slightly towards each other like those dolls with magnets in their heads.

Now why, I thought with a shake of my own head, why is it Mel who is sitting out there on that tractor with her instead of me? How could someone else have already snapped up the very girl of my dreams? *My* dreams!And I must have grunted aloud because when I turned back into the kitchen I found three gazes upon me. I'm sure I flushed though how could they possibly know my thoughts? Yet I knew they did. It wasn't going to be easy keeping my new and torturing secret. I'd have to be careful.

I swaggered over to the table, proffered my left ear to Rune and said gruffly, "Where's that needle and spud?"

Five

To warm up my cabin for Viv, I made a fire in the cookstove, and the room took on a glow of comfort it hadn't seen all winter.

With my bare feet up on the lip of the stove, I sat back in my old rocker, stuffed my pipe with some riff as I waited for the fire to get going. I loved that cookstove, an old, and long obsolete cast-iron Lennox. The only reason it still functioned was that it had been stored in good condition for over fifty years in someone's barn. The few cracks turned out to be mendable. And with new tiling inside it was tight though the oven a bit unpredictable. What I liked was that ornate lip, inlaid with steel, extending from one end to the other just below the firebox and oven. And what I really liked was the door of the firebox itself which had Torrid Zone molded into it in big block letters.

Once the very centerpiece of Blue Corn, that stove was truly my one and only stable relationship, having moved with me. And don't think I haven't sat there many a late evening having hard-fuck fantasies, double-fisted and all thumbs. You betcha it was Spence who gave me permission to liberate my fantasy life, the night she was loading up the fire box, moving a piece of wood in and out suggestively for Rune's and my benefit. Rune groaned, I recall, and not out of arousal, as we sat around bare-breasted and stoned. But Spence kept on with a wicked gleam in her eye, saying suggestively, "Don't you wish, baby." Leather cuffs on her wrists (so it had to be late Blue Corn era.) I think she had just come back from her shopping spree in the city, and everyone was appalled as she flaunted them. She said, "Get over it."

Which I did, oddly enough. Why repress fantasy, I told myself, and I still load up the old cookstove suggestively. Put my feet up and fantasize away to the roar of the fire and the hiss of the kettle. Yeah, so watch out, even the most unlikely looking lesbian can have the wildest, outrageous fantasies in front of her hot stove. And then if she's really lucky, one day she meets the woman who has just the right stuff to bring it all out. Like Gem. "Who would ever think you'd be so adventuresome in bed?" she'll say, looking me up and down. And she says it with dreamy satisfaction too, especially when we lie entangled naked in the sheets late at night.

"You." I usually retort.

Meanwhile as I smoked my pipe, Viv sat on the futon couch, the gas lamp shining on books she had spread out on the low cinder block-and-plywood table in front of her. I wondered if she was writing up significant notes or plotting out her next barrage of questions.

How come I didn't have the ovaries to ask her about her sex-life. It's true I didn't really want to know, did I?—so, do you practice 'safe sex'? Do you like sex for a good time, or do you get all romantically involved? Do you have sex at all?

If she seemed so nonchalant about sexual questions, maybe she thought I was either safely out of age range, or I simply held no appeal. I somehow preferred the former. Made me think of when Fortissima gives one of the others a whiff, then stretches her neck way out, curling her upper lip back in distaste. That's what I was puffing away on when she looked up and found me giving her a direct gaze.

"Do you have any pictures?" She smiled as I looked blankly at her. "Pictures of you all back at Blue Corn."

"Somewhere, some box," I said unhelpfully, "...I have maps though." I tilted my head suggestively, removing the pipe from my lips.

Now she gave me a blank look.

"Maps. Maps of Blue Corn, to show how we used the land and all. For a cut-and-dry twenty page paper, a few maps would surely be of help." My feet dropped to the floor and I heaved myself up, stuck the pipe in my mouth, shuffling over to some corner shelves. Secretly, maps were something I liked very much and I knew exactly where to look for them. What a good solution. In a long white box which had once held roses (from Gem to me!) in our early days, I displayed some rolled-up papers, held with rubber bands. Checking the corners of each, I selected one. "I think we should roll it out on my kitchen table. We can weight the corners with rocks—yeah, bring a few from that shelf there. Bring the lamp."

I walked to the table and discarded the pipe to one side, unfurling the map lovingly. This was one I had carefully drawn to scale from the surveyor map. It showed the boundaries. I had also marked the existing stone walls that ran though what woods we had; numbered the old pastures along with those we had changed over into gardens and corn fields.

"*Too* much, " Viv said in satisfaction. "I'd like to copy it, not necessarily to scale, but good enough for an appendix to my paper. Coop...er is always telling us how important systems are in collectives. How does a group organize its physical space for the work it does? Since cooperatives uphold team endeavor, the separation of individuals becomes obsolete. Work spaces have to accommodate meeting areas too, and work stations are geared to shared tasks.

Usually its offices or warehouses, so this is way cool."

"She does, huh?" I remembered certain discussions clearly when Gem must have been working out her thoughts for classroom lectures. Funny, never thought of it that way. I just thought we were talking. "Then maybe you want a plan of the farmhouse too—living space for a collective."

"You bet!"

So I unrolled another paper and placed it on top of the first.

"Wow. This is to scale too. Jeezee peezee, I was wondering how you all fit in."

"Well, Kite and Mel shared what used to be the dining room, here, and Elsa had the traditional morning room or birthing room which was large—she had to fit her canvases in somewhere. She painted on sizes up to ten feet either way."

"How'd she get them out of the house?!" Viv exclaimed.

"Here. We cut a door to the outside on the gable end. It was really a narrow panel on hinges, insulated. It bolted shut and was only used when she moved paintings in or out. Sometimes she rolled up her canvases too."

"Did she give shows?"

"Yeah, she worked at it."

"What did she paint?"

"Big giant vulvas. Red and purple, of course." I watched her jaw drop. "Gotcha kiddo. No, she did landscapes—abstracts. Stuff that she thought corporations would buy—lawyers offices, banks. No messing around."

"Good, coz vulva pictures are getting kinda trite." Viv smiled wanly at me in rebuke, relaxing her shoulders and face. Then looked back at the map. "Okay, go on—upstairs."

Trite, huh, I could remember when it was radical. I sniffed, refocusing. "Just wait a minute, here's the kitchen and living room—the common space—bathroom off the kitchen. Just a teeny tiny window in it. The old farm houses always had a central room that could be kept very warm for sick people in the winter. And it was really warm. Guaranteed you could be naked in it even on the coldest night in winter. We always wanted to fix up the bathroom, and run pipes upstairs too, but we really didn't have the room. Or the money."

"All eight of you used this one bathroom?"

"Yep, sure did. As Willa always said, 'One bathroom for five to ten people is a health necessity, any more than that is self-indulgence.' You have to understand in our collective vocabulary, 'self-indulgence' was a dirty word—politically, that is, not sexually. Okay, so off the kitchen here...well I don't know what its original use was—maybe it had been added at some later date—was a closed-in porch which faced west. No door to the outside. For laundry to dry? I dunno. We insulated that, closed off the end windows, and that was Kristy's room. Really too cold in the winter, but that's okay because she went to sleep with Elsa unless they had a fight."

Viv leaned with elbows on the map. "Okay, so that's four downstairs—four up?"

"Yeah. We tore out the wall that separated the living room from the front hallway, so that heat would go upstairs. We used the cookstove—that one I still have here, that old Lennox right there—and a big old Riteway in the living room. Okay so, go upstairs—over to here," I pointed to the next drawing of the second floor. "On the west end, two small rooms. I had the coldest room, the northwest corner. Rune had the south room so we were neighbors. Less than half the roof was high enough to stand up in. Then you went through the 'tunnel' which must have been where kids slept around the chimney in the old days. Then through a door into a large room which Spence and Willa shared."

"Hm, I guess you were all lucky to have such a couple thing going. What if you had all been single?"

"Then I suppose we would have rotated sleeping arrangements."

But Viv wasn't going for a straight answer. "No bed hopping? Did you guys all sleep with each other or stay in the couple thing?"

"Ah, I should have known you were driving at something," I cuffed my forehead with an open palm. "You want us to have been the hotbed of lesbian sex? You want 'Torrid Zone—lesbian utopia' as a title for your paper? For one thing you'd have to be so quiet making love to have any privacy at all, and then you'd have to face everyone at breakfast who knew exactly what you had done—"

"Oh, what? Come on?" Her eyes were widening.

"Is that all you want to know about? Isn't there something besides sex?" I shrugged. "I hate to disappoint you. I kinda had a lover once who was not part of the scene at all."

"Kinda?"

"Well, it wasn't very successful. I like forgetting about it."

"In ten years?" Her head nodded like a turkey's in her disbelief, her mouth exaggerating the words.

"Sorry, kiddo. I was a late bloomer, a Latter Day Shaker. Simply celibate. I fell in love with the wrong women or at the wrong time. What can I say?" I shrugged again. "I cultivated a reputation."

"I don't believe you." She almost sneered, except it was coquettish at the same time.

"I'm flattered. Look, I'll untangle that another time then, but it's largely true. And no I didn't sleep with anyone in the collective."

"Not even Spence?"

I laughed. "Spence, the big bad butch! Spence, the one who told me I didn't want it enough because if you want it you get it? No, she was too tough for me. She liked real femme women though we did not talk about it that way then—we were all into being lavender Amazon wimmin with labryses between our bare breasts. That whole time while we didn't know all about the roles we were playing, Willa was really totally femme, a tough, heavy duty femme. They liked it rough, those two—that's all I knew about it at the time. Uh, Rune gave me a bit of a low-down on what that all meant, but I did hear them on occasion. Usually if I did, I'd slip downstairs, embarrassed, put on a record and get stoned. I'm sorry, I didn't like it. I didn't like hearing others fuck, you know?"

Viv pulled back slightly from where she had been leaning on the map, as if retreating from Willa and Spence's room.

"I think Rune was the only one who slept with everyone—except me. 'Gotta know,' she'd say. I'd argue with her because I couldn't see it—just sleeping with someone whether you were attracted or not, or even just because you were stoned. But she was like that—*light*. Always wanted it light.

"But sleeping with Spence—well, something was different there. Once Rune had a black eye and bite marks, and wouldn't talk about it for a long time. Tough on me because I thought we pretty much shared everything. I know it was a summer night when she was talking to me about it, and we were out on the stone wall I had just about finished building in the front yard. Full moon, air soft, just enough wind to keep the mosquitoes down. And we were stoned, of course. And she was getting bitter in her talk, her mood. We were talking about how we couldn't grow a crop anymore, it was getting too tight with the legal crackdowns, airplane crop-spotting and all. And that if you were found growing dope on your land the property could be confiscated, and since we didn't even own it—well, it belonged to Kite's great uncle and it was a family deal that involved many relatives.

"Kite didn't want the risk anymore—this lucrative dope crop. She was still hoping somehow we could own the farm—she'd inherit it somehow. She didn't want to hurt the chances. So odd—it was the one crop we were really good at, mostly because of Rune. Oh, you know, she knew the male plants from the female, and just what to do for pollenization. She talked to the plants as though they were family, real beings. And the thing of it was that whenever we were really hard up for cash, if something came up like a hospital bill or tractor repairs that exceeded our budget, what did Rune do, but go into the hidden stores, pull out her trench coat with all the hidden pockets in the lining. We'd weigh out the portions into zip-lock baggies—hey, we even had little labels which said, 'Blue Corn Organic'!

And off she'd go on the night train to her city contacts. I went with her a few times but stayed clear of her dealings—didn't poke my nose there. She didn't want me to. And she'd come back with the cash. So when we got busted—"

"Busted?" Viv said, solemnly.

"Yeah, well we got busted. All so stupid." I stretched out my back and went to throw another stick of wood in the firebox. "See, Spence paid for the lawyer who took care of it. Someone—of us— had put some weed seedlings which were always hidden among other seedlings in the green house…put them in with the tomato sets when we went to the farmer's market one Saturday. And even though Rune whisked them out of the way and hid them in my truck, someone must have noticed and reported us. Cops showed up that night, you know, as in just after we had all gone to bed.

"Do you know what it's like to have the police breaking down your door and yelling 'Open up!' just after you've gone to bed? You don't get over that. They arrested Rune and me because we were the ones at market that day and it was my truck. Luckily Rune had been sharp enough to get rid of all the plants. Every trace. Bye bye dope crop. That was the last of that. They didn't find anything, but they did find a roach in my truck ashtray. Off we went. Spence, I guess, did some routine, what Rune called 'outrage as only the privileged can pull off.' I don't know, I wasn't there. I was in a daze about it all. But Spence was the one who bailed us out and got it all settled— something about the search warrant saying only 'plants.' She basically stopped them from ransacking the house. You can bet they came and scoured our property in daylight. We had to watch their every step and yell at them if they so much as disturbed our seedling beds. They trampled stuff anyway, just to hassle us. We were let go due to insufficient evidence.

"Anyway, that night when Rune was talking to me, she said something about having paid her debts. She had paid Spence back in kind, as Spence had requested. They were even. 'And after all the times I went and got cash for us,' I can remember her saying. 'What did it amount to?—squat. Spence with money in the bank all the fucking time.'" I sighed. "I don't know what kind of sex they had, Viv. I don't think it had to do with light recreation, more like settling a score."

"I'm sorry I asked." And she looked like she meant it.

"A loose thread you pulled at. Watch out. And not for your paper."

"So Spence was *into* S and M."

"She's out about it now. Leather butch. We had no such definitions then."

"What's this little one?" Viv pulled loose a sheet of writing paper clipped to the corner of the house plan.

"Look at it and give me a guess."

She turned the paper this way and that, finally determining how she should look at it. I could see her puzzling. "Looks like stars or something...North is here, then South..." She shrugged at a loss.

"It was a calendar built with stones. From this exposed rock in the top field, looking south, I plotted sunsets and sunrises on the Equinoxes and Solstices. So, even without a clock or a watch on, we could calculate time out in the field. Well, I did, devoutly. Planted these neat rocks I got from the old barn foundation we had near the house. I have one here on the farm too. I'll show you...in daylight...Perfect for your paper—'wimmin's time'. "

Viv was leaning on the table again, fingering the last rolled map in the box idly.

"You can open that, if you want."

She unrolled the last map. It was really the rough blue-prints of a house. I stared at it while I moved rocks to hold down the corners—goddess, it had been years—and I noticed that she looked at me quizzically, waiting. I was strumming my lower lip with my forefinger. "That sure ain't worth the paper it was printed on."

She read, "*Blue Corn 1981.* Wow. I was barely starting school."

"I spent the whole winter working towards that plan. What can I say? Kept me going. Dream house for communal living. I wanted to tear apart the old farmhouse down to the frame. The roof needed replacing, and the sills were rotten. This is when I thought we still might get enough money to buy at least half the property, at least the tillable part. Okay, so the house is torn out to the frame, foundation fixed, water pipes and electricity are accessible to reroute, add to. First I was going to put in this large bathroom downstairs, a double-sided bathroom, two of everything but the plumbing kept to a minimum expense. But we consulted a bank agent hoping to borrow money, and she said I had to think of 'resale value,' family house and all. That we had to put a bathroom on both floors. Anyway, what we were going to do was extend out on each side, see, private, good-sized rooms. Greenhouse in front. We had meetings over it—what did we want, looking at sketch after sketch. But it was my design project, really. I tell you, the biggest desire was to have a bathroom for each bedroom, or at least one for every two rooms. That was the fantasy, one's own bathroom! Self-indulgence sure was hard to get over, huh? So this all went nowhere fast."

Tapping the plan, Viv said supportively, "I like it—this plan. Has possibilities. Visionary."

"Well you can have it for your commune then," I teased.

"Seems like thriving lesbian communes or retreat centers would be interested. You could design a *retirement* community."

"Great, you mean if I just hang onto it for a few more years? What is the term for it nowadays—Affordable Assisted Living?"

She helped roll up the papers, put them back in the box, asking if I could leave them out for her to look at again. I was already on my way back to my rocker, pipe in hand when she said, "Would you take me there, to Blue Corn?—Can we go tomorrow—it's Sunday, isn't it?"

I gulped, "Uh well, Lorraine and I were going to put up the pea fence, and then—"

"Don't you get time off, not even on Sunday?"

I chuckled. "Time off? That makes me think of Kite—she always joked about time *off*—"

"Please?"

I sighed, a hollow feeling grabbing inside. "I haven't gone back, you know. I just haven't."

"You'd have me along. Please? Or could you give me directions?"

"No, no—that wouldn't do because I don't know what you'd find. I suppose if you could help me with the pea fence or help Lorraine work the horses."

I thought she was going to throw her arms around me—I could feel myself stiffening—but she just grinned.

Six

Sunday was supposed to bring rain but when Viv and I set out for the old homestead in my pickup it was still sunny, May in its prime. Trillium and jack-in-the-pulpits were in full force in the woods as we headed down the farm road, fern beginning to unfurl. It was as good as being in love. Peepers singing in the wet places. And yet I had a sinking feeling too—about going back.

How I had avoided it, like it didn't exist on any map of mine anymore. A part of me couldn't believe I was doing this now. And yet, there sat Viv in the usually vacant passenger seat, peering expectantly through the windshield at everything, wearing my Beacon feed cap on backwards.

I decided to take her, not on the Interstate, but through the back roads; I especially liked the winding Skunk Hollow Road—except what had they renamed it now?—Sugarhouse Road or something.

Bouncing over the gravel, we passed the Jersey Cow farm, an old established place that gave me a sense of stability in a fast developing region. The barn, grey with age, its silo leaning, had to be well over a hundred years old.

"Kite and I bought a calf there once." I slowed the truck to a crawl, enjoying how the cows hung about chewing their cud, "It was late in the Blue Corn days; we only kept her a year, never did breed her or milk her which was the whole idea. I think Kite was missing her 4-H kid days when she raised a Jersey or two. By the way, this guy has a handsome team of oxen that I saw him training when they were scarcely six months old—taking them for a little walk in a training yoke. All grown now. I've seen them at ox-pulls—maybe you'll get to see that."

"Ox-pulls?" She gave a poof with her lips.

"What?" I scowled. "What does that mean?"

She tilted her head, used the cap to brush back her hair before re-adjusting it. "Not something I ever thought about, that's all. What the hell do they pull?"

"It's a contest. They pull weights—logs, maybe a huge cement block. Livestock sports! That's what they've been reduced to in the last fifty years," I finished ruefully.

"Don't sound so sore about it." She eyed me in disbelief, a slight shake to her head. "It wouldn't have been so easy being a dyke back

43

then wearing long skirts, hair down to your ass and all. And you wouldn't have been working the oxen anyway."

I did a brief double-take on that one. "I suppose so. I'd have been the milkmaid with cowpox, huh?"

"Yeah," she said looking at me meaningfully.

I shrugged. We were passing the new-fangled place with its cute barn, llamas and angora goats. The old farmhouse had been retrofitted with windows à la eighties—that arched glass in the gable ends, the skylights. I figured I had better not start ranting about this place and about what it had been.

But just beyond the small dip in the road I screeched to an abrupt halt.

"Damn," I cried in spite of myself, leaning over the steering wheel at the 'For Sale' sign by the side of the road.

"What now?" Viv sounded peeved.

I pulled off the road a bit and turned off the engine."Old man Wheeler must have died this winter. Well, goddammit." I slammed out of the truck and strode around to inspect. Some kind of track had been started. Now, was it a logging road or the future driveway? I began walking up the track, noting the pink surveyor ribbons, noting the boulders which had already been dislodged here and there.

"Hey, where you going?" Viv was leaning out her window.

I'd forgotten her in my split second of rage, and simply motioned for her to follow as I walked on. The road was muddy and maybe a skidder had left those deep tracks. Pretty steep too. One hell of a driveway for the happy summer buyer to find out about in winter. Had to be the picture perfect house-site above the ledge. Yup.

The sunny glade had already been roughly graded, signs of it being a logging landing, but whatever timber had been taken out had to have gone before mud season.

Viv came trotting up behind me. "Don't tell me you know this place too."

"I haven't been on this road for awhile. This was a farm until about ten years ago. The old man got too feeble. Pastures are all going to pine. His kids must be selling it off."

"That's the land you should buy!" She said as we headed back to the truck.

I snorted. "Right. This is fancy prices here—we're just across the town line into North New Boston. And that site is on ledge surrounded by woods, no pasture nearby. If I could buy land—which is out of the question—I definitely want farmland. And I have that. I don't need to own it—"

"Yeah, yeah." She waved her hand at me dismissively.

I stopped in my tracks and she bumped into me. I pointed to a crumbling stone wall running through the woods. "Take a look at that, Viv. Want to know what that is? A gold mine. No, I don't want this land, but I could sure use those rocks. I'm not only a squatter but a scavenger. Come on, let's load up."

"You serious?"

"Nah. Maybe just five or six. I have some shapes I need for the wall I'm repairing. No, what I need is a big truck, and that means talking money and permission."

* * *

When I pulled onto the old Blue Corn farm road, a new sign read Bradamont Hill. Oh hell, at least Kite had something memorializing her, even if it was her family name. The road was paved now, a real town road with a Stop sign and row of mailboxes. I counted seven. Hmm, either someone had bought a double lot or there was still one floating up there on the ridge, the granite outcropping where I went to mourn the death of John Lennon one snowy day, stoned and depressed. I guess that's when I 'discovered' it, my mourning rock, because I went there over Rune too in early April once. And I heard the geese honking way up. Looking and looking. At last I saw them, formation upon formation, their wings glistening in the sunlight. For a moment I know I believed in heaven.

Then lastly, of course, that bitter November day in my orange vest (to alert hunters) when I had looked down from the ledge over the farmhouse, my pickup already loaded up with the Torrid Zone Lennox.

About fifty yards up the road, I pulled over and stopped. "The road used to end just beyond the farm house, in the barnyard where the barn was once—before our time. The farm track went up the old pasture. We had our fields cultivated on either side, the corn over there." I pointed to what was now a sloping front yard and site of a large modern house. "Let's get out."

I have to admit I was choked for a minute. I hadn't been here since the day I moved out of the house, taking not only that old cookstove, but some solid window frames, the hand-churn ice-cream maker, Rune's artwork and her empty beehives, besides various garden tools which I had split with Kite. And that only after I had tumbled all my calendar rocks, shoveling dirt over them for bulldozers to bump into. 'Take anything you can pry loose,' Kite had said, 'the salvage company is mostly interested in the beams and the wide oak flooring.'

On the same foundation where the farmhouse had been sat a large cape—natural wood siding and a deck with sliding glass doors facing south where we had had our makeshift greenhouse. The lawn spread out level and very green to the terraced stone wall which in turn, had steps leading to a lower area where dwarf apples trees flourished, just beginning to bud.

"Welcome to suburbia." I leaned against the front fender because my knees were weak, and folding my arms, I fought the queasiness. And it was as though I could smell the hemp in the air, could feel the echo of being stoned. "There Viv, is where I used to live but I never saw this house before. And that, that's the first stone wall I was telling you about last night, the one I built using rocks from the barn foundation. What a job. Drainage seems to be holding up. I don't see any buckling or leaning. Holding up well."

I could see her eyes getting bigger, those heavy brows going up. She pointed, nodding approval. "I'd be very proud if I were you."

"Nice to see the irises are thriving below. Kite and I planted them." Yeah, I was proud. The wall was about fifty feet long making an alcove in the center about ten feet wide where the three steps were set in. How I had sweated over those steps having dragged them with chains and the tractor. Kite directing me where and how to position them. Then I sandblasted the center of each one, gave it a well-worn effect. We sat on them afterwards drinking cold beers, plastered with dirt and sweat, feeling absolutely terrific.

I went on, "The trees were planted by Rune. She had a thing for trees. She had a thing for weed too, but trees—well, you knew trees were what she'd have to get into."

"And did she?"

I rubbed my neck and chin, scrutinizing the dappled sky. "Nah. Computers. But we used to build a make-shift brick hearth right there at the foot of the steps, hang sap buckets on that line of maples over there, and boil down sap into syrup during mud seasons, getting stoned and star-gazing. It was our hang out."

A woman came out on the deck at that moment. Maybe she had seen us through her glass door. Slightly plump with a short, blunt haircut, thirtyish and wearing one of those low-waisted print dresses, she made her way almost hesitantly out into the middle of the lawn. Then I thought, rather than wait for her approach, the best thing would be to smile broadly, give a wave, and stride towards her. She obviously thought we were out of place.

Besides, that way I got to leap up onto the stone wall and stand there.

"You...you need directions?" She asked tentatively.

"No no. I used to live here, that's all. Was in the neighborhood and thought I'd take a look."

"Oh." She relaxed slightly. "We bought this house a year ago. My husband's a doctor. So...you must be the previous owner?"

"No before that. Before this house. There was another—"

46

"She wanted to show me this stone wall she built." Good old Viv, right there beside me, had jumped up too. She walked along the top gracefully there in her tank top and baggy shorts, arching into the alcove and leaping, true dancer form with arms in fifth position, across the steps to continue walking the length of the wall.

"You built this?" The woman sounded incredulous but at the same time, pleased. "It's the thing that sold us on the place."

"Oh good," My head jerked involuntarily at that. Sure must've added to the property value. Someone had made good on my effort.

"I can't believe you built this." She shook her head. Viv was heading back. "I had the impression it had been here a very long time—the worn steps."

"No, sandblasted. If you know anyone around here who wants a stone wall, I'll be happy to give you my card." I reached around into my back pocket, pulled out my beat-up wallet, and presented her with one of my dog-eared cards. "The name's Ida Muret—here. And I can give locations of work I've done. I mean, if you see someone looking at it again someday, they probably want to know what I've done."

"Oh, thanks." She took the card politely. "I didn't know we had bought a showpiece." Why was she eyeing me so oddly? I didn't like it. Was she trying to place me? Did she know me from before?—how could she…she said she just moved there? Did I look like such a hick old dyke now I didn't even know it? I actually looked myself up and down, taking in the sensible shoes, the worn (but clean) jeans, the faded T-shirt. Was she admiring how butch I was? Hey, maybe I was actually intimidating—being older and more creased around the edges.

"I think you've lost an earring," she said finally.

I immediately reached for my unpierced ear. "Oh dear, did I?"

"I got to walk on your wall, Ida!" Viv returned triumphantly. Then to our hostess, "I made her bring me here to see it. It's her art form, like, she's a sculptor in rocks. So what you have here, see, is a permanent exhibition. Three worn steps leading to a now vanished temple, perhaps one to which a procession of priestesses danced and sang their way with a lute, a temple to Aphrodite, say, on the island of Lesbos. Layers of new housing on the old foundation. The beauty of it is that it's so subtle, using methods which became a tradition of New England as people cleared the land for pasture. It's a statement of history because she recycles, see, taking stones that others have already used, mostly from old barn foundations. Like she's really into that. Her signature stone is a key stone, so if that goes, it means the whole thing has crumbled. Let me see—a long flat rock vertical to a short horizontal one meeting it at the center. Let me find it Ida."

Dammit, if I could actually feel myself flushing. Our late night conversation, long and drawn out, about my love for rocks had never been explained so succinctly, so sweetly…so at the wrong time. "I didn't do it on this wall."

"Oh," The woman said again with that mix of stand-offish politeness, cautious interest and maybe a hint of disappointment. She looked from Viv to me, and back again, then smiled, "You two *must* be related! You look so alike, but surely not mother and daughter?"

I choked silently, rocking back on my heels as I shot a look at Viv.

"Cousins." Viv smiled sweetly, her hands behind her back.

"On my mother's side," I added quickly. "Well, we must be going now. Thanks for coming out to talk to us and letting us walk the wall."

"Oh, anytime." With a wave of her hand.

"Great!" I meant it. "Come on, Viv."

Viv leapt off the end and sprinted after me as I hurried with huge strides back to the truck.

I turned the ignition key, scrutinized Viv as she climbed in. "Can you believe that? She thought we looked alike."

"Can't be our hairy armpits because she couldn't see yours," she offered, her chin puckery as lips curved down in thought.

I snorted, still looking for some mirror image in her face, her physique. Her hair was darker, and I was graying at the gills. We were indeed about the same height and weight. I was bonier but only because of age. She had round cheeks, wide set eyes. Was it the nose? No mine was different, definitely broader. The lips? Yeah, we had full lips, the both of us. But altogether, hey, I just didn't see it.

We hardly know each other, I wanted to tell the woman over again. Is it because we're dykes—the way we move? Our auras or something? Hell, we aren't even lovers.

"And what was that about my lost earring? Seventeen years ago a gold ring in my left ear may have been radical. Now even heterosexual men wear earrings in only one ear. Hasn't she ever noticed?" I drove on up the paved road slowly, giving us each a chance for a look at either side. So much for our 'tribal thang,' Spence. I could hardly recognize that this place had ever been under cultivation. Each yard had been landscaped—big back hoes had been up here. Places leveled, regraded. Trees gone. Other trees put in.

As I anticipated, we came to a cul-de-sac. There as always was the only thing still familiar—the old, rusty metal gate that closed off the upper pasture with its granite outcropping. Except now there was a sign that said 'No Trespassing.' I thought for a moment I'd take Viv up there, then let it go. I was done with my grieving there. Finished.

"Would you mind—" Viv began tentatively as we headed down the hill again, "I mean, what do you think about me interviewing all the members of the collective? Do you think you could help me get in touch with everyone?"

My fingers played on the steering wheel. "Kite and Mel are the easiest. We can swing by their place right now on the way home, see if they're into it, maybe set up a time you could talk to them. They have a kid now—Kelsey."

"Kelsey? That sounds so...so..."

"So?" I goaded her.

"So vogue. A little girl who should live in that house with that woman we just talked to."

I laughed. "What did you expect?"

"I dunno. Something...*different*. Did they artificially inseminate, the whole bit?"

"Yeah, actually they did."

"Who?"

"Mel gave birth to Kelsey."

"*Too* much!"

"I like to have Kelsey come up to the farm whenever possible. She's a scream, let me tell you. Skinny little thing with big brown eyes and braids. Mel and Willa both wanted kids even back at Blue Corn. But artificial insemination wasn't as accessible then, or you know—same sex parents. Willa went back to the city. She has a kid now too with her new partner."

"What? You mean Spence isn't in the picture?"

"Ah no, Spence—no." All I could do was shake my head. "It's kind of a tangle of thread there again. Can't unknot it right now."

She nodded her acceptance and we headed off to see Kite, Mel and Kelsey.

"By the way," I added. "Her second name is Maude. Kelsey Maude. They had a big fight over whether to call her Mel's choice—Kelsey, or Kite's choice—Maude. Mel wanted her to feel normal at school, especially if her family was different. She can always switch to Maude someday if she wants to. I kinda hope she does."

Seven

Kite and Mel's house was right on a main road, mostly because of Mel's massage business. A small post and beam house with an attached garage for two cars, no less—the upstairs of which was Mel's massage room. The place belonged in organic, alternative, passive solar *Better Homes and Gardens*—well, especially the garden. Kite's expertise was in evidence with tulips and daffodils heralding the delights of the upcoming season. Later there would be borders of iris, lilies, foxgloves, hollyhocks, you name it. What better business card for a career landscaper?—Come over to my place and see what's possible to make out of a pasture gone to berry bushes and pine.

I could tell that Viv was instantly charmed, especially when that skinny scream of a kid came running out, wearing a green velvet skirt and a stained purple T-shirt, "Eeda, Eeda, big mosqueeda! Ayeda Ayeda, big mosqueda, Ooda, Ooda—"

I coughed into my hand as Viv's eyebrows went up and down, then swung out to grab Kelsey up.

Mel appeared at the door then, a towel in her hands. And oh my goddess, wearing a long-waisted dress cut along the same lines as that 'doctor's wife' we just saw. Now this was a disconcerting new development. I mean, sure Kelsey wore cute little dresses and as I put her down, she was running around on the lawn going, "I'm so excited, I'm so excited!" à la Pointer Sisters, finishing with a beautifully executed pirouette at which point she lifted up her skirt to reveal her pink underwear.

"I used to do that when I was a kid too," Viv remarked over her shoulder.

"Hm. Do you think it's inherent?" I remembered doing that too. Right in the family photo album there is proof.

Mel hailed us or me anyway, "Well, if it isn't the stone dyke!"

Hardy-har. Old joke, trust Mel—except the times had changed and the 'd' dropped—really, I used to think it meant stoned dyke. For years the joke was on me. Anyway, I avoided looking at Viv on that one, proceeding up to the door.

Mel continued, "Long time no see. Definitely must be spring for you to show up. Except usually you come to announce the geese are flying over."

"Been busy. Hi Mel." Hug hug. "Where's Kite?"

"Out back. I guess you must be okay since you haven't called me again. You know you should really come on a regular basis not just when you're in spasm."

"I know, I know. I just can't afford you anymore, kiddo. This is Viv, by the way. She's up here on a research project."

"Yeah? Hi, Viv."

We proceeded into the house which was much on a plan like my own but far grander. I was waiting for Viv to say, '*Too* cool.' But she didn't, just did a slow turn, taking it all in, Kelsey walking around her curiously.

Mel went on, "Kite's planning the stone terrace. She'll be real glad to show you."

"Wow, maybe I'll stroll out and see." Which I did, going through the open French doors, deciding to leave Viv to her own devices.

Sure enough, there was Kite out back having already dug a trench about twenty yards long. I could see the stakes and string measured out. Shovel sticking out of the ground.

"Well well, look what blew in," Kite looked up at me from where she stood in the trench. "Now we can be the same height, see? Like in the movies. You can be the short butch and I'll be the tall, leading lady. Come over here and give me a kiss."

Which I did. Are you kidding?—Kite had never given me such an order before. Never. 'Come over here and kiss me!' I thought my knees would give in. I mean, I think we were black belts in the art of not touching, much less kissing. For fear of…well, simply for fear of it signifying too much. And now she was boldly calling me over. I leaned slightly towards her, my lips brushing hers. It was more than I could stand. I stood back too quickly, inspecting the trench to cover for my old shyness.

As usual she wore her stained chinos and open-collar, cotton shirt with short sleeves, that same old labrys resting against her collar bone, her arms tanned and muscular. Always good to see Kite with her short sandy curls, her charming smile, but didn't I detect some kind of strain? There was something different about her, the tightness to her mouth. I knew Kite well enough from the old days to know when something was eating her which wasn't often, but when it was, she got this distracted, furtive way of looking around as if she had lost something.

"So, you're going to do it…the wall. Good for you."

She shrugged. "Yeah. I was just thinking about you—maybe I could use you on a consultant basis."

"I'd be glad to help, you know."

"Yeah, yeah, but I can't afford you."

"Hm, I was just saying that to Mel. Maybe we can trade, muscle power for massage."

"Well, I can't," she sighed. "Unless she offered. It's not my trade to make."

Now this was different talk. I mean, weren't they married and all, a collective of two? No, three?

"Well, I'd help you anyway."

She sat down with her booted feet in the trench. I joined her, ready to ask her about moving stones when I saw that lower lip trembling.

"Funny you should come today." She wiped her face, staring off. I waited. I thought she was going to burst into tears but she restrained herself. "It's so crazy, Ida…Mel's in love with someone else."

"No." I muttered under my breath. How could that be? They had been together so long, through so much. I just couldn't see how anyone could do that to Kite, the beautiful amazon, generous to a fault. I looked at her winsome face, those creases around the eyes and mouth, the laugh-lines defined by time. Not that young face I always expected. Haggard around the edges now as we aged, so that the passing of a few months made me see more clearly what we were becoming. And I thought of how often I had been jealous of them—meaning that Mel got Kite and I didn't.

"Yeah," she sniffed. "But this is different. Harder." And stifling a sob, she wailed through gritted teeth, "She's in love… (gulp)…she's in love with a…*man*. She's going *hetero* on me."

"Shit." I must confess I was reeling. I mean, *Mel*? "How? Who?"

"Some client."

"I thought she only did women."

"Nah, that began to change over the last couple years as women wanted to refer their 'nearest and dearest'. Plus there's been more competition now since she-who-will-remain-nameless started up."

"You mean Sadie?"

"Shh. Anyway, she's been doing this guy for about a year. Now it's…love." That last word was almost inaudible. "'Doing this guy,' listen to me! I never knew she was wrestling with her bisexuality. Must have been repressing it for years—because of our relationship. Now it's cracking open. Makes you wonder—who is this person I thought I knew inside and out?"

"It'll pass. Surely."

She shook her head, wiping her nose, shaking. "I dunno. It's a biggy. Too much for me. It's like ever since she, we, had Kelsey, she's somehow wanted a dad around. The family she never had. Wanted the whole *picture*. It's just she's sort of taken it to the…extreme. Next she's going to want a real wedding, invitations, white dress and all. And no butch playing the groom."

"Have they…I mean…how far—?"

"Yeah, I think so. She won't talk about it. We walk around doing the usual stuff, you know, Kelsey and all. But like zombies. And Kelsey's no fool. She's this barometer, you know, kind of bouncing off the wall. There are nights when Mel has been out real late. Then Friday she didn't come back at all. Left a message on the machine while I was picking up Kelsey! Not till Saturday morning. And there's Kelsey and me chowin' down our pancakes. I thought I was going to gag. And Kesley just kept stuffing her mouth fuller and fuller and fuller till I thought her eyes were going to pop out of her head. Mel came home *in a dress*, pulling more out of shopping bags, some for Kelsey. I just can't… I just can't bear to see it all fall apart…like this." Her chin was down on her chest as she struggled with her turmoil.

"Oh hell." I put my arm around her shoulders.

"And I'm supposed to be building this goddamn wall like everything's *normal*."

"You're going to have to ride it out, Kite, ride it out. If you stay solid, she's got to come around."

Kit dhook her head. "He's well off. He has a marvelous house. His wife left him—"

"Yeah, just listen to that last bit, would ya? His wife left him. That's got to mean he's a real creep. Out for conquest. Wants to see if he can lure her away from you. After that he'll make her miserable."

"Yeah, well how come Mel's a sucker for it then? Don't I do well enough by her?"

Using a tactic I had learned all too recently, I blurted, "Yeah, but what about *sex*, Kite. Do you? I mean has it still been fun for you two? Or is it—"

She looked at me shocked. At least I had knocked her out of her collapse. "I dunno! We haven't, well not since she…oh, what the hell. You know? I thought we were adventuresome. Round about the time we were trying to get pregnant there, she got this real thing for dildos. I mean, at the time, I thought, okay okay. But now, now I see it…it all differently."

This was probably the most frank talk about sex I'd ever had with Kite. I had to refrain from exclaiming, "Dildos, woah!"

She flushed with embarrassment. "I well…I couldn't…get the hang of it…I mean…" And hiding her head she began laughing or was it sobbing?

"Kite—" I thumped her on the back. "You're too special, Kite, too special. If Mel is going to be so stupid as to foul this all up with you—" I didn't finish, I couldn't finish. "You have to ride it out, babe. She'll have to come round. Seventeen years you've put into this! Can't knock that. You've got a rock solid base, come on. So maybe the drainage needs reworking or something."

"I don't know, Ida, I think the key stone kinda fell outta this one."

"She has to come around! You're just going to have to give her the space and the time to. Maybe it's something she should explore, get out of her system."

"By then she'd be totally contaminated."

Oops. "Then we'll send her on a purge, okay? She'll probably beg for one."

"It's not that simple these days."

"You mean about safe sex—" I stopped because it looked like she was going to explode in tears of wild rage and frustration. "Look, hard as it may be, you've gotta keep on keeping on—for yourself, for Kelsey."

She sniffed. "Ever thought of getting into mediation?"

"Aw, Kite. Do you think you'll have to find that sort of help?"

"I dunno. We aren't talking right now, that's for sure."

"Listen, let me help you build this wall. Let's get to it. It'll keep you going. Hey, I was just up to the old place, saw my wall for the first time again. It adds to real estate value, don't you know."

She half-laughed at that, rallying. "Aren't you…aren't you still working over at Stintson's?"

"Yeah, yeah. But I'll get it done over the next two weeks."

"Oh god, how'm I going to get through the next two weeks?"

"I could come, say, Tuesday afternoon. I could come, say, half days here and there."

She looked at me sadly. "Oh, Ida, will she really leave me for him?"

"Listen, how about you come inside with me and meet Viv." I explained briefly about Viv, how she seemed to be all fired up to investigate what Blue Corn had been about, and that since I was only an eighth of that experience, I couldn't be counted on to explain the whole, as true and accurate as I thought I might be. I almost got a chuckle out of Kite on that. I also explained that so far Viv was in the dark about Gem and me.

"Uh oh, we'd better get in there then," Kite picked herself up out of the trench, gallantly offering me a hand, "if you want to warn Mel in time."

I gulped. "Even more so about what happened to Rune…I haven't gotten into that."

Again, "Uh oh."

"Let's see that plan of yours, we need a prop here."

She handed me the piece of paper diagramming her wall.

If I had learned one thing from Blue Corn it was that whenever there was a crisis or you had just had this heavy heart-to-heart with someone, you always had to go back and face the crowd. And since the heart-to-hearts were usually about each other, you had to apply some quick 'make-up:' everything's cool, everything's fine. I mean, of course everyone else knew exactly what you had been up to or else they didn't care. But there was still this effort to put on the game face and go mingle. Which is what we were going to do now, walking through the French doors together, the paper in my hand as I noticed particulars out loud, and questioned her about the drainage on the western side.

In the living room area, Kelsey was dancing to an old Mamas and Papa's tape of all things—what was the subliminal message in that choice? (And whatever happened to their theme song by the Roches: 'You're the two that I wa-a-ant'?)—exclaiming to Viv, "Look at me! Look at me, look at me." Growling it out just like a Laurie Anderson clone. Spence woulda loved it.

Yes, uh-oh. I saw that they had been busy. There on the coffee table was the Blue Corn family photo album, no less. Sheesh. I know my own pictures were stuffed in a box somewhere pretending to be well forgotten. There was Viv leaning over, Mel pointing at something.

"She doesn't look anything like I imagined." Viv was saying.

"Who?" I squeaked.

"Spence!"

"Ah."

"When you called her a big bad butch, I pictured some six foot hunk. She's so scrawny."

"Sorry." I glanced down over her shoulder. Harvest picture. Spence's self-timed camera on a tripod took it. We, the collective, oh what a motley crew, posing with our pitchforks. And Rune, there on the end, that wispy blond hair swept back from those high round cheeks by the late September breeze. That wide toothy grin. And bare-chested. Rune was always bare-chested because she said her breasts didn't show much anyway.

There was Elsa, big, round, heavy bosomed, turbaned, bracelets up each arm, Kristy of the 'long dark hair' nestled against her. Mel of the very short hair (especially compared to now). And Kite in oversize coveralls and bare feet.

Yours truly was sitting in the wheel barrow, Willa and Spence with matching bandannas pretending to push me.

"I mean nobody looks like I thought they'd look." Viv shook her head.

"What did you think we'd look like?"

"I dunno—bigger?"

"Well, that's just a very small photo." I pointed out.

Mel intervened, "Larger than life?"

"Yeah," Viv nodded with that turkey waggle of hers.

"Amazons, of course! If you want larger than life, it's Elsa's painting she must see," said Kite, then, "Hi. I'm—"

"Kite, yeah. Hi." Viv nodded some more. I think I was imitating her in a sort of fascination, then out of the corner of my eye, I caught Kelsey doing it too.

"So, I hear you're up here to separate history from myth which I see you are already doing," Kite continued. Oh brave Kite. "If it's myth you want, you have to see Elsa's painting."

"Is it still up, Kite, you think?" I queried, not believing the bank would still have it up after the recent merger.

"I was there last week, but you're right, it could get rotated into storage any old time."

"We'll try and get there in the next few days—it's only one of a series, Viv. There's another in a Boston law firm—women partners. And one is supposed to go up in the Women's Museum in Washington."

"Wow, who's in it?" Viv's eyes widened.

"All of us!" Mel glowed.

"Well…" Kite shrugged.

"It's almost abstract, you see," I jumped in. "We're there but you can't tell it's us unless you knew—from our postures. You can definitely pick out Rune and Spence. And Kristy is hard to miss with her flowing brown hair—a wig!"

Kite snorted, "The babe with the boobs, you mean, it'll sell a picture anytime. Nude in a field with women working."

I elaborated, "You might think it was men because it's Spence and Rune from the back. They do look very androgynous—"

"Are you going to keep talking about the old days again?" Kelsey's face twisted up in dismay while she stood on one leg.

"Not now, honey," said motherly Mel, and then for the benefit of everyone else, "We all know that life began with Kelsey."

"Yeah," Kelsey said, pleased.

"Oh, I thought it began with me," Viv pouted at Kelsey, so that I knew they were going to get along famously.

Kelsey giggled.

"Well, we better move on outta here," I said to Viv, then to Mel, "but I'm coming back on Tuesday afternoon to help on the wall."

"Great," said Viv turning from Mel to Kite, "maybe I could have an information interview with you then?"

"Sure," Mel smiled, and rose from the couch. "I'll have clients but maybe I can squeeze you in. That's the afternoon Kelsey is in day care till three-thirty."

"Maybe Kelsey could come home with us up to the farm?" I suggested, wondering if the space I was offering them was wanted.

"That's a thought," Kite said slowly. "We'll let you know."

"Yeah, yeah." Kelsey promoted.

"Cool," said Viv.

As we made our way out, I hung back with Mel, whispered, "Uh, I haven't told her about Gem and me yet."

"Professor Cooper?" Mel grinned. A forced grin. "No, I didn't happen to say anything."

"I haven't explained about Rune either."

"Oh—" She stopped cold. "I...I was waiting for her to bring it up, because, well, *I certainly couldn't*. Then, thank goddess, you and Kite came in. Anyway, she was too busy asking about Spence."

"Hm, yeah...funny thing how it's Spence, huh?"

Her smile was rueful. "Yeah. Tuesday...maybe you should explain by then."

I gulped. "Yeah, it's just...hard. But I'll talk to her, and I hope you and Kite will try and *talk* to each other too—how to work things out from here on, and not be too hasty or hard on yourselves."

Her face really fell then, but at the same time I could see all this glow about her, sort of 'born again' beatitude. Gave me the shudders.

She said flatly, "Well, I knew she'd have to tell you. I knew that. I'm not a monster, you know."

"Monster?" No, I would have simply called her 'weak'. "How long have I known you, Mel? I don't know exactly what you're going through but you're not a monster. It may seem as though you're way out there to me right now. I can't say I understand, or even relate. I just hope you remember how long Kite has been there for you, really been there, and that you don't throw it all away, grabbing for something else you may regret later, or find out you didn't really want."

I thought she was going to burst into tears now as she whimpered, "Yeah, okay." Then she tugged me on my arm, "Please don't tell any of this to Viv."

Oh dear. "Of course I won't."

Snively, "Thanks."

We passed into the front yard where Kite was throwing a miniature football for Kelsey to catch. "Here you go, Buster!"

Retrieving the ball, Kelsey threw it back, yelling, "Busterama!"

I called across the lawn, "Wow, what a *dad*!"

Sorry, I couldn't help it.

"Yeah, her name is Butch!" squealed Kelsey.

Kite fumbled her catch.

"Butchorama!" yelled Kelsey.

I hustled Viv off to the truck and we split.

"Cool family," said Viv.

I drove in silence thinking how secretly and madly I had been in love with Kite for many of those early years, how stilted and bottled up I had been because of it, how damned *respectful* of them as a couple I had been. Well, they had been enthralled with each other, after all, and I had been in awe of that. It was also why Rune had been able to sleep with one or the other or both of them, and come out seemingly unscathed while I knew I wouldn't.

Even now when kissing Kite in the trench like that, after all these years, it was a kiss that lingered all too powerfully. Her lips were too close to being her naked body pressed upon me, our slow, blended yet urgent movements making up for time lost in other lives. *Wait a minute!*

She had gone and broken a taboo. The thing was—why?

Could make a girl get confused.

Eight

I needed to stop at a store but I still wasn't too keen to roll up at my local stop, Hatch's, on account of Viv having gone in there with her 'dyke' hat on so recently, so I stopped at the one on this particular route home. We were at the cash register checking out when the older man leaned over the counter at us, shoving over the bag. "You two must be related," he said with a nod, then leaned closer, giving me a big wink. "You must be sisters."

During my split-second double-take it dawned on me what he was saying: I couldn't possibly be her mother because I looked so young. I rallied and gave a big grin. "As a matter of fact we are."

He went back to his register, satisfied. As Viv and I were walking out the door, she said too loudly, "Mom, did you hear that, he thought we were sisters!"

I slammed into the driver's side. "I don't believe it! That's twice in one day. I'd better not hear that we look alike again or I don't know if I can be held responsible for my response."

"All dykes look alike," she said with a shrug.

"Then don't call me 'Mom' ever again."

"Butchorama?"

"Stop it."

"Oh, don't worry," sniffed Viv. "You're not at all like my mother. For one thing she's older than you are and an Episcopalian priest!"

"Oh?" I started up the car, interested. "I thought...well, I guess I hadn't thought...when you said you were a preacher's kid that you meant your mother."

"My dad is too though he's a counselor now. But my mom is really into it. All my childhood that was her big driving ambition. To get endorsed by a church, to be ordained! And suddenly, when I was thirteen and I had to be in church watching her, I thought why? Even though she was into all this Mother God stuff, it all seemed ass backwards. I mean, I didn't figure that out for a few years. Eh, you know, my big act of rebellion in high school was to spout Mary Daly at her. She listened. Turned out she'd read Daly's stuff while I was in grade school."

"So, what does she think about you saying 'Jeezee peezee' all the time?"

"Well Jeezee Peezee just means Jesus is pissed off."

"I suppose you're right."

"What can I say instead? I don't want to blaspheme the Goddess, right? How do you take her name in vain?"

"Hapshetsut."

"Bless you."

"Or is it Hatshepsut?"

"Bless you again."

"Very funny."

In this way we got home. I found Lorraine digging in the garden. "A message for you inside," she hailed me.

"Lorraine, do you think Viv and I look alike?"

She stopped, looked us over. Made us turn our heads to the left, to the right. Then, "No."

"Good."

I left Viv to explain, and went in to find that Gem wanted me to call. She sure was getting into a phone thing. I dialed her office, hoping I wouldn't get her blasted answering machine. She answered, "Hi, wait a minute, I've got my hands full here—"

"Oh dear, I wish I was there to help," I crooned as she covered the receiver and called out some directive to a departing voice.

Then she was back. "Don't be an ass. I'm talking literally."

"Well then, maybe we should get something else going for our sapphic code—" I was stung.

"Yes, yes. Now listen, I'd like to fax you something. The Dean's been giving me a hard time about it, wants to question Viv. Not pleased, not pleased at all. She may have to come back down here, unless she wants a permanent suspension. I guess the boy's parents are threatening some sort of suit against the college."

"She just got here! How can they expect her to do that?"

"I know, I know. I need you to talk to her. There's a poster that appeared all over campus this weekend, causing more problems because it just happened to feature a particular guy from the fraternity so much in question these days. For the first time there is some very obvious fingering here, and listen, I can't take the heat for her. I have too much else to do. So talk to her about it and get back to me."

"Wait a minute, I don't know how this fax thing works."

"Just press the fax button after we hang up. It'll be automatic. Don't forget to reset it afterwards, though. Gotta go."

No love chit-chat for Gem and me. I wasn't pleased, not at all. Hanging up, I hovered over Taylor's machine nervously trying to figure out which button was for the fax. Pretty soon the single ring came and then all that grinding noise. I tore off the paper which was a crudely done-up poster: WANTED in bold letters, then: *By the*

Feather and Tarnation Court. Then a terrible photocopied photograph of a smiling male face. Underneath: *George 'Joker' Atwell, Rapist.* At the bottom: *Maids in the Shades Squad.*

I sighed and went to find Viv who had already walked down to my place. I could see her sitting on the front cinder block step.

"Hah! All right!" Was her immediate response when I showed it to her. "Cool. See, they just carry on the work."

"Yeah, and you're in more hot water. Your professor back there is going to bat for you with the Dean again, but she wants an explanation. Did you have anything to do with this?" I said forcefully as I sat down next to her. Maybe I got a bit heated because I was defending Gem.

She hedged. "Yes and no. I mean I did give out the copies of scanned photo I made from his fraternity album. But they've blown it up. Went through the 'zine, see, with instructions to take that page out and post it wherever convenient."

"Who's they?"

"Don't know exactly. Anyone can put something in a 'zine or try and sell it."

"Anyone? No editor or contact person?"

"You're asking me to name names!?" She looked at me incredulously with that head waggle of hers.

"No," I said too defensively, "but you may want to explain yourself out of this or take the heat."

"Duh," she shrugged. "There is no *editor* on the 'zine. It's just girl-talk. We always display pictures and write-ups of guys who cause grief. Usually on weekends. Usually someone who has gotten hassled or has a friend who was hassled. Or knows of a guy who is an out-and-out woman hater. And we've posted them before in dorms, at the sororities, light-poles, wherever anyone wants to. It's a service. I don't see why the Dean should get all uptight over this one. Duh. Except that Joker's dad is some alumni big wig, and someone must have seen it and gone 'uh-oh.' I don't believe he'd sue, but worse—he could influence alumni not to come forward with money for the old Alma Mater. He's some hot-shot lawyer. You know what Joker wants to be?—a lawyer just like his Dad…George Atwell *Senior*. Some slimy corporate lawyer for a chemical company. And with a nick-name like 'Joker' you know who his role model is, and it ain't Batman. Sheesh."

"Don't you think this is a bit vigilante? It says 'rapist' here when it should say 'on charges of rape.' I mean, aren't there avenues of complaint through the women's center or police on your campus?" I stood up and opened the door, but lingered there, leaning on the doorpost.

"Like I said, it's a service no one else is giving us. It's guerrilla tactics. He's the guy who stalked me and shot at my car to make his point, right? The only way guys are going to see the light is by noticing we're onto them and won't stand for their shit. Public humiliation has its benefits. And besides most of the women on campus know about the 'zine or have seen it." She jumped up and brushed passed me.

"But how do you put it together? How do you distribute it?" I was curious now as I closed the door behind us and she made for the couch. "The paper for it has to come from somewhere, the nickels and dimes for the copying."

Sitting with her arms on her knees, chin in hands, she shrugged again. "I dunno. You pass along something to your friend. If she likes it she makes a few more copies, adds something—sometimes poetry or cut-and-paste art making some comment on whatever subject she feels like. Passes that along. So every few copies the 'zine *mutates*." She laughed then. "Like a virus. For the poster to get put up means a lot of the kids liked it, you know. We always like to put up posters. It's easy to get free copying done if you have a friend in an office. Sometimes the English lit. students gather all the stuff they think is really neat and make a more formal issue which they number over the year."

"I'm impressed, I have to say." I began to lay a fire in the Torrid Zone as the cabin had a chill to it, and also I wanted to cook potatoes, make a potato salad to contribute to supper.

"Oh 'zines...anyone can do a 'zine. If the Dean wants to do some really good work, he should be looking in the trash buckets and finding out what the boys chuck in there. Top Ten Girls. Cut and paste bodies of women. And I do mean cut and paste. Sometimes headless. Let him see the real horror show. He'll also find skinhead stuff, socialist stuff, economics, computer info., gay stuff, music, you name it."

"Well, that's what you should tell him then."

"What, tell the Dean to go stick his head in a trash bucket?"

"You don't have to put it quite like that. But yeah, tell him to haul in some trash, get some research students onto it. Get himself informed."

"Yeah well, he'd better get with it on his computer. More and more students just talk through their computers. Stick his head in a modem." She jumped up and came over to look in the shopping bag, wrestling out the salsa and chips she had bought. "I'm starved."

"How about opening us a couple of beers, kiddo," I tossed at her as I stuffed more kindling on the reluctant flames. It was then, as I turned that I noticed Gem's picture gone from the wall.

"Sure thing, hon." She winked at me, relaxing a little as she got the bottle opener from a hook above the sink. "But you shouldn't serve alcohol to a minor."

"Oh dear, I forgot about that. It used to be eighteen when I was eighteen. Sorry, I didn't buy anything else." I filled a pot with water and put it on the stove.

"I won't tell."

"Sure, great. Look, would you just talk to Cooper, and tell her you'll talk to the Dean soon, as in tomorrow."

"Aye aye, Capt'n."

I shot her a dirty look as I took a long swig of the cold stuff and smacked my lips. "You might want to remind the Dean that you did not name anyone in your article about the rape—victim or rapist."

She nodded. "Sounds like legal advice."

I shrugged one shoulder and poked the fire again, having noted that Gem's photo lay on the coffee table next to Viv's lap-top. "You may also want to try and reach your friend again, let her know what's going on. If this boy has gotten some pressure now, she may feel more like pressing charges."

"I doubt it, but I'll see what I can do."

"Grab a knife, come help me peel these spuds."

Nine

On the phone again with Gem. Oh, it was becoming a nasty habit. That after getting her 'voice-mail' three times. Okay, so the first time I said, "Just checking to see how many birds you wanted in your pie." Next time I said, "A bushel and a peck" By the third time after I had seen to the horses, mucked the stalls and called Viv to be on hand, I said irritably, "This bird's tired of singing, and has flown the coop."

There, I guess I told her.

And I was only calling her to hear her sweet voice on the line before handing the receiver over to Viv so they could discuss the poster. I was also getting antsy to leave, first for the bank to show Viv Elsa's painting, then to work on my stone wall before chores again. Lorraine was gone, of course, back to her job as a school counselor.

Finally I just left Viv in the living room to work on her essays due by the end of the week while I went to change into my steel-toed work boots and load up my truck tool chest with the heavy chains I'd be needing for the day. By the time I got back Viv was talking to Gem in earnest; she looked up at me with those eyes lit up.

She motioned me over, "Listen to this—she's here, hang on a minute." Then to me, "The other fraternities are putting pressure on Joker's brothers to do an in-house investigation and clear up his name and their image. Apparently Joker Sr. did indeed get informed. The poster worked! Big daddy wants his kid's name cleared up, except because of the poster the police got a search warrant and found Joker's gun which was the one that fired the bullet into my car! A gun his dad gave him! For Christmas probably, along with his conspicuous red Mustang."

"Wait a minute," I interrupted her enthusiastic outpouring, "this isn't about rape anymore. This is Joker getting heat for shooting at your car."

She shrugged. "So, it's a start." Then she went back to saying "mm-hmm, mm-hmm," to whatever Gem was saying to her. I paced but I didn't want to get on an extension so badly as to tromp upstairs into Taylor and Lorraine's bedroom. I never went up there except to check on frozen pipes (once) or on mouse traps in the fall (once too many times).

Viv was talking to me again, "Uh-oh. Senior is flying up in his helicopter to post bail for his son."

"He was arrested then?"

She nodded. "But something stupid like discharging a weapon recklessly. I may have to go back down at this rate."

"Now?"

She shook her head at me, listening to Gem, then, "It all depends what happens next. She'll call back. She wants to talk to you."

"Hi Gem," I said flatly. "Where will I be?—we were going out for a while…this evening. Okay we'll hang out here and watch a video or something."

She sounded tired. "Look, the police down here want to know where Viv is. Natalie who has kindly taken on her legal representation and I stalled them because she isn't a suspect. They say it's a safety thing—because she was a perpetrator as well as a victim. We say it's a control thing. I said she was in a safe-house. I think it's absolutely essential that no one down here knows where she is."

She'd brought Natalie into it, hm?—her gorgeous lawyer friend I had taken an instant dislike to the one time we'd been in the same room. A threat?—you bet. All in *my head*, Gem like to says. I rallied to the moment. "Why should they have to, honestly?"

"Exactly. But they insist she may be needed for a statement. Obviously Natalie knows where she is so that makes them fairly happy. But they still want you to let the police know where she is."

"Forget it. I don't touch police with a ten foot pole, you know that damn well."

"Baby, don't you think I know that? I was thinking more about your town constable."

"Ah." She was referring to Elwyn who was also the dog catcher. We first met after I had managed to shut two loose dogs in the barn once till he could come get them—two beautiful house dogs who had killed a few sheep on a nearby farm. Perfect. I said, "If I have to let someone know, Elwyn's the one. I guess I can deal with that."

"Okay. Nat will go by that then."

Nat? She was calling her Nat?

"Also, I've asked Viv to contact her friend to come forward."

"But—"

"Now don't you start too. Look, it's been a real drag down here. Please keep those birds in the pie—I want to hear them sing."

How could I resist that plea in her voice? "You can count on it, dear."

We hung up and I called up Elwyn but only got his machine: 'Out chasin' dogs and lead feet. Keep your dog on your prop-erty and observe the speed limit. Thank you,' his voice said in broad Vermont.

"Come on, Viv. Enough of all this. Let's get rolling." I motioned her out from under her books on the couch.

She rose more lazy than studious as she mumbled, "Right behind you, Capt'n."

Our moods definitely brightened as we headed to town and got to the business of the day though thoughts of Gem lingered in the back of my mind. Sure, Viv and I could filter out our morning's most personal news broadcast, but Gem was in the thick of it. I was glad she would be off for the summer even if it did mean no income for her. Sublet her apartment and she'd do fine on the farm with me. It would be quite the experiment living together for eight weeks. Had we ever done more than three?

While we drove I told Viv a bit about Flo who was the great personal curator of Elsa's one local painting. Long in the banking business, she was also on the Board of Directors of the local gallery. At Elsa's first major local show she'd said, "Oh, this one's going to go big time." I remember being taken aback. We all saw ourselves as struggling artists, Spence with her welding torch, always on the look out for old copper water pipes; Willa with clay—oh and that big struggle she had getting an out-door kiln together; Kite with plants; Elsa with oils; Rune with weed—no, her real medium was 'needle-point' on screens—she wove and sewed all kinds of things like wire or string into window screening, determined to make lasting, basic home decor because everybody used screens, right?; then me with stone; Kristy with her body—no, no, no, I mean fabric, costuming; Mel with her hands on muscle—she liked practicing on bread dough which had a great side effect for the rest of us at meals. And we were all taking part in some grand experiment, supporting each other and our collective independence on the land.

So, when Flo said this about Elsa, I thought, oh hell, and the rest of us are just screwing around, mere pretenders, because I knew she was right. After all, I hadn't walked into the dilapidated farmhouse demanding my room double as a studio with northern light. (Oh yeah, I mean, I did get the small, northwest bedroom with a teeny tiny window upstairs so I shouldn't complain but I couldn't sculpt there, now could I?) It came down to Elsa thinking big, painting big, demanding space, demanding shows that involved renting a closed moving van and enthusiastic volunteers.

One of the reasons I got involved with stonework had to do with a significant day when I sat on the rubble of the old barn foundation. I'm sure I was high. And those rocks were humming, buzzing, vibrating something, maybe the sunshine, maybe the garter snakes lazing in and out. I stood up and began to roll some aside. Someone carted these here, I thought, someone piled them in order to hold up a barn. And there they were again, slowly inching apart, tumbling into the disarray of natural order. But of course! This was it, *this was it.* And I began my first project of banking up the front lawn and making a terrace wall. Kite was especially supportive. And I have helped her here and there, got a paycheck here and there in her current business. You get paid for labor not for the piece. Only Elsa gets paid a thousand or more for a painting, but I suppose for the cost of material and time, it comes out to the same, if not less. I think her loft studio in New York is a lot more humble than the birthing room of the old farmhouse at Blue Corn. And how the hell she gets her paintings out beats me.

Okay, so all this I was explaining to Viv on our way to town as I anticipated Elsa's canvas again. It had been years since I had gone to see it, but maybe I was ready now. Maybe it wouldn't hurt.

I gave a sigh of relief to find Flo still at the bank.

"Well grrrls, I haven't been laid off…yet," she said with her usual no-nonsense manner, "but just because I survived the last merger doesn't mean I'll make it though this one. The cuts this time will be deep. So it could be a matter of days and I could be out."

I hesitated to offer any words of encouragement such as, she had been so effective as personnel manager all this time, they'd be crazy to let her go. She had already made it plain the last time that preferences in management styles change. Instead I said lamely, "I brought Viv here to see the painting before that goes."

She sighed. "Yeah, good thing. They already had an art appraiser in taking stock. Has the painting gone up in value or what?— almost double, triple! I'd make a stab at trying to take it with me, but I don't think my severance pay would cover the bid. I'm afraid there's no telling what will happen to this Elsa Matthau." She gave a slight wink because she was really very proud that she ever got one of Elsa's paintings as a bank acquisition. "But I'm damn sure going to try and keep track of where it goes. I fought for it to stay the last time when they wanted it out of the lobby, had it brought to this floor. But it just represents money—well, good money now that her name has accumulated such respect. An early Matthau pastoral. It will be just as valuable in storage."

She left her desk to escort us down a hallway to a sedate waiting area with vaulted ceiling, high walls and high-set windows. Perfect gallery.

"Well there it is, Viv," I nodded up to the expanse of wall. "It still has some distance here but it did better in the big lobby for viewing."

She looked up at the large canvas in silence for a few minutes, then walked over to take a seat on a small couch, leaning back.

"Gotta go," said Flo. "Enjoy."

I sat down next to Viv, scrunching down in the seat as she did, my head well supported by cushions.

"It's not as I imagined it."

I looked up at the picture sentimentally. I couldn't just see it as a view of a wide, plowed field with figures bent over the furrows. In the foreground a woman sat leaning on her straight, right arm next to a water bucket, facing away from the viewer, her left hand holding up a dipper. Beyond her were two figures, bare backs. One might have assumed they were young men. But the red splash in the back pocket of the first could only signify Spence to me in her Amish pants and with her trademark bandanna. And the other, with a burlap pouch slung from her shoulder, could only be Rune working bare-breasted as usual. In the distance three figures clustered around a tractor. It was Willa in the seat, Kite and I looking into the engine. Mel was not as obvious in this painting. It was her turn in the kitchen that day, and she stood, a small figure, in the doorway of the distant house.

The biggest impression one got was of the expanse of earth—moist, well-worked loam, and the distant hills in new spring green. Come to think of it, the season was May, just like it was now; the golden light suggested a long, bright afternoon. Hot even, because of the lack of clothing.

"What did you imagine?" I asked quietly.

"Well, a nude woman for one thing. From what Kite said about Kristy—with boobs. But her boobs aren't showing at all."

"Well, there's a suggestion just below her armpit."

"Yeah, but that's not the focus. She is looking where we should be looking, at the two figures just beyond her."

"Most of her others in this series have Kristy front or side view. And because she is turned away in this one is why it can be in the bank."

"It's kind of odd, a nude in a field. Well, I see she is sitting on a garment of some sort, so she's not right in the dirt. And her hair is back in a kerchief, evoking another era. Except for the tractor you'd think we were in the 1800s. It should be a horse."

"Yes, it should be a horse!"

"What are they doing?"

"Planting rows of corn."

"By hand?"

"We did many measured, small plots of different varieties, rotational, so that the supply of corn would last over some weeks for continuous picking. Yeah, it was tedious and we did have a planter that you pushed on wheels. But somehow we got a better job done this way. A bit at a time."

"What's with the tractor?"

"We had almost finished spreading compost and the engine

stalled. Dirt in the fuel filter. I was learning about the tractor from Kite and Willa. Kite had learned how to fix it with help from her cousin—times when we'd all conveniently be scarce...well, except for Willa. Good ol' Willa. So, since I was so stupid as to be as sepa-ratist as I was, I thought I'd better pay attention to Kite when I had a chance. Anyway, this is a composite from quick sketches Elsa did sitting on a rock in the pasture above. The rock that was the center point of my calendar. Usually we were all out there sweating it together."

"That's a meager water bucket. No wonder she's sitting there, tired out from hauling water."

"It's for us to drink! She's getting a drink."

"By stripping and sitting nude. Hm. Well, I have to say I do like the texture of the painting, how the earth colors bleed into the can-vas. You can feel the moisture. And the figures, well they are nice—those three backs in a row."

"Yes, Elsa did like backs, especially those three."

She shrugged. "But, I feel cheated. If I didn't know what I know, I'd think a man did it. It still feels very male. The fact of a nude in the foreground. Why can't we just have workers? I mean, the field is so beautiful—I don't need a nude in it! I think I see what Kite meant about Elsa's use of Kristy, like she couldn't get past her."

"But you're absolutely right!" I nodded. "Elsa definitely had a thing for her. Now in this series, there are five paintings, yes, and they all feature a nude woman in the foreground. But, to be fair, most of Elsa's paintings are indeed landscapes. They have sold well. She has good technique with thin coats of paint washing in, blend-ing, building up. But these—I don't know, she was definitely push-ing some boundaries because these are what started to get her name said in hushed tones. And maybe she did use Kristy as the ticket...or the match to the tinder."

"So male." Viv said in disgust, sinking lower into the couch.

"Hm. Knowing Elsa, it's hard for me to see it that way. I had always thought of what she did here as a reversal. Because ulti-mately, viewers would understand that these are women working on their land. It's one of those things that you have to look at again. Dykes who have seen the painting gasp in delight to see images of themselves. Right here in the bank. It's a riot. I mean, it's kind of a legend already that this painting is here. Women come from all over to see it. Flo says she could always spot the pilgrims in the lobby. And the one advantage of having moved it up here is that she can see who comes and chat them up. And we all have a bit more pri-vacy for the viewing. She had to notify everybody of the move in the statewide lesbian newsletter, and she sent word to as many news-papers as possible—like *Sojourner* and all. I mean, the very image in its invisibility is our invisibility, its revelation is our revelation. That's not just a nude woman up there. That is a woman-identified-woman. She isn't gazing at two boys or distant male figures around a tractor. She's looking at the rest of her collective. And that teeny tiny figure there, that smudge of blue bending over to look inside the tractor is my great claim to immortality." I looked over at her as she took careful stock of my words in her continued inspection of the canvas. I didn't expand on the fact of my happiness that Rune was a prominent figure, that it always gave me shivers to come and see Rune again here. I nudged Viv. "Go see what the title is on that little sign."

She hauled herself out of the soft cushions and made her way over. *"Women in the Field."*

"Yup. Not 'woman' but 'women.' Flo says she has actually heard people puzzle over that one—some of the three-piece suit types who walk through here for their meetings. They're drawn to that figure of Kristy, sure. Then they're stumped, though there have been the jokers who try and peek behind the canvas to see if Spence or Rune have breasts. Hardy-har-har." I stretched my limbs and yawned before hoisting myself to my feet. That was a dangerously comfortable couch—I knew I could take a nap in it without even knowing what had come over me.

"Hardy-har," Viv snorted in chorus. "Jokers, yeah we know about *jokers*. Well, I still don't like the fact that they see her as a bimbo, or fertility goddess."

"Ah well, the artist can't dictate what the viewer will get out of the work."

"But she can! I think she damn well can. And she still shouldn't have used Kristy like that in a very traditional male way. She could have worn clothing just as effectively. What about the one going into the Women's Museum? What's that one like?" Viv asked as we made out way slowly to the elevator. We couldn't say good-bye to Flo because she was totally involved in something, but even in mid-sentence she gave us a wink.

"In that one we're picking corn, coming down the rows. So it feels very lush and tropical. What we'd call the Torrid Zone because it was such hot work there in late August you could never believe you'd ever see snow again. She really got into the feel of the green corn leaves just turning to yellow, the light and shadow, the heat. Kristy is in the foreground to the left like this one, except she is standing, front view, just coming out of the corn row with a basket. I think Mel is in the next row over, a side view wearing a sarong around her waist. When she still used to cut her hair really short."

Viv's eyebrows went up at that. "And bare-breasted, right?"

"Right."

"Shades of Gauguin in Tahiti…"

I said nothing.

"Huh…I think I shall have to interview this Elsa someday. What about Kristy—where is she now?"

"Let's see, last I heard she had moved to San Francisco. School. Costume design, I think, though maybe she's working by now. She always did love clothing, all kinds of get-ups, the trappings and trimmings."

"And yet she's always naked in the paintings? *Too* much." Viv gave a sharp nod of the head so that her hair flounced.

"She was Elsa's model. That's how they met. That was the basis of their relationship. Her nakedness was costume. The long dark hair—a wig. She liked being in the paintings though ultimately, yes, she did want to be free of Elsa. And she did leave. She went back to the city and modeled all over again for a long time—for both female and male artists. But she was only a star in Elsa's paintings. That's where her fame will endure. There is a whole series of smaller oils that are of her too."

"Well, I hope she gets some kinda royalties." On that irritated note we found my truck in the parking lot. Damn, it had a ticket. I always forgot about the heavy meter patrol in this upscale town, the dense parking. We hadn't been gone that long. I was getting to be like an old-timer, refusing to acknowledge that parking meters had swarmed in to stay ten years ago even on side-streets, and that even my chosen haunts were getting either scarce or metered.

I was feeling pissy, definitely pissy. As much as I thought Viv's perspective interesting, and true, it really irritated me. Like Fortissima with ears back, I wanted to bite her.

Anyway, I guess we had all been too sacrosanct about Elsa. Blinded. Someone I was real proud of in an awfully sentimental way was getting knocked down by an upstart out of the blue, and with a totally heretical criticism.

"Have you ever had reunions?" Viv asked as I stuck a couple of bucks in the ticket envelope, looking around for one of those red ticket bins so conveniently placed all around town. And which I could never find.

"Reunions. You mean as though we were a high school or college?"

"Yeah, why not? Do you think you could get everyone back together?" She made it sound like a simple, obvious plan.

"You're kinda talking along the line of getting the Beatles back together. Sometimes things are just over. Like certain love affairs. Finis."

"I dunno. I just thought it would be neat to get you all in the same room. Bound to be old jokes and memories. It would be neat."

"Dream on, kiddo. Everyone in the parlor: was it Elsa in the studio with her paint brush, or was it Spence in the back room with her vibrator?"

Viv's eyebrows flew up. "Spence had a vibrator?"

"You bet. I always relied on Spence to be at the forefront of everything, bring home the latest."

"She let you see it?"

"She always left it in the top drawer for anyone to use."

"No way!"

I braced myself for the next question. Sure enough.

"And did you...borrow it?"

"Some secrets a girl just has to keep." I snapped.

"Oh I had one," she said with a limp-wristed flick of her hand. "Someone stole it from my room. I think it was this girl I got it on with a few times, and it was in my bed and she got all excited. I think it's the vibrator she wanted, not me. Kinda tough on the old ego, eh?"

"Well..." I said for lack of any astute comment, driving out of town.

She found a remark for me. "Yeah, kinda pisses you off cause first, she doesn't want to see you any more and second, she's taken your means of consolation. What a bust."

But I was thinking of Spence, the big bad butch.

She may have been scrawny but she had presence all right. Like the time I was up in my hot airless room on a muggy July day, the first summer. I had been weeding and mulching for hours, taken a shower and retired to my room to be alone, a small fan in my window blowing air across my nearly naked body. I was wearing my pokadot boxer shorts, lying on my cinder block, plywood and foam mattress of a bed, reading.

"Ah, there you—wow, look at them *melons*!" All of a sudden this voice booms out, and there's Spence leaning, no leering, in my doorway, still filthy in her sweaty, grease-stained tank top and cut-offs. She and Rune had been working on the tractor, putting in a new carburetor.

Taken completely off-guard, I hurled my book at her. It hit her in the belly then dropped at her feet.

"Ooh, is that an *invitation*?" She said, pretending to dust herself off.

I retorted, "Spence, for crying out loud, you've seen my breasts a hundred times over."

"Not lying down!"

And now since I felt thoroughly exposed without my book, I had to hold up an imaginary one. Licking my finger I turned an invisible page, looking at her over the top. "You know perfectly well

I am waiting for true love."

"What a waste." She faked a bored yawn, scratching herself under her tits before she wheeled around to leave, muttering over her shoulder, "Missing out on a lot of fun."

I rose and stalked grumpily to retrieve my book. "I can wait."

Ten

Don't that beat all if Elwyn wasn't right on the spot when I rolled up for my Stintson job, chatting up old man 'Stint' who was waiting for me with his tractor. As tall and stooped as Stint was, Elwyn was short, square and straight-up, even though he was leaning against the big rear tractor wheel, arms cross over his chest, his beer belly hanging out the front of his red-checkered shirt just a little. It wasn't a bad paunch the way beer-bellies went in these parts. Maybe it was that he was more barrel-chested.

With a three-day-old beard, crinkles around his smiling eyes, he greeted me with a slight tip to his greasy old, leather cap that looked like he'd picked it up off the road after somebody ran over it. Or maybe he was adjusting it.

I unloaded my first chain without saying anything as Viv jumped in the back of the pickup to keep the tool chest lid up for me. I dragged the chain over to the tractor. Stint and I were going to pull up some large slabs of rock that had slipped way down the nearby bank to the edge of the river. The river had probably put them there in the first place but we hadn't been the first to pull them up the bank for use in a wall. In fact we were fixing the wall that ran at the crest of the bank from his house up to and along the road, finishing at an ancient maple way past its prime, and more like a relic now. I had seen the old photos of the place, back when the main road was still a dirt track and all the hills around still clear-cut, overgrazed sheep pasture. The majestic maple there, and the neatest wall. We wanted to fix it to match the photo again though the maple looked as though it were sighing over the whole idea.

He had wanted to fix the wall all his life, Stint had said, and had done a bit here and there but never seemed to have the time. And now he was too old to do all the lifting. Oh, he would never have considered me seriously for the job if he hadn't seen what I had done over at Selma Treetor's place. He was skeptical when we began, but over the summer—because we worked at it slowly when we could—I think he came to appreciate the fact that I knew what I was doing with my crowbars and chains. Maybe my enthusiasm was catching—I made a point of making plenty of time to work on it, eager for his stories and all that. A job that took its own time. Building stone walls—it's a people job really.

"Wahl," said Elwyn, not budging a bit, "looks like you brought your sis-tah along, a regular family outing."

"Must be." I grinned broadly and let it go at that, pointing for Viv to lay out her end of the heavy chain so it went down the bank. I hitched my end to the tractor and instructed her, "We'll need the other one too. Stint, maybe you could check out where best to wrap the chain around the rock. I may have to pick it up a bit. Watch out there for that moss."

"How come?" asked Viv.

"I don't want to scrape it off. Moss takes a long time to grow. When the stone is in place, it always makes the wall look like its been there a long time."

"Really? That's important to you?"

"Absolutely. My one ambition in life is to see moss on all the walls I build." I marched up the bank again, hoping to get a few words with Elwyn alone.

"Wahl, must be going anyways," Elwyn adjusted his greasy old hat again and walked towards his truck.

"Say, Elwyn, I need your advice on a matter," I said hurriedly, quietly.

"You do, huh?" He stroked his bristle as he opened the door which squeaked on its hinges.

"Yeah, kinda delicate. You see, my sister over there—well, I'm trying to help her out, keep her in a safe place. Some guy took a shot into her car...no, no, she wasn't in it at the time—down at school, see."

"Not her boyfriend then?" He looked like he'd need real convincing to the contrary.

"No, no. Some guy who raped a friend of hers, and she confronted him. No proof he was the one, that is, the police don't know who it was for a fact. Anyway, the police down there have been putting some pressure to know where she is. Her lawyer has to have an official contact up here. And that's where you come in."

"Outta state then?"

"Yeah. They would be happy if I had someone local aware of the matter—"

"Not the state police? They should know."

"No, no!—just in case they need a statement. She said he just did it to scare her—he's not going to bother her, really. It's not that...I'd rather you were the contact than the state police."

He looked at me and nodded. "Not worried about her then? Lorraine got a CB up there on the hill?"

I shook my head.

"Too bad. I prefer the radio." Reaching into his truck, he pulled out a phone, "But I just got me a cellu-lar though. Call me anytime.

Don't have to leave messages on the machine. I'm round the clock as of today. Here's the number." He handed me a small, handwritten card.

"Gee, Elwyn, I don't believe it. Weren't you against that new tower coming in at town meeting?"

He shrugged. "Got voted down, didn't it? Tower's up for all them Interstate folks passing through. Not doing me any good fretting over the spoiled scenery. There'll be one on every hill before we know't. People don't seem to mind all them satellite dishes and phone towers. You can reach me any time."

"Thanks, Elwyn."

"Sure he's not a boyfriend? Nothing do-mestic?"

I shook my head. He spent many an hour on his own time settling disputes in the home before they exploded…and plenty after the fact too.

"Awlright then." He adjusted his hat at me as he drove off, and I went loping back to my pickup for my heavy crowbar, some serious rock moving to do. I wanted to get three great slabs up and in place today. Oof, urk. That would make me happy. I most certainly didn't think I'd ever need him.

* * *

We were sitting around the Torrid Zone that evening, rain having moved in. I was smoking my pipe and reading the newspaper, my feet up, Hecate on my lap. What I call bliss.

But I noticed I didn't have a happy camper in Viv. She was clicking her ballpoint pen. A notebook on her lap, seated in the rocker next to me, the gas lamp on the three-legged stool between us.

"What are you working on?" I queried.

She sighed, "Still on his ten page essay for my class in Capitalism, Government and Unions, on a hypothetical union's strategies for negotiation. I'm used to working with music."

"What, those peepers singing in the bog out there not enough for you?" I tilted back in my chair so that I could feel Hecate's claws dig slowly into my thighs. I liked that—one of my sick things. As I came forward she retracted, her ears still back even though her eyes were closed. "Listen, listen, hear that tree frog just come in? I don't know, how can you beat that?" But then she hadn't been up here in all the stillness of a stark winter in the country.

She nodded her exaggerated way. "Yeah, it's cool. Guess I'm just in the mood for something else, okay?"

"Say, I have music here, if you want. See those shoe boxes on the bottom shelf?—full of tapes. Take a look-see, be my guest. I'll warn you—it's strictly archival—all those are from Blue Corn."

"You haven't listened to anything since?"

"Not much." What I meant was that it would have been unbearable.

She went over and brought a couple of boxes back, her curiosity piqued enough she couldn't hide it behind her careless motions as she sat down again.

"See, Willa and Spence came with boxes and boxes of LPs. I mean, I was shocked—I'd never seen the likes of it. They built cinder block and board shelves for them all along the living room wall. Willa brought her life's collection—all her Motown 45s from when she was a kid. Music heaven. Living with her was a course in popular music history from the Miracles to the Vandellas, from Stevie Wonder to the Jackson Five. Spence was into the up-and-coming punk rock plus anything in between. She was the first to bring home the B-52s, The Pretenders, Patti Smith. Cyndi Lauper! Also jazz!"

She shrugged. "I like Vega, Crow, DiFranco. But how did they get all that music—I thought you guys were some poor collective. Oh, I know—you used money from dope."

"Not at all! We had agreed when we set up the collective—and this is definitely for your paper—that we each would put in forty hours one way or another towards the farm and feeding ourselves, but beyond that could work part-time or scrounge odd jobs for our own cash—that was supposed to cover clothing and personal items. So, Willa went and got a job as a weekend manager in the best local music store. She had worked her way through art school doing that so it was nothing new for her—an asset for the store having this hip Black, urban kid's influence. So she got to play all kinds of stuff in the store, brought back the demos of what she liked. Spence helped out some weekends and brought stuff home too. So we were rolling in music. Rune and I were like vultures waiting our turn to pick something out, and make our own tapes. I have this collection as a result. Most of it is compilations. Take what you like—you can dub 'em up at the house."

Her eyes brightened as she began to inspect the titles. And I laughed, more like a snort, tilting back in my chair, Hecate's claws slowly digging into me, the farther I tilted. "Remember I told you how I used to go downstairs and put on music when Willa and Spence got a bit too rowdy in their room. Well, they were onto me pretty quick. One time as I was heading down, Willa stuck her head out their door and said, 'How about Armatrading—we'd like that!' Now if she'd said something like that to Rune, Rune would have said, 'Fuck you.' But not me, so damn compliant. I went down and put on some Armatrading. Hey, I like her, so it was no big deal. Got to be though, every time I headed downstairs, I got some request.

"Sometimes everyone else came and joined me in the living room, eyes rolling, groaning. Elsa would say, 'How can anyone work around here with that going on?' But then, she and Kristy could always go to Kristy's room—and they did. But Mel and Kite would come out of their room and hang out on the couch, falling asleep. And Rune and I would light a joint.

"And Willa would laugh at us and say we must have been brought up in suburban white tight-ass houses without upstairs or downstairs neighbors or small apartments full of people. Spence would just sneer at us quietly. Rune said that's because Spence grew up all alone in a mansion. Well, I don't know what she grew up in—

"Hey, she, I mean Willa said it was nothing new for her to live collectively. The only thing that was different was that now she was with a bunch of uptight white girls out in the middle of nowhere. She'd always say it with a laugh, kind of like patting us consolingly on the back. Willa always laughed, got us to laugh at ourselves. She was a tease, but easy, not abrasive like Spence. Totally different styles. You could swallow it from Willa whole and beg for more while Spence left you gagging and sputtering.

"What was it?—yeah…Rune said Spence could put you off while Willa could put you on! As if you had caught Spence in the act of doing something really wild and kinky, but hell if she was going to let you in on it—smirk, smirk. While Willa wore a smile which made you know for sure she had some great secret, something up her sleeve—and wouldn't *you like* to know, baby?

"Then, of course, the owner sold the music store on its upswing—no thanks to Willa, right? New owner took an instant distrust in Willa and laid her off. That's when she and Spence started being sound techies at east coast women's music festivals. They'd be gone at least a month every summer. Left the weeding and hoeing to us. Hey, we got into some music festivals through them, so I'm not complaining…"

The image of Willa flashed through my mind, radiant and proud in those days. Blue Corn's hopeless ending was so miserable it had eclipsed that earlier beauty.

My throat tight, I couldn't talk any more. Never mind music and fucking. Willa was the one who hit on the idea of making corn relish as a way of using what we couldn't sell fresh on the cob for the dinner table. She also perfected the recipe, and it became a real means of farm bread and butter. All because we found a stash of old canning jars with glass tops in the barn. New rubber rings from the general store, and we were in business.

I remembered the time just the two of us were canning relish— no room for more than two for that job. How glowing she looked, pleased that the product was catching on. The general store was carrying it. I must have been basking in her light because as she asked me for a wet sponge from the sink, Willa said, "Ida! See how happy you look right now! Sometimes I see the light in your eyes. Odd times. Like when we were pressing apples. You got all jumpy and I was thinking—what's the big deal, we're just making cider? And sometimes when I think you're going to jump out, you don't at all—not even when that jazz harpist was flirting with you backstage that time, what was her name…?"

"Oh dear," I had said as I scrubbed the sink, definitely avoiding the embarrassing memory. I hadn't even known the harpist was flirting with me.

Willa lined up the sealed jars on the table. "You keep your real self so hidden away, especially around Spence and me. Don't you feel safe?"

I looked up at her, handing over the saucer with its wet sponge, and said half-joking, "You kidding? I can't tell when I'm coming or going."

"Oh hell, we're just wise-asses." But she took me seriously then, really. "We should be more careful of you, huh?"

I fumed, "I'm not fragile."

"Good, because it's so much fun—you set yourself up so well," she teased me with her wide grin.

"That's me, a set-up. The straight for you cut-ups. I don't mind. I think it's more that you and Spence have urban savvy—you know how to deal—and I can't even cut the cards."

"So? Elsa is urban! So is Rune, right outta steel-city, Ohio."

I shrugged. "Rune kids me, but it's different…I do feel safe with her—we're on equal terms while you two blaze away, often at our expense. Rune gets rip-shit all the time, Kristy sulks at you—well, she sulks anyway, and I just go undercover to preserve myself. Besides, I only think of clever come-backs days too late."

"Serious!?—But I want us *all* to be blazing, you know? I remember the very first time I went to Cauldron Books—and I was so excited to be going to this great new women's bookstore. And just as I was about to go in, these two pasty-faced, dumpy, down-in-the-mouth dykes came out, really badly dressed, you know? And it was such a downer I couldn't go in. It was weeks later before I could get myself to go back. Hey, why couldn't I see two glorious amazons come out? Luckily they were there the next time I went. But that's the key, see? We're in on the great secret, right? Lesbians need to be out, dazzling, making everyone jealous! I mean, I see it at the festivals—the women throw off their covers, come alive. It's so great to see—exploring, going to the edge, because they have the space to do it. Not to say they can't also screw each other over without even try-ing.You can't protect yourself too much though. You got to get out, get hurt, beat someone else up too. Fume, spit, get your anger out! Whatever. I just want us to be blazing, chests out, muscled shoulders back, ready for action. And funny! I want us all to be funny and clever. Proud! Faces all lit up. All the fucking time, not just at music festivals, but take it to the streets where people see you. Now that's activism. Otherwise, what's the point, may as well go be a repressed wife in the 'burbs watching TV and ironing, yeah? You say you're slow on comebacks, well then, be the strong silent type! Do it with your *eyes*—give a knowing glance. How about a wicked twinkle. C'mon, you got the eyes for it, girl!"

That was Willa. I wanted to be like her. Don't think I didn't work at walking proud after that! And that's what she wanted from me, from anyone. Willa—she must be very happy about the nineties. Many more happy dykes out and about—Gay Pride Marches, Gay Games and all. I mean, what's the main book we had in the early Blue Corn days, our little bible of language, of image—Monique Wittig—all that raw amazonian anger. Look what we have now— the lesbian library grows. I can't believe the range and choice—a bounty of images, of finding our own way of thinking, of speaking. Glossy magazines portraying us in color. We even have our own comedians now, for chrissake.

* * *

"Look, I found Armatrading...Ida!" Viv cried, snapping me out of my daydreaming, "Come on."

"Sorry—?"

"Let's go up to the house and listen to some old Armatrading that Willa and Spence used to fuck to."

"Oh goddess..." I moaned, hand sliding to cover my eyes and forehead as my head sunk.

"Hatshepsut," she corrected me.

"Fuck you." I tilted forward in my chair, feet smacking the floor, so projecting a miffed Hecate onto the floor. "And I knew you'd capitulate."

"What?"

"Going up to the big house."

"Oh that." She shrugged.

With that we took the boxes of tapes up to the big house to *Walk Under Ladders* with Armatrading.

Eleven

After mucking stalls together, I took Viv up to see Curley's Ledge, the quarry, because I wanted to find some white rocks among the refuse there. Mostly refuse there. Hard to believe it had ever been worked though you could see traces where dynamite had been used to tear apart the granite ledge. What was left was a steep rockface, slightly concave, like a satellite dish, except I always tell Kelsey when I take her there that we're 'tooning intada stahrs.' The reason I liked the place other than all that rock, was how it looked like the ruins of some ancient amphitheater. Maybe even an oracle's temple.

"Listen to the acoustics." I demonstrated for Viv by standing in the center of the dish. "Voices, voices." I whispered, "If I whisper here and you're over there by those rocks, you can here me clear as a bell. Then you answer, see what happens."

Good old Viv, game as Kelsey ever was. She hallooed me and her voice echoed off the rock and bounced around.

"Willa and Spence would love this, wouldn't they?" Viv declared. "Can't you just see a concert here. Camp across there in the old pastures. Have a three day festival. You've got to get them up here."

"Yeah," I said vaguely, handing her a pair of gloves. Conversation stopper in a nutshell—good hard work. We set about looking for whatever white rocks we could find—that we could carry—and put them in the back of my pickup, the two of us lifting together. Oof, urk. I covered them with a tarp against the rain expected overnight, because it's never a good idea to work with wet rocks.

Job done, and seeing as it was sunny and warm in the quarry, I went to find a perch where we could sit awhile as I smoked my pipe and leaned back against warm rockface. Believe me, I like to enjoy my moments of pure laziness, especially after heaving a few rocks around. It sweetens the laziness almost to unbearable. Precisely the kind of torture I like.

Maybe Viv noticed I was relaxed, maybe that's why she said, "Okay, I think it's about time you leveled with me about Rune. What did she do that was so terrible nobody wants to talk about her?"

"I talk about her," I said defensively, puffing on my pipe so I wouldn't lose my moment of bliss.

"You and Kite and Mel just sort of look pained, and change the subject quickly when I ask about her."

I sat in silence for awhile reflecting on whether that was true.

"See, you have that look right now—and she was your best friend, you've said so yourself, but she doesn't come to visit you—"

I snapped, "None of them come to visit me. After we all split, that was it."

"But—"

"Okay, okay. She's dead," I said with more vehemence than I intended. "That's a strand that was severed."

"*Oh*," she said too quietly. "I...I didn't even guess that. I thought she had dealt you a really bad hand or something. That you were all mad at her."

"No, no, not mad at her. Just *sore*. The kind of pain you think has finally gone, then it hits you again. Chronic."

"What of?"

"That's much harder...she was killed. Under mysterious circumstances. The killer has never been found."

I heard her sharp gasp. "When?"

"...The last year...not around here, back in Ohio. She was supposed to come back by summer. Except she had gotten a real good job computerizing her uncle's hardware stores. Computers had replaced dope for her. 'All day and totally high and legal,' she'd say. And it looked like she wasn't so interested in coming back. Meanwhile Kristy left too."

"Why didn't you tell me before—?"

"What, right away? Oh by the way—? Sheesh it's hard enough now. I was waiting for the right moment...but there never is one."

"Can you talk about it? Now, I mean, is now—?"

"Barely. She was found...in the trunk of her car which had been towed from an Interstate rest area because the police thought it was abandoned—flat tire, back window smashed."

"Not because of drugs!" It was a statement, definitely not a question.

"No! No, no," I said in appreciation of that assessment. "Rune wasn't a drug dealer. When we stopped growing it, she stopped selling it. And she wasn't into anything else. You have to understand that weed was a sacred herb to her. The police asked that. It was late at night and she had seen her mother at the hospital and was taking the city by-pass route home. Apparently she had stopped to fix a flat, had opened her trunk to get the jack and spare. Someone came up, and killed her with her own jack—well, the police never found it. Hit her in the head. Stuffed her in the trunk, and removed the license plates. Thing is...the thing I cannot get over—she might have made it if someone had taken her to the hospital but she froze while unconscious with a concussion. Do you see why it's so awful? She was reported missing by her uncle because she didn't show up for work. The car had already been towed away as an abandoned vehicle, so that really screwed up any investigation. Hell—

"And I've had to deal with my own guilt—of encouraging her to go when her mother was so sick with cancer. She was hesitant, and as usual with us, came to me to talk it over. And me saying yes, yes, go, of course you must go.

"See, Rune was super friendly and good with people. She was above all, somehow invincible—someone who could take care of herself. She was savvy, knew when vibes were wrong and didn't stick around anything like that. That's why this was so...so peculiar. And why I'm baffled over and over. And so unsettled. If it could happen to Rune, then, well, it can happen to *any of us*. It unleashes that fear, that unshakable fear of your vulnerability."

"Strange...makes it seem more personal than random. You said she went back to her hometown? And the police couldn't figure it out?"

"You'd think with the plethora of dyke detectives we have these days, someone could get to the bottom of it, don't you? Don't you? Believe me, I've banged my head against the wall many times over it. Unsolved mystery, freeway killer at large...many unexplained homicides...difficult to trace in such an anonymous setting as a freeway or rest stop. Late at night you aren't supposed to stop and fix a flat."

"Did you ever pursue any leads, ask any questions?"

"No, why would I? I'm not a budding P.I.," I hissed too bitterly.

"Come on—just to know?"

"Because I was scared shitless, that's why! I was bone-fucking scared shitless."

"What about her family? Brothers, sisters? I mean, could it have been a family thing?"

I looked at her, stunned. "Touché. Nail on the head. *Bulls-eye*. You want to talk family. We were the family under suspicion. Get it?"

She gulped, "No shit?"

"Believe me they went through any possible personal motives. They interviewed all of us, grilled on both sides, for chrissake. Radical lesbian separatist collective. Had to be it, right? And Spence! They were sure they were onto something there with that bad girl. Like Spence would chase Rune down in Ohio, cause her to have a flat and kill her. We were *all suspects*! Like we'd be carrying ice-picks under our shirts. Detectives descended upon us. Interviewed us all separately, see who they could trip up, who was lying! Kept asking us who 'Isis' was, which one of us was Isis. Apparently Rune had written a note in her pocket calendar—it was found on her body—for the day she died. It was Elsa who got that bit out of the police or we wouldn't have even know that much. She had taken out five hundred bucks from the bank that day. Written 'five hundred dollars, dash, Isis.' No wallet or money on her."

"Never mentioned this person to you? Didn't she ever call or write?"

"She had only been gone since October. She called a few times. Talked about how this job was developing for her. She went to take care of her mother who had to be in and out of the hospital for her cancer treatments. She went to be with her, advocate for her at the hospital. She and her mother were close and all because her father died when she was little. I think she would have stuck around here otherwise. She was making good money, saving it up, threatening to take me traveling with her some day, an Olivia cruise! That's what she wanted to do. She thought it would be such a riot. Take me off in style. Not saving for a rainy day—hey, we were going to the Torrid Zone because of course we'd have to go some place hot, and she was going to pick up hot women all the way there and back. I told her we'd better not share a cabin then. And she'd say, was I kidding, we'd have a suite. But she obviously wasn't going anywhere till after her mother died."

"Has her mother died?"

I shook my head, my lips in a tight, ironic smile. "She went into remission! Rune and I would have taken the cruise by now, I'm sure. Me on a cruise, ah, can you picture that?—only with Rune.

"Anyway, the investigators couldn't shake some feeling about Spence and that our alibis weren't meshing because, hey, we weren't *thinking* about what we were doing when. It was winter and we were all doing separate things, and we weren't so close-knit anymore, to put it mildly. Elsa had gone cityside to see to some gallery shows—as well as to see Kristy who, as I said, had already left us, and Spence had made the trip with her, then split off to do her own thing. Just a couple of days.

"They came back together the day we heard the news. And the police were convinced Spence went out to Ohio somehow because some witness had seen a woman with shaved hair talking to Rune on the day she died. Maybe Rune was *dating*…the Isis in her calendar. Great, so the police see us at the funeral and pick on Spence right away—she'd just gotten a new do in the city—left side of her head shaved. It left a bitter taste to our whole ending, let me tell you. The final blow that sent us scattering. Hell of an ending to Blue Corn. You want talk about reunions!—I don't think so."

"I see," she said, subdued. "I see. But you and Kite and Mel—"

"Yeah, the survivors clinging to the wreckage."

"And yet you grieve for those days."

"Yeah, yeah hell I do. Some sort of lesbian utopia lost, hardy-har—lost in a hurry after almost ten years! I was happy then, well, as happy as I knew how to be...I *believed* in my lesbian family. I was like the lover in a relationship which dissolved in front of me, but I was too attached to recognize that it was over. Rune's death was something we should have been able to rally over, instead it was the last straw." I shrugged, "Hey, just because I wanted it... I thought the three of us left would move to another farm and build again, bring other women in, but it was like we were cursed by then.

"It was Lorraine who told me it was over. Not in so many words, but by giving me another way to be. A place to recover. I'm someone else now. My whole life is completely different, you know? And I've realized, hey, I'm amazed with it—like a cat landing on all four feet somewhere totally unfamiliar after a long tumble. It's just different, that's all."

"She knew all about Rune?"

"Yeah, I cried a lot on her shoulder." I wasn't past wiping my nose on my sleeve now. I laughed to recover my regurgitated pain. "Now she waves good-bye when she leaves and tells me to watch Fortissima for signs of heat. She makes sure I have things to do."

"So do I," Viv said, almost primly. "I give you things to do."

I whacked her on the arm. "Yeah, I'm supposed to keep you out of trouble."

Twelve

Even so, I didn't have to tell Viv everything, did I? About the down side of Blue Corn and its demise. I didn't have to drag her down into that. I didn't have to tell her how we waited for Elsa and Spence to return so we could all (without Kristy) pile into Kite's van and drive out to Ohio, mostly mute and stoic, for the funeral. The funeral. I still can't admit whose.

Rune's older brother, Tom, said we could stay at the house—her mother wanted that. I was the only one allowed to see her mother in the hospital for a short visit.

"I haven't been home…" she choked, shifted, oxygen tubing in her nose, "since. All her things, Ida…all her things are still there. Would you?"

"Of course," I said, holding her hand as I sat close beside her hospital bed, watching the I.V. drip.

"Her personal things…take them with you. You decide."

So we took our sleeping bags and camped in the den that night, glad to be warm, tired after the long drive which we had done non-stop, switching drivers. Spence the most because she was a marathon driver.

So I went to Rune's room. I wanted to vomit. Her bed was unmade the way she had left it the morning of her death. And in the middle of my nausea I wanted to laugh and cry; there in the corner was her pile of dirty clothes. She always did that, had one corner of her room she threw her clothes into. And when the pile was big enough, she'd pick them up and go do laundry. So that's what I did, but I didn't wash them. I put them in her duffel to take home, wash and sort later. I just didn't want to do it yet.

From the bureau and bedside table I picked up her piles of books, pens, a letter I'd sent her, a few items of jewelry she didn't happen to be wearing, and put them in a box I found. Packed the clothes from her closet. The others would poke their heads in the room, see if I wanted help, bring me a drink. But I did the task alone, and it didn't take long. She had left most of her stuff back at Blue Corn, still boxed up in her room.

We didn't talk about death much, Rune and I, no more than anyone does when they're young and full of life. Oh, in a literary way we did, I suppose, but that was in college. By the time we had arrived at Blue Corn, we were advocating 'Life!' as in 'Bless Mother Earth.' None of that death-wish crap brought on by living in patriarchal alienation, right? But I do remember Rune saying once that if she died—I remember she didn't say 'when'—she wanted to be cremated and have her ashes scattered in the field. We were sitting on the back doorstep sharing a joint. I remember how she squinted through smoke on the inhale, gesturing towards the sprouting crop. "Out there, see? Have it fertilize things, at least neutralize the soil acidity, ha-ha! Yeah? Oh, hey, I doubt we'll be here that long, but on some wimmin's land somewhere—won't matter as long as it's wimmin's land. Just so long as I'm not stuck in a box in some hole in the ground in the family plot." And only then, exhaled.

But there she was in a fancy box going into a hole in the ground next to her father whom she hardly had a chance to know. I tried to talk to someone in the family, somebody—not her mother then, she was still too sick in the hospital and sedated because of the shock. It seemed indelicate to approach anyone at that point, but I did stammer something to Tom about how Rune had expressed the wish to have her ashes scattered, and not be stuck, a battered body in a grave. And he looked at me aghast. "Our family doesn't believe in cremation. Besides, it's too late, the arrangements have all been made here."

Too late. Totally caught off guard. Too late to be of help to Rune even in this, her burial. I was so choked I had to leave the graveside service and roam the perimeter of the blasted cemetery, cursing and crying until the others came to find me, put their hands all over me, around me.

We went to the rest area—no facilities—where she had been killed, to stand beside her spirit there, days too late. She wasn't there, no sign that she ever had been. I lit some incense that Willa had had the foresight to bring. Well, she always had a bag full of supplies.

"These are your ashes," I said, saving the ashy stick in my trembling hands as it burned slowly down giving off the sweet smell of lavender. "Good choice, Willa. We'll put it on our cornfield."

We stood, huddled in the bitter cold of that February day gathering the ashes in the ashtray taken from the back seat of the van, flickers of smiles playing on our faces just beneath the disbelief of loss. Bundled in our purples and blues, we were all wearing the knit caps Rune had made for us a few Solstices before. Amazon hats, each trimmed and shaped differently. Except for Spence, bare-headed, new brace of earrings up and down her ears and underdressed in her leather jacket.

A simple thing we did, because we didn't know what else to do before heading home.

"We'll play lots of music, all the stuff she liked," Elsa said, teeth chattering. "Let's party all the way—"

And that's when two police cruisers pulled up, flew into the parking area, no sirens but blue lights flashing, each blocking the access lanes, followed by an unmarked car from which emerged a man and a woman, not in uniform, but buffered against the cold in trim wool coats—no, not trench coats. Both of them approached us, flipping IDs at us, their faces impassive while police stood at a distance, hands on their holsters.

I remember standing there, my jaw chattering uncontrollably, my legs trembling. This was not like being arrested at an anti-nuke demonstration along with fourteen hundred other people. Nor did we have our supportive Vermont neighbors and political allies, much less Kite's buffer zone of family connections.

The man said, "I'm Detective Sergeant Findley. This is Detective Daniels. What are you doing here?"

"Holding a vigil," snapped Spence, immediately our spokesperson as the rest of us stood dumfounded.

"Well, we'd like you to accompany us back to the station for some questions."

"We're on our way back home and it's a long trip," she stated flatly.

"That will have to wait," he said curtly.

"Why? If you want to talk to us, you can reach us there."

"That's true," Detective Daniels cut in smoothly, going woman to woman with Spence, "but it would be better if we could talk to you before you go. We know you were at Renata Bullock's funeral, and that you are from the farm where she lived before coming back here last fall. Now, we'd like to ask some questions, just routine, to help with our investigation."

"But we can't," Kite said frantically, looking around at the rest of us. In our haste we had left without plugging in the electrical wrap on the pipes. "I'm already worried the pipes have frozen. It's supposed to go below zero tonight. We need to get home."

Yeah, we needed to get home; we wanted to be home badly. We still had it then.

"We really have nothing to say," Spence insisted. "Rune, uh, Renata, came here. *Here* is where the problem is. The whole thing is senseless. We have nothing to add."

They just looked at us; moved away to confer. Why did they keep glancing at the rear of the van? Our bumper stickers? What was wrong with those?—LOVE YOUR MOTHER, FARMS NOT ARMS, NO NUKES, our small interlocking woman signs in the rear window, our *Madeleine* political sticker which couldn't mean anything to a non-Vermonter—she was the first woman governor. The vanity plate couldn't possibly be of interest either. Rune had paid for it as a birthday present for Kite: ISIS

"I don't believe this shit," said Willa. "Come on, let's get in and start the car. My ass is freezing."

"I didn't know her last name was Bullock all this time," Kite said as she opened the sliding door. "Did you, Ida?"

"Yeah, way back in the recesses of my brain," I said as I climbed in.

"I thought her last name was Cowan," said Mel coming in behind me.

"Joke. That was her little joke. I remember she refused to go to graduation because she didn't want to hear her name—she was already known simply as Ren to everyone. You can get that by professors but not when it came down to official stuff. Then of course she called herself Rune when she met you all."

Kite came and squeezed next to me. "I just don't believe I never knew."

"C'mon Kite, it wasn't important—she was on wimmin's land. She worked on a cash basis. She reneged on her school loans, never paid taxes."

But Kite was really taken aback. "Renata Bullock is not anyone I know, that's all. Makes you wonder what secrets we all have."

"Oh Kite, I don't think of you by your legal name either!" I protested.

"Yeah, but I deal with it all the time—my mail comes right to the house—"

"That's coz your name wasn't Bullock for chrissake."

"Are they going to let us out or what?" Willa was asking Elsa as they took to the front seats.

Just then Daniels came back. We were throwing sleeping bags over ourselves while we shivered, not from the cold so much as the intensity of the whole ordeal. Elsa was at the wheel, volunteering for the first stretch. Daniels stuck her head in the driver's window. "You can follow us to the station or we can impound the van and take you in the cruisers, hear what I'm sayin'? You choose."

So blunt, so hostile! So unnecessary. Luckily, I guess, Spence wasn't the driver or surely she would have told Daniels to 'Fuck off.'

"Why are you threatening us?" asked Elsa, not about to be strong-armed. "Look, we came to lay a family member to rest. You may not see us as family but that is what we are."

Daniels cocked her head slightly, perhaps to look understanding yet unrelenting. "Surely, you must know, Miss…?"

"My name is Elsa Matthau, but then I bet you know that already."

"Yes, as a matter of fact we do. And you must surely know that

89

in a murder investigation, family is often the very first people we question."

"Then why the theatrics?" Elsa jerked her head in the direction of the cruisers. Lights were still strobing. "Why didn't you talk to us at the funeral parlor?"

"We have reasons we really can't go into here. Now, are you going to come with us?"

"It's not my decision. I have to have consensus." She rolled up the window almost taking the detective's nose off, and turned to us. "Well, you heard the lady. Must know something we don't. Or so it seems."

"We don't have much choice but to cooperate." Willa was working it out for us.

Kite wrung her hands, knuckles white as she leaned, elbows on knees. "I just want to get out of here as soon as we can. It can't take long...can it?"

"What do they *want*?" Spence hissed from behind.

"So. We go?" Elsa looked at each of us.

I waved her on. "Go."

She rolled down the window. "Okay."

She shifted into first and roared onto the freeway as best she could considering we were under escort. Lights still flashing, one cruiser stayed ahead, the unmarked car behind, and the second cruiser in the passing lane.

"God, they really do seem to want us, don't they?" said Willa in a tight voice.

"What's it all about?" I chattered weakly from under the blanket between Kite and Mel who had taken on the role of being extra protective of me. (Maybe my jaws were also shivering because Kite had put her arm about me. I was teetering on the edge of a rocky precipice anyway but with her so close I don't know how I kept my equilibrium—Mel on the other side?) Spence who was sprawled on the rear window-seat where she had intended to rest before taking over the wheel later, simply groaned.

Willa turned around to me. "It doesn't look good. It doesn't look good at all—their investigation, I mean. It means they don't know what the hell happened to Rune."

"But what could we know?" Mel whispered anxiously.

"Fuck," yelled Spence, thrashing around on the back seat. "It's called police harassment. Get used to it. After all we're the lesbo-separatist commune Rune left. They're gonna want to know why? 'Why are you here?'" She mimicked Findley. "Why do you think, asshole? We're visiting the scene of the crime. Isn't that what fucking killers do?" She kicked the side of the van.

"Let's just take it easy," Elsa's quiet voice calmed us. "Come on.

We did what we came to do, let's not let this ruin things more. Find us a tape, Willa. Let them talk to us if they want. It's their time and money."

"No, it's not," Spence fumed, "it's taxpayer money, wasted taxpayer money."

* * *

The only thing I can say positive about the police station is that it was warm. Otherwise it was overwhelming it its starkness, the fluorescent lights blinding. True, we weren't booked, no finger prints or mug shots. But we weren't so dumb as not to know we were being watched, or to think that our van wasn't being pawed through. Thank goddess we weren't dopeheads any more.

There were other things we worried about silently. Our copies of *Lesbian Connection, Maize, off our back*s, *WomanSpirit*, the Judy Grahn, Olga Broumas and Audre Lorde poetry books we'd been reading aloud on the trip.

They gave us coffee from a tray. A woman officer took down basic information on each of us: Full name, address, employment, income.

"Were you ever arrested?"

"Yeah, Seabrook."

"What?"

"Seabrook. A nuclear construction site. 1977."

The dope bust in 1984 completely slipped my mind until later when I was too scared to say anything.

How could we tell them they were looking in the wrong place? All we could do was wait it out. What looked like a couple of derelict men sat on a bench down the hall smoking. Derelict? I realized the officers saw us much the same way.

I was a street person, a drug addict, a thief, a whore. A dyke. I was a murder suspect.

It still hurts beyond words.

Detective Daniels—could you say she was just doing her job? Did she know or even care that she was driving the ultimate wedge into the heart of us? Dividing us? Making us feel unclean even when we had nothing to hide? Almost dykey-looking but not quite, not in her otherwise savvy eyes. Dressed casually—corduroy pants, one of the first polar fleece vests I had ever seen.

They called us in one by one. Wanted to see if we'd corroborate each other's stories. My interrogation session was with Detective Daniels—me, Mel, Kite. Findley took Elsa, Willa and Spence.

"Want some more coffee?" she asked as she sat opposite the table from me. I shook my head. My stomach was already raw from being unable to eat. Why couldn't I get warm?

"Well then, let's begin." The woman officer stood at the door. I saw Daniels shake her head and the cop left. I couldn't help but notice the video camera in the corner. And I knew what the mirror-mirror on the wall was.

Questions, questions: How would you describe your relationship with Renata Bullock, the person you called Rune? How long did you know her? When was the last time you talked to her? Know of anyone who might have had a grudge against her enough to harm her? Was she in any trouble here with anyone? What about drugs? Did she mention any trouble at home? Why is the word 'Isis' on the van's license plate. Does the word or name 'Isis' mean anything to you? Is anyone in your collective nicknamed Isis? Are any of the members of your collective having problems with each other, or any personal problems you know of? Are you in an intimate relationship with anyone in the collective? Do you know why Renata Bullock whom you called Rune, would withdraw five hundred dollars on January the twenty-eighth? Where were you on January the twenty-eighth? Have you been on any trips? Where? Who is the head of household? The leader? Do you know what Joan Spencer was doing in New York? Was Spence, as you call her, was she into drugs?

Rhetorical questions: I can see that you're angry and upset—don't you think we want to see the killer found? Don't you think we want to see justice done?

And that one statement—direct quote as best I can remember: "If anything comes to mind, anything, if you find something that could be of help, please, give me a call, day or night, any time." With these her parting words, she gave me her card.

But where did I put it?

And why do I remember her questions so vividly pounding into me when I can't remember how I answered them? Sullenly, I'm sure. I want to remember precisely.

Rune was my best friend. Best friend. Do you understand? She was the very one who first got me to join her at Blue Corn. I've known…I've…known…her…No one. No one. No one would hurt Rune that I know. I talked to her before Christmas when her mother was going through surgery. *Computers*—she was into computers, not drugs. Isis. Well, she's a goddess. Rune gave it to Kite for a birthday present. Yeah, she got the proper form. They filled it out together. Why Isis?—I don't know…Isis was the Giver of Life. No! I simply don't know. Rune never said *why*. She gave it like a blessing because Kite had bought the van so we could all fit in and go places. No. Nobody went by that name. Problems. Our only problems are whether we'll get enough money in from the farm to pay taxes. We worry about our wood supply. We worry about the ice dams on the roof. The pipes bursting while we sit here. And no, we didn't ask her for money. She was under no obligation to help if she wasn't there. She worked on a cash basis! I'm surprised to hear she even had a bank account. We were stuck at home in a snowstorm. Schools were closed. We weren't plowed out till afternoon. It's a collective! We work by consensus. No, I don't know what Spence does in New York. She likes the city. They're all my intimates! And no, I don't sleep with any of them. Never have. Okay?

That's when I broke down and sobbed. She had to call out to the woman officer to get someone. Kite came to get me, but I didn't want her to touch me. I bit my lower lip and went to sit on the bench again with my face and body turned into the wall.

We waited. Exhausted, uncomfortable. Those bright lights. The hard benches. The cigarette smoke. This was the true mourning of Rune. Our loss of innocence. Our loss.

Why were they keeping us like this? Why not put us in a cell where at least we'd have a bunk? I looked up, bleary eyed. I felt battered. The others waited with me. All except one.

Spence.

We waited for Spence.

Why were they keeping her so long? What could be wrong?

Why was I so cold?

If I began to nod off I'd wake up with the horror of Rune slowly dying in the trunk of her car. Freezing to death—was there any mercy in that?

"Do you think you can talk on the phone?" Elsa's voice broke into me where I huddled.

"What?...Maybe. Why?"

"Could you call Tom and see if we can stay at Rune's again. I know you gave him back the keys today, but we're so beat. I think we need to sleep tonight and drive tomorrow. Kite says if the pipes are frozen, they're frozen."

"Sure." I fumbled in my jeans for a change. "Why are they keeping Spence so long?"

"I don't know, Ida, I don't know. They must be working on her attitude. Willa is a mess."

Trembling, I punched the buttons on the pay phone, biting my lip so I wouldn't cry out of relief when Tom answered, looking for fraternal protection or something.

"Hello?" He seemed far away. Out of reach.

I began to explain.

He cut me off, business-like. "Look, Ida, we know. The police have been here. Under the circumstances you can't possibly expect us...look, if it were just you, Ida...but we just can't—"

"What do you mean? Tom! You and me—we used to play backgammon together! I was Rune's best friend."

"I know, I know, Ida." His tone was barely less cold. "I don't know the others—"

"We came from Vermont!" As if that were a magic formula.

"Look Ida, I can't help you. It's bad enough you were all in the house last night. To think—"

"You think one of us did this? All the way in Vermont?"

"I can't help you, Ida. I really must hang up."

Shit. I hung up numbly, turned slowly to walk back to the others. I had gloves on, two sweatshirts, long underwear under my jeans, boots with felt liners, and I shivered while sweat trickled between my breast, down my spine.

Just then Spence flung herself out of an interrogation room, catching herself on the opposite wall. At first I thought she had been shoved. But it was her own energy like the stored energy Kite always warned us about in machinery—I thought I finally understood it. I thought I would see anger blazing in her eyes but she was pale. Like the death I felt in me.

She was heading for the door. Rallying, we all fell in behind her even as an officer told us we could go. I could hear Findley's voice bringing up the rear, "Directly home, you hear me?"

Tom's voice still in my ears, I turned around stupidly, "You mean Blue Corn?"

As we walked out of the station, camera lights flashed in our faces. A hail of questions hit us like bullets from a firing squad. Pushing reporters out of the way, Spence led us to the van and jumped into the driver's seat.

The void of our silence on that fourteen hour trip was filled with music on the tape deck for the sole purpose of keeping each driver going. A lot of blues, Willa chose, and gospel she'd never shared with us before.

Our fear pursued us. Every time we stopped for gas and snacks we wondered if cops would descend. Didn't we see that blue sedan at the last stop? We didn't think we'd get home.

* * *

Someone had been in Blue Corn when we arrived around noon the next day. This was obvious. Not ransacked, just things moved. Drawers left open. You could tell. It was like having been burgled. We would have thought so under other circumstances. Our cars too. The door of my old pickup wasn't quite latched, leaving the cab light on. Luckily the engine started up fine.

The only reason the pipes weren't frozen is because someone had used the toilet and didn't know about jiggling the handle to stop the water from running.

We couldn't find anything missing. Nothing we could deter-

94

mine. If anything had been lifted it would have been fingerprints. Like with the coffee cups offered to us from a tray and taken back with a tray almost before the last sip.

Go for it, I remember saying to myself. Take our fingerprints. By the way, did you get Rune's too, over here at the foot of the stairs? There where her sooty hand print is left on the wall and I said she was next to repaint the kitchen?

"They can't come in here without a search warrant!" Kite fumed.

"What are they looking for?" Mel whined.

"Oh yes, they can," Spence growled. "They can do anything they want. Don't think they didn't plant something so they can bring a search warrant for it any time they damn well feel like it."

"Don't start getting paranoid here," Elsa cut through calmly, laying a fire in the Torrid Zone. "We've got to stay calm."

"I thought I left this short of shit in the city," Willa said, putting a blanket around me, pulling off my boots, bringing a tub of hot water for our feet.

I said nothing.

That evening after bathing and fitful attempts at rest, we all gathered for supper—something Mel had thawed out and heated. Spread on the table was the local afternoon newspaper, opened to the page that said: 'Lesbian commune questioned by police in suspected link to the murder of a member in Ohio.' The picture was only recognizable to us because of our distinctive hats as we poured out of the station, hands up against the flashes. The last line read, 'No arrests were made.'

"Shaming us in our own community for no reason," Willa crumpled the page in disgust.

Kite paced. "How could that get in the paper faster than it took to get home?"

"Goddammit, why did I go to New York? Why then? Why, why?" Spence lamented.

"Why *did* you go to New York?" Mel asked, serving the slop up. "I mean, you might as well tell us what you told them. Why should they have *all the dirt* on us? Why don't we all just tell each other what we told them?"

We huddled around the kitchen table. We were having a really hard time eating Mel's notorious, undercooked black bean stew.

"So, you want to know what I was doing?" Spence looked all around at us. "You want to know why there's a hole in our perfect set of alibis, and why I won't say what I was doing? If they want to try and pin something on me, let them. They can't—"

"Spence," Willa tried to calm her, "forget it. It doesn't matter what you were doing—"

"No, I don't *mind* telling you all! Findley wanted to know who I saw, where I went, down to the hour and minute. Okay, so I went to the bars—all the women's bars and some of the gays too. Okay, so that'll take five minutes to check out. I picked up somebody, okay? Okay? Does that bother you? Or rather she picked me up—we went to her house. I was there that night and all the next day and night. Oh, big shock, isn't it? Well, I can't get any kicks here, can I? Real kicks is what I'm talking about—stuff you don't want to know about or care to do at home, well not with this bunch listening in. But Findley didn't think it was enough. Why is that? Someone—" She swept her index finger like a knife at us and collectively, we flinched—"*someone* here said there was bad blood between me and Rune. Well, thanks a lot! He wanted to break me down, get me to confess. 'Come on, we know where you really were and how you did it. Why don't you just get this over with. Were you into kicks with her too?' Leaning on the back of my chair and breathing down my neck! 'What was it, sex or drugs or both, hm? You're through, we can throw the book at you.' So I thought, let them, I gotta see this to believe it. Then Daniels came in and asked it all over again. What, the soft touch was going to do it? So, you know what that bitch—" (Hey, we never used that term in our household, cardinal rule—you did not say 'bitch', you did not say 'whore', you did not say 'bastard'…no such words in the matriarchy) "—that fucking bitch wanted to know?" Spence punctuated each sentence with a finger jabbing the table horribly close to the hole made by Kristy in an outburst before she left, "Who was I with? Name, address and presto, I'd have my alibi, and all my 'friends' waiting out in the hall could go home too. Come on, is that so hard? You bet it is! You think I'm gonna tell a fucking detective who I slept with and where she lives? Get real. You think I'm gonna do that to some innocent sister who gave me a good time. Jesus-the-fucking-Christ. That's what she wanted from me. And so, ladies, I don't have a fucking alibi. And until they find some other reason to strike me from the list, I am a fucking prime suspect! And they'd like to nail me real bad. How do you like that?"

"Come on, get ahold of yourself." Willa's voice rose. "You did good. You know I don't care. I mean, I don't." She turned to the rest of us, "Spence and I have an agreement." Turning back to Spence, "No one's blaming you, okay?"

"Yes, you are. You are all looking at me and there's this...this smell of doubt. I can see it—"

"No way," I blurted adamantly. "No way! We're all fucking suspects." (I picked up her language real fast.) "The four of us were stuck here in a snowstorm. What kind of alibi is that? Maybe we all aided and abetted each other. Until they find the killer, that's what we'll be, suspects. Because we're lesbians and our van has 'Isis' on it. You just always startle us, Spence. That's nothing new. This is all just too much all at once, all mixed up. You would never tell us what you do in New York under normal, everyday circumstances. And we'd never ask. We might hazard a guess. We aren't stupid. But this now, since…well, it's like a poison…Rune's death just ripples out, affecting us. Let's be careful with each other."

"Hear, hear," Elsa said as she cleared away the uneaten servings. I could hear her scraping the plates into the compost.

And Mel began sobbing over how we'd wasted good food that was supposed to nourish us when Spence sprang up from her chair, kicking it over with a sharp crash, "Well, I've had it, babes, with the nourishment. It's over for us, see? You simply don't understand! I'm leaving as soon as I get all my stuff packed. I *do* not *want* to *be* here any more. Waiting for the other shoe to drop.You know what they told me? Better not try and vanish or we'll really come after you. Did anyone say that to you, Ida? I will not be harassed, I tell you. I'm going, what they call, Underground. Better believe it."

"Spence!" Willa called to her, a command that would have stopped her in her tracks before, but something had broken in Spence. Her heart? They went to their room. Door slammed, but no thumps or bumps. Deathly still.

Mel, still sobbing, ran to her room, slamming the door too; Kite hesitated just a moment, her hand on my shoulder before heading off in pursuit. That left Elsa and me doing the dishes in a ritual of silence. When we were done she gave me a long hug.

"Ida, it's like this—I've been thinking all winter that I should go join Kristy. It's not sudden, any of this. I've been aware that Spence really wants a big change. And I think Willa will want to go too, even if it doesn't end up that they stay together. I don't think they will. Did you see Willa's face?—like hell they have an agreement. Oh well, maybe they had an agreement as long as Spence never talked about it, one of those deals. I think it took everything Willa had to keep it together in front of us. Look, I know things are really over with me and Kristy too, but it's a link, a stepping stone back to the city where I really should be for my art now."

I just snuggled in her big arms against her big chest knowing that when she released me I'd enter a profound loneliness, and yet I didn't cling. I knew it was all true. We had all gone hellbent for home just so we could leave it.

* * *

Daniels told Spence she'd need to give an address where she could be found if she were going to New York. Spence gave her a bogus lesbian bar address in Manhattan, said the bouncer would know her and she'd be going there on the weekends as a DJ. This part only came out days later as she and Willa were packing every-thing, boxing up all their records, renting a self-moving van even though I offered to drive their stuff down in my truck. It was the least I could do, right? But she said no, it would be too hard on us. Elsa made a going away breakfast of potato latkes with one of our last jars of applesauce from the previous fall crop.

Elsa was right about them splitting. I heard from Willa after about a year. Said she and Spence weren't together any more, that she was living with two other dykes in a small apartment, working at the co-op part-time and trying out her music contacts for some sort of job. Getting back into working with clay.

Strangely silent about Spence, she was. Another time she wrote to say she hadn't seen or heard from Spence at all, but heard through some friends that Spence was into S and M in a big way, had become a techie for rock concerts and was doing something called 'sound sculptures'. As for herself, Willa said she had fallen in love and wanted to have a baby, a family with this most beautiful 'yellow gal' whose brother was gay too and was going to donate the sperm. And so he did. I have yet to see her son—a bit younger than Kelsey. What does he know of his mother's previous life?

All I know is that she wanted to be a mom again for a long time—she would have loved to have a kid be part of Blue Corn. Of anyone, I still had faith she might come visit someday because she writes to me every so often, keeping in touch. Funny—I always felt closer to Elsa. Well, she sends cards announcing her shows but I don't go see them, do I?

Meanwhile Kite, Mel and I hung on for another summer, but I was lost. And then Lorraine took me in like a foundling, telling the story like this: "Thing is, it was you I saw standing there that day with those pumpkins. I didn't know what had happened, not really, except for the newspaper article, that something bad hung over you. I noticed that from one summer to the next most of your collective had disappeared. I had really admired you all—great produce, a consistently festive stall. When three or four of you used to come, always a party. And the lesbians rolling in during the morning to see you, sitting around in the back of your pickup. Lots of laughing. Then where did everyone go? That last summer you came most of the time on your own, sometimes with Kite, and even less often with Mel. Such a cloud over you. Such a shroud of silence—if your com-munity did come, it was in dribs and drabs, low-key. And then you alone, Saturday after Saturday with your jars of relish, with the kale, beets and acorn squash, the pumpkins.

"It's not that I hadn't been straining over my own farm, what to do, what to do? I already had Fortissima and Mosey from that farm that went bankrupt. And Juniper was looking like a good buy. But how was I going to do it? I didn't know. Until I saw you standing there. I think it was like a lightning bolt, I was so jolted—some vibration from you saying, 'Here I am.' Call it what you will. You know what I mean? After all, you didn't say, 'no, I'm busy,' did you? No, you looked me right in the eyes—I love those dyke looks. You were already agreeing. When I asked you if you knew about horses and you said, 'About as much as they did in *Desert Hearts*, maybe even less,' I knew it would work out. It was a truly amazing moment...for me. A magnetism.

"Must've been a karmic thing, Kid. Oh, I knew it wouldn't be the same, but I thought you could help me define something here. Something good and true, because you're the one I saw—"

"—standing with the pumpkins," I always finish the story along with her.

I found out much later that the producers of the farmers' market, due to Lorraine, had written a collective *Letter to the Editor* expressing their disdain at running an article like that about a group of people who worked hard, were honest and caring, and had lost a member of their family to senseless violence far away. Why were they being publicly branded?

I know none of us wore those distinctive woolen hats again, what with their charms woven in—temple bells, I-Ching coins and small silver venuses, the tribal ones Rune had made for us to wear with pride.

Thirteen

I must have dozed off there on the sunny rock in the quarry, because I came to suddenly as my cold pipe clattered down to rocks below me, the sun hitting me full glare, the light in the quarry sharp and painful to my eyes. Flies buzzing about. I shifted stiffly, moving to retrieve my pipe.

Shit, I had been dreaming. All the talking just made me dream that recurring bad dream I get. Ever been in a place that should be full of people but it's deserted?—a church, a school, a street—Blue Corn. The Blue Corn house was always empty in my dream like those last days I stayed there on my own, my ears alert to every creak and groan of the old place. Always empty, in ruins. I was like some priestess of a religion that had died, hanging on to the temple before its sack, wandering from empty room to empty room, trying to keep minimum routine. I'd wake up in a sweat. Got so that I slept in the afternoons and early evenings, paced around in the dead of night.

This time in the dream I knew who the killer was, without a doubt. I was handing out 'wanted' posters for him. Except they were playing cards. And I knew he was out to get me, there at the old Blue Corn house which was slowly falling apart, cracks in the walls I could see through. Half demolished, the windows taken out. I found a jack in the middle of the debris-littered kitchen floor—the jack from my truck. But when I went to pick it up I saw that it was a card—a joker.

I woke with an awful sense of foreboding which I couldn't shake. Too much stirred up. I hate the way dreams jumble up symbols and elements from waking reality. And now I had that same heavy knot inside me that I had taken so long to loosen, though as Gem says to me whenever I feel it again, "At least now you know how to undo it—you can untie it much much quicker each time. You know your way out of the maze."

"Ahoy there!" Viv waved to me from the top of the ledge. "What a fantastic view from up here—you can see over the treetops. All the mountains. A bit hazy."

"Hm," I replied groggily, looking about, relieved to find her nearby, to hear her voice. The forest had that light green of new leaves, making me feel light-headed, but new summer does that to me. Maybe I was hungry. "We should go home for lunch."

She came down the far side of the quarry, a more gentle slope, holding onto strategic trees growing between and out of the rock. I like trees that have their roots wrapped around rock like that. Ending with a light jump into a plié, she ran gracefully towards me and the truck.

"Thank you," she said, "thanks for telling me."

"It was your shoes—" I said, stowing away my pipe and tobacco in the glove compartment as she waited for me. "I dreaded it when Gem wanted you to come up and talk to me. Gem knew that too, but she thinks I need to talk about it. I get these…breakdowns. But then I saw your shoes—just like Rune. Not only sneakers just like hers..but without socks too. Like a sign. I thought, okay, I can talk about all this with her. But that last year sort of destroys all the years of work—the way we just scattered to the winds."

"Well, until you told me about this I was getting a different picture, of…possibilities. Now that I know, and that's clear, can we go back to all the work? Except for one thing first—I was thinking about it up there on the ledge. I need to know more about Kristy. That last year… I mean when the detective talked to you, was she a suspect too?"

"No…no, I suppose she wasn't. She wasn't around and didn't go to the funeral with us. The detective must've talked with Elsa about her."

"Well, what put her so definitely in the clear? I mean, why give Spence a hard time when Kristy is totally unresolved?"

I had to laugh—a snort. "She was lucky enough not to be there, that's all."

"Yeah, and yet there she is featured in Elsa's paintings, looming, always in the foreground, like Elsa couldn't see past her to the rest of you?"

"True, she probably couldn't. That's because Kristy was only there because of Elsa. I don't think she would have been there at all, otherwise. And they fought the whole time. Elsa definitely into the control factor, Kristy responding by walking out and slamming the door, fuming underneath, sulking. For days! Somehow Elsa cajoling her back. Over and over and over. And yes, sometimes she'd slam around, things like ramming a screwdriver into the kitchen table, or throwing the can of paint-thinner Elsa put her brushes into, right onto one of Elsa's paintings. The first couple of years it kinda got to me—then it was a matter of habit—'Oh, there they go again.' That's the beauty of collective living. You have others to buffer you, distract you, keep you busy. And that's why they lasted. That, and because Elsa wanted to paint her—she did have a thing for Kristy."

"Did you think she was beautiful? Does *Women in the Field* do her justice?"

By this time we had gone the short distance home and sauntered into the kitchen to rustle up some food. "She definitely was naturally chiseled—strong body shape. But for all that excellent build, she didn't move well. And yet, maybe it was that quality that enabled her to stand still for long hours at a time—perfectly immobile. She could do that, freeze, be a statue. Here, want some mayo?" I shoved the jar across the kitchen table to her as we each built a cheese sandwich with thick slices of new bread and some of the cold-frame lettuce. "But I don't think I ever got anywhere with her in a conversation, and she never helped us think things out about how to do the land. To be fair, she pitched in with whatever had to be done. She just wasn't thinking about it. I don't know what she was thinking about. Half the time she was fuming at Elsa.

"Got to hand it to her, she had a thing about cleaning windows, wherever she could conveniently reach. Hey, she had that place gleaming, hung crystals in all the windows for rainbows—uh...downstairs, that is. She never had any reason to come upstairs. We were on our own up there."

We had taken our sandwiches and iced mint tea to Taylor's patio. I had helped him lay the slate there and build the wide, waist-high wall, perfect for sitting on and taking in the view of the horses in pasture—except they were in their stalls for awhile. I loved how the land eased gently down towards my cabin against the woods, there where I had planted all kinds of perennials just waiting to burst forth over the summer. Daffodils were coming, the black tulips, and jack-in-the-pulpits which came up on their own account along the edge of the old track.

Brushing crumbs from my mouth, I laughed. "I remember her great contribution now—to be fair. She always scrounged at yard sales, brought things back for the house—chairs, things like that, useful things but also total trash sometimes too—something for Kite to clean up later—and...and oh yes, all those canning jars—dozens—for our corn relish. She started a five cent bottle deposit at our market stall. Customers used to bring us boxes of jars they didn't want. Kristy had recycling down ahead of its time. Oh yes, and the dishes, how could I forget about those dishes?

"Thing is, when Kristy left she took her dishes—these beautiful blue-glass dishes she had bought at some yard sale. Sheesh. A full set—eight dinner plates, five breakfast plates and maybe five saucers. You eat off dinner plates like that for years, day in, day out—and we never did break a single one, not a single one—it's part of your very *identity*," I looked down at my plate of the moment, one of Lorraine's solid grey and brown stoneware. "So anyway, there you are time and again staring at that empty, blue-glass plate after you've eaten every last slickin' separatist-lesbo vegetarian dinner, then suddenly!—poof, they're gone. Deal with that, kiddo."

* * *

That night Gem had sent a fax. I woke up in my room and heard a grinding sound. A fax! Sure, it was a letter but what a zap.

No usual opening endearment. Just two items:

1) Good news. Sort of. Amazing actually—though I heard it through a confidential source. There has been an internal fraternity investigation. Joker Atwell has been suspended from his house! Rumor has it—from what the kids tell me—that his buddy told all about the assault. He has been required to do 50 hours of community service, and then will face peer review. Meanwhile he is also on academic suspension and will not be graduating with his class. I am sure he is devastated. Since he can't leave the state until his court date and he can't stay at his House, he must be in an awful limbo. Needless to say it does leave me with an unsettled feeling. I keep kinda watching over my shoulder. Don't like to be in my office unless other folks are around.

2) Now the bad news. Don't know if all this has bearing on me and my part in advocating for V., plus the rape awareness and accountability campaign I have helped the students with or whether I went over my bounds and stepped on somebody's money, but I haven't received my contract for next year. I should have signed it by now. Silence. I don't know whether I should go to the chair and ask outright or wait a few more days. Surely she would tell me if there was a problem unless she can't...I've been part of designing next year's courses and in staff meetings my courses have been determined, two of which I helped design and am supposed to co-teach. Remember the one about women heads-of-state in the last thirty years, Meir to Bhutto? No, it can't be my big mouth—the chair herself says that all the strident women are in this dept. so it wouldn't be anything new. It'll all boil down to unforeseen budget cutbacks, won't it? There has been plenty of buzz about that. Just warning you—in case you find me on your doorstep not just for eight weeks, but unemployed. I'm winding things down here. If I haven't heard before my last day, I'll have to find out. Will Lorraine still be picking me up on her way on the 27th?

I really miss your Thai pie. Especially your hot sauce. Gem

For Gem to warn me!—she had to be down. And really worried. For Gem to land on my doorstep for more than eight weeks and no job prospects had to be a fate worse than death, so to speak. It's not the fact that she'd have to come to me, it's that she loathed the idea of being dependent in any way. She would want to come as an equal—just because it would be fun and romantic to summer together. A treat—helping hay and working on her upcoming courses, easy togetherness.

103

But this development—oh dismal, dismal—I didn't want to think of a summer with her lack of employment hanging over our heads. She'd be dashing off resumes, chewing her nails, running to every possible hint of an interview as far away as Kentucky.

Hell, what a state of nerves she had to be in.

Then I began wondering about mine. Any talk about Rune always undid me. At the time in broad daylight it had been fine. Viv had been fine.

But somehow double-exposed with what Gem was feeling right now, I was right back to that awful last year at Blue Corn. The unsettling feeling was like the fear I had that someone was watching me, following me. All those times when I was so afraid of police descending on Blue Corn still gripped me now. Irrational maybe. But we had been exposed in the papers, identified, labeled, under police surveillance.

I could still feel how I was all alone in an empty house jumping at every creak and groan. Never could get it warm, even though I had closed off the upstairs, stapling plastic over the stairwell, my bed in the living room. In fact, to conserve wood, never mind oil—I had a half a tank left over strictly for emergency back-up—I was living solely in the kitchen and living room.

I could not stop shivering, even when wearing long underwear and layers of wool, huddled in front of the Torrid Zone which did its best to warm me. I remember thinking how I was the *only* one in the Torrid Zone—a small bubble of warmth in a cold landscape.

It was because Rune was gone that I was so cold. It was because Renata Bullock had been stuck in a hole in the ground. And so where indeed was my Rune, really?

In the end I had taken the incense ashes up to the rock ledge above Blue Corn. I didn't put her ashes in the field like she asked, but spread them on the rock that time I looked up and saw the geese. That had been in April. The summer was a blur of dull activity as Kite, Mel and I carried on without heart. We felt very exposed over the aftermath of going to the funeral. True, we weren't bothered, but we were jumpy. It was with relief that they packed and moved to their land. And then, there I was alone. When you're alone, those fears eat you, eat the warmth right out.

So I shivered in my fear as fall came.

Sure, I could've run to Kite and Mel in their trailer, camping out for the winter on their land. But that wasn't a solution. We weren't a threesome. And if Kite was torn in any way, Mel had the upper hand there. They were going to start all new themselves, give themselves a go as a couple. That's how Kite explained it to me—how she and Mel had never really had that chance yet, always being in a collective household.

They wanted to have a family.

I never begrudged Kite the fact that she was given five acres by her great uncle's eldest son. Kite deserved it. And the family was doing halfway right by her since they were going to let Bertie's land slip away from them. She had lost a lot when she lost Blue Corn, more than any of us. Her consolation prize was five measly acres of land, four of it scraggly, second growth woods, the one 'open' acre full of thorny blackberry bushes.

And I was just stupid because I hadn't found a solution for myself, instead I sat in a condemned house worrying about someone out to get me. It wasn't the police after me but economics.

Meanwhile what Gem was going through now was real. What Viv was going through was real. If I was afraid, if I shivered now as I went outside to smoke my pipe and sought reassurance from Hecate, even as a drizzle took hold of the night as forecast, it was because those close to me were being threatened. And keenly, it brought back the nightmare of what had happened to Rune—my Rune whom I couldn't help when she most needed me.

Fourteen

Inspired by Gem I decided to make hot Thai peanut-sauce 'lasagna' in the big kitchen, a small pan for Viv and me to eat fresh that evening and a larger one to heat when Lorraine arrived the next night, knowing that she would bring a bottle of exquisite wine.

"You must be expecting company, huh?" Viv said, almost dreamily, her chin cupped in the palm of her hand, notebooks spread open in front of her on the kitchen table.

"Sort of," I muttered noncommittally. The water was boiling and ready for the stiff lasagna which I put in one at a time, enjoying how they softened into the water. When they were done I would brush them with hot and spicy sesame oil.

"Not the mysterious lover?" tilting her head slyly.

"No such luck," I sighed for myself.

"Then tell me about her."

"Haven't I already?"

"About how you met and stuff."

"Forget it about the 'and stuff' part—I ain't telling you any of that. But okay," I offered grudgingly though I liked talking about Gem, even if it was difficult with the imposed restrictions which I was growing more annoyed about. "I'll tell you how we met. I was supposed to go to a party, see, and I didn't really want to go because it was a good hour's drive. And what would I do there?—play volleyball and drink beer. I just didn't have the heart for that kinda deal anymore. I liked it when we all went as a group piling into Kite's van, a party all in ourselves. What can I say—I liked the *group identity*. Lesbian Sorority. Home Team. Besides Rune and Spence were always good for a laugh. But hey, I went. And the usual sort of extended dyke community was there, a pick-up game of softball in the works. The mood was good but I wasn't. And I went to sit down by this woman—didn't even look at her—I knew she had—"

Ooops. I paused suddenly, realizing I was just about to describe Gem's silky locks. How I do love the way her hair sweeps back, always well cut. "I knew the reason she wasn't playing was because she had a broken arm—her right one. And she looked unintimidating I suppose, if not miserable, where she sat in a lawn chair, her arm in a sling. Nice sun-tanned legs stretched out. I figured a good looking woman like that was probably watching her beloved out on the diamond so that made me even more comfortable.

"She says to me, she says, 'So what's your excuse—how come you're not out there playing?' And I say, 'I'm no good at throwing.' And she says, 'That's a pity…What if they were dancing? Would you say you were no good at dancing?' 'Not at all,' I say and then I don't know why but I blurt out, 'and I'd probably ask you to dance since you don't have a broken leg.' She *laughs*—this wonderful naturally sexy laugh, and says, 'Good. When there's music, please fetch me.'"

"Wow," Viv stared at me all starry-eyed so that I was a little worried. "You came on to each other in broad daylight?"

"…Come to think of it—but I didn't know it at the time, did I? Thank goddess, or I would have run for my life and that would have been a big mistake."

"Didn't you ask her about her arm?"

"No, actually I didn't. And she liked it that I didn't. Turns out it was a mountain bike accident. I only found out way later."

"When did you know you were in love with her?"

"Heck, I was a goner pretty much right then and there, really, I think I was…but I kept watching to see just who would come up and claim her—in that *tiresome* way lovers do if it's not you—you know, so I could get ahold of myself really quick and stop being foolish."

"And no one did?"

"No! Amazing, huh? That was before I knew she drove hard bargains romantically. No cozy couple stuff. Monogamy, yeah, okay, even honest-to-goodness love, but no other strings, all the baggage that bogs down into habit…"

Not my Gem; she wanted to experiment, defining new lesbian relationships, not—as she said—reverting to patriarchal, traditional form, something she saw happening again and again. She didn't care if it was couched in charming ceremonies like jumping the broomstick and all. The more experimentation the better, she always says, and why she thought testing out role playing, butch and femme stuff was okay…just so long as you made nothing a lasting habit. That you could switch roles, change. That motto: Always innovate! She said her philosophy was a sure-fire turn-off—except no one would believe her, it seemed, and so she had many loves and many disappointments. No one would take her on, not seriously. But I have to say, I was fascinated. I didn't believe her either. I was only one more brazen hussy who thought she could handle this girl.

"So?" Viv broke through my long, self-absorbed pause.

I rallied, straightening up as I gave the noodles a stir. "So anyway, I figured out pretty quickly she was 'not attached'. Then I got really nervous because I didn't want to look like I was on the prowl.

Ha—me thinking that. And I certainly wasn't! I kept talking in great circles around her, talking to everyone else, that is, when really I wanted to talk to her. Dykes, honestly, I have found us all to be painfully shy and awkward, for all the talk. Turns out she was feeling the same way. I was only going to stay at the damn party for a couple of sociable hours because Kite and Mel were going to be there, and they thought I ought to meet new people, my hermit ways not having escaped their scrutiny. Anyway, I found that I couldn't bear to leave without somehow talking to…um…her. And finally it was late evening and someone started putting some hot party tunes in the tape deck. Tina Turner, I think. Or was it The Go-Gos? No, Laura Brannigan…I finally summoned the courage to walk over to her—to this day she says I positively swaggered which I swear I didn't—and asked her to dance with me. She said, 'I thought you'd never get here.' And she said it to me as though we had been together for years—do you know what I mean?—the way you say things to someone you really know. I was floored. And she begged me not to dance slow coz she couldn't put her arm around me. I tell you I was a goner. I wanted to take her home and lie next to her and just let her be miserable with her broken arm while I…well, while I consoled her, you know." I finished lamely. The noodles were ready and I fished them out, glad to have something else to focus on.

Hm, this is difficult I thought, because I couldn't very well mention the conversation I had had with Gem that evening, how we had talked about back-to-the-land utopias, and how she had laughed at my claim to be a Latter Day Shaker while her eyes flashed with passion, rebuking me. And how she had told me she was an Itinerant Women's Studies Professor with a particular interest in history. No, no, all that would have given too much away.

Instead, poor Viv, got the short, steamy version.

"Did you?" Viv was asking me.

"Did you what?"

"Did you take her home?"

"Oh no, no, but I did get her phone number. And I invited her to come up and see the farm."

"Oh." She looked dejected.

"What's the matter?"

"I wanted to know if you got to make love to her while her arm was still broken."

"Ah. Yes…yes I did. Do you think that was too quick? I was scared if I didn't act, nothing would happen at all. Think I should have waited?"

"No, no." She shook her head. "I was just wondering—"

"Yeah, I bet you were," I finished tersely. But no way— I'm not going to tell you how to make love to a woman with a broken arm, kiddo.

It simply has to do with thinking vertical. And that can be a considerable challenge if the walls are slanted, as they are in my barn loft. But no challenge was too great for that exquisite first time with her, especially since I had a hunch it wouldn't be the last, and especially since I had suffered for an eternity of two weeks until I knew she wanted me too. I had thought Gem was just one more mirage in the heat waves of my desire. Instead she broke through the surface of my fantasies. And how she did.

No way was I going to divulge how I leaned into her nakedness against a wall of moonlight, how I traced over her skin with my fingers and lips. No way would I reveal how she shivered in the echo, groaned for more as I sought out her full breasts—first with my mouth, then with my tongue—her nipples tight in anticipation.

And when I found her swollen labia, wet to my fingers as she opened to me, I let my body slip down hers until my tongue could take her too, slowly, my mouth growing rich with the taste of her. Grabbing my hair with her strong hand, her tension grew slowly, oh how slowly. I thought she'd pull my hair out and I wanted her to. Slowly. I braced against her, wallowed in her. Slowly. Then she thrust her hips against me for more, demanding more. I wanted to make her cry out and she did. More. I wanted her to call out my name, and she did. More, *more*. I wanted her to writhe, break over me, and she did. I wanted her to tighten her thighs against my head, and she did. I wanted her to let go as if she were plunging away in a dive—and then, back arching, my arms around her, she did. And how she did.

I wanted to write to Spence afterwards and say, well gee, maybe you weren't having rough sex all that time, really. Maybe it just sounded rough to me coz I didn't know squat, when maybe it was just vigorous. But I didn't write to Spence because in my heart of hearts I knew the sex I'd had with Gem wasn't rough, just vigorous, and I knew in my heart of hearts that Spence knew the meaning of rough sex first hand. And I was tame by comparison. And I most certainly didn't want to think of my lovemaking with Gem as tame. Because it was wild, I thought. So I never did write to Spence about my true sexual arrival.

Besides, after Gem's arm was better, did I ever find out how aggressive she could be! Whewee. And all the time I thought I was the top…'Always innovate!'

And of course I wanted to write to Rune but I couldn't. After all, she of all people really wanted me to find true love and true sexual enlightenment, mostly because she knew that's the combination I wanted. 'Can't wait till I meet that woman who will do that for you,' she had said with a shake of her head, 'I'm gonna get such a kick out of it.'

It bugs me, still bugs me that she didn't.

All the while I was preparing the layers of lasagna, the noodles first, then the bean-curd and coconut milk mix, then the peanut sauce which I had simmering to the side of the stove, after first sautéing the scallions, next adding the finely chopped cayenne peppers, then the peanut butter diluted with boiling water. And I was lost in the process so that Viv's sigh roused me with a start.

"I'm in love," she said mournfully, leaning across the table, her head on her arm, "But it's hopeless."

So, now it made sense why she was asking me about love. Aha. I turned to her, eyebrows up. "Well, well. Oh dear. You'd better tell me about it."

A statement I was soon to regret.

"Yeah," she sighed. "I'm in love with Professor Cooper."

"What?! Are you sure?" My ears went back, my teeth were bared.

"Yeah," she said curtly and sat up. "Does that shock you? Do you think she's too old for me. Don't say the age stuff to me, puh-lease."

"Uh no, I certainly wasn't—"

She pouted. "I thought you'd understand or I wouldn't have told you."

Irritated and flustered, I sped up my slow cooking, slapping that sauce around. "No, no, I think it's fine you told me. I mean…" Slap. "…well, I don't know quite what I mean." Slap, slop. "It's just a surprise, I guess. All this time…you pining for her—"

Woah, and wanting her, to say the least. Slop.

She brushed a hand across her face. "No big deal. She's involved with someone else anyway."

"Oh." I nodded with great understanding, raising the spoon so that peanut sauce splatted down the front of my shirt. Hey, I always did that, a regular messy cook.

"Yeah, I saw them together at a lecture."

I stared at her warily. What, who? Who the hell is Gem seeing on the sly? Oh sure, she must mean Natalie, that's who Gem went to cultural events with when I wasn't around. And sometimes when I was—Gem isn't the kind to butt out on a friend just because her lover is in town.

"Yeah, gorgeous blond. Wears silk shirts and power suits."

Yep, that was Natalie all right, a lawyer and mediator focusing on cases of violence in the home, many within the dyke community. And I don't know why, but for a moment there I was greatly relieved to know that Natalie was supposedly Gem's lover when so often I had to fight my jealousy.

Viv went on, "Yeah, I should have made sure she wasn't involved before I fell for her. But I couldn't help it, I guess. She's just so dynamic, and so fierce as a teacher. Inspiring. Anyway, I'm a student and she's a prof. She is too cool to cross that boundary, even if she did like me, which I know she does. I mean, she doesn't flirt or lead me on or anything. But, I mean, the whole way she helped me out, giving me her *car* to come up here, her camping gear, *everything*."

Mmm. That camping gear was the clincher, huh? And sending you to me, don't forget. I licked a bit of sauce from my fingers—ooh, hot enough—and put the final layer of mix on top of the mess of lasagna, finishing with a generous sprinkling of sesame seeds. "Yes, she did get you out of some hot water, and is still taking the heat on your behalf." I know my tone was most removed.

Viv began to walk around the kitchen; she came to investigate my project which I was sticking in the oven. She took the wooden spoon I had been using and licked off the sauce and curd mix as she paced. "See, that's the thing, I know she cares. Waah, this is hot." She beelined for the kitchen sink and a glass of water, panting, "And...and that almost makes it worse. Because I want to please her. I want to do this project well. I want to get myself together. I have to get beyond the student thing with her. I mean, who knows, by the time I graduate...She wouldn't care about the age thing if we were meant for each other. She always says in class, 'Test the waters, look out for your blinders. Don't assume the definitions you get handed or accept complacency just because everyone else is content with the norm. Maybe the norm is what is off the wall. *Always innovate!*'"

I let the oven door shut with a bang. Be still my beating heart. I rallied, voice dead calm. "Uh, but she's involved, Viv. Get real."

She held the spoon in midair. "I know, I know. But things do change. Three more years?—anything could happen." Suddenly the spoon dipped as she flung it in the sink. "Who am I kidding? I should have done like you—waited around to see if she was involved with someone already, not let my heart take over so soon."

"Oh well," I gulped, "I don't know if that would have done me any good in my case either."

No, no, no—we weren't talking about the same woman. Surely not.

She looked at me with those sharp eyes, so sharp I was wondering how come she couldn't just read my mind, discover the truth about Gem, and settle everything. "You're so right. Things like that don't really matter if you get hung up on someone. It just complicates things. Anyway, I should have known such a hot, intelligent

111

woman almost twice my age would be involved. Happily married, for all I know, from the way things look."

Married, ha! Hiding behind a facade of coupledom, is she? Interesting. I guess she has been careful not to tell her classes just how married she isn't.

Which is why we don't live together in a happy, settled little couple situation. Cozy cottage with climbing roses and the picket fence, cats and dogs at our feet while contemplating children. She always brings up the cases Natalie talks about, always talks about how couples and families torment each other. Nuclear families, that is. Even well-meaning ones. Too insular, too habit forming. That's why we often talked about the idealism of communes and extended family. We have wanted something, both of us. But what? Family, yes, but in an extended way with lots of diverse points of view. 'How do you create that besides out of blood-bonds, religious cults or political single-mindedness?' she'd ask repeatedly in one way or another. 'All experiments fail. We (meaning the lesbian community at large) don't know how to be truly tribal and you can't trump it up.'

From my own personal experience I had to agree, homesick as I was for those Blue Corn days, and now watching Kite and Mel break up—with a kid in the middle of it. Or did I dare say that those relationships had lasted as long as they could, and that part of the breaking down was innovation? Like recurring music festivals. We just didn't know how to strike the stage and clean up very well.

I shook myself free of remorse to face the present problem which I didn't want to deal with either. What a fine fix. Gem and I were going to have to have a serious chat. And soon. I would write her a letter immediately. When she had said she didn't want me to reveal my relationship with her to Viv, I had accepted it as a reasonable request because Gem was always reasonable. Now I wondered. Part of me wanted to sit Viv down and tell her." But I knew I had to be careful. If Viv hadn't been told right off who she was coming to stay with, it was going to be horrible to level now after she had confided in me. I had already blown it.

I had to know first if Gem had a clue that her star student was in love with her. I liked to think of Gem as with it, so of course, I couldn't believe she didn't have an inkling. Why ask me to remove her picture?

But the letter would have to wait. While the lasagna was in the oven, I had to see to the horses. It was a good way to excuse myself abruptly.

I took each horse in turn out to pasture, dutifully checking Fortissima for signs of heat. When I released her, she kicked her heels up and Mosey, the only horse we put out with her in the same pasture, kept his distance. I wondered if this would be that night I'd hear her make squeaks outside my window. There's something very particular about a mare in heat making those squeaks, like no other call.

When I finally sat down to dinner, gulping my cheap, sharp wine rather than sipping it, and toying with my lasagna as I waited for my tongue to cool after each bite, I decided I should try and wade into the subject of this love. "What about acknowledging this love you have for what it is, uh, subliminal? That the passion comes out of, uh, the *inspiration*. Maybe your prof. there is very careful not to encourage you because she hopes you'll be happier, really, with a peer, that you'd have more fun with someone your age."

Viv, fanning her mouth and taking a big gulp of seltzer shrugged, "Whatever."

"Whatever? That's too easy."

"Well, I'll say this," she pointed her fork at me. "What do you know about it? You've been there, right? Did keeping things chaste work?"

"And if I slept with the woman was it a disaster?"

"Yeah, like that. Even one night."

"One night with Professor Cooper would be enough?"

"I don't know. You tell me." She poured herself more seltzer.

"All I know is I was once in love with someone a hell of a long time too long. While part of me was telling myself to get on with things because she was involved, another part truly thought I could wait the situation out. I even used to save notes she wrote me—things like—'Would you please pick up a can of gas' as if it were a love letter! Meanwhile time passed, see. She obviously wasn't the one for me because we didn't have a chance to realize it…or find the right moment or something like that. She was busy and otherwise engaged. And we never, never talked about it. Somehow, on some level I knew it was just taboo—it would wreck things…whatever we did have." I chugged some wine to cool my burning throat. Shit, I always made the lasagna too hot. "We became friends, solid friends. And so maybe I shoulda waited it out. Things did change but by then, well, by then I had moved along and found what I call pretty damn true love. Maybe not quite how I expected it, but there you go."

"Blue Corn—you were in love with someone that whole time at Blue Corn?" She screwed up her face at me incredulously.

"Well…actually, yeah." I put my wine glass down so hard some splashed out.

"Jeezee. Don't tell me…let me guess. No, wait a minute, I'm going to have to think about this."

"Good, you do that." My words came out a bit pissy. I was glad

113

on the one hand she had something to ponder, but then I didn't think I had made her realize how foolish it was to be ga-ga over Gem. I changed the subject. "By the way have you contacted your friend again?"

She sighed like I was hassling her, said wearily, "She's not going to come forward. I already wrote to her. I thought of calling but I don't think I'll get far if her family is around. She won't talk."

"You should try anyway."

"I don't have any money to—"

"Consider it part of my bill." I jerked my head towards the living room. "At least give it a go." And I began picking up the dishes as she stuck all her notebooks in her canvas bag. "And then you get to do dishes."

She rolled her eyes at me and went off to the phone. "You'd better come along and hear what I'm dealing with."

So I followed and sat on the couch going through one of Lorraine's catalogues. Always got stuck in the men's section thinking this or that shirt looked nice, then suddenly I'd land in the women's part among the prairie dresses. Woah, right there, that was like the one Mel was wearing the other day.

"Hello, may I talk to Serena, please," Viv cut her eyes at me, realizing she had had to let slip the name she was withholding from everyone; her finger pointed at me in warning. "It's not really her name anyway, just the American version."

"My lips are sealed," I countered.

She covered the receiver, whispered, "That was her mother. Not good." Girlish now: "Oh hi, Serena. This is Viv. I wanted to see you how were doing…your migraines and all…"

Code. I tell you, it's part of the language.

"…oh, well sure, let me give it to you. Call me anytime—you can call collect."

"Thanks," I muttered as she looked at me apologetically.

After she hung up she came and sat heavily next to me. "She was super friendly, said that she was feeling much better, probably just all the stress of school and she thought she'd be much better off at the community college for a semester or two. That means she'll live at home—just what she needs, right? Then she said she was busy and could she call me back sometime which means no way could she talk because her mother was right there. She always told me she went out to the convenience store down the street to call friends, so I'm pretty sure she'll be walking out the door before too long having thought of something she needs there."

* * *

True enough, just around the time Viv had washed up and

114

tidied the kitchen, the phone rang with a collect call. I decided Viv didn't need me hovering around any more than Serena her mother, so I took the opportunity to go outside and smoke a pipe while I talked to the horses—Cloud and Hepp—who came up to the fence to see me. I didn't have anything to give them except a little tobacco which they lipped off the flat of my palm each in turn, cats coming from the barn to rub around my legs, always led by Hecate.

I was just about to head back because of the mosquitoes when I heard the screen door of the kitchen slam. Huddling with her arms folded about her because she was still in a tank top and the evening was cool, Viv sprinted towards me, shaking her head. "No go, no way. At least she got her period—she's so relieved about that, but now that she knows she's okay, she has even less interest in reporting it. She's just putting it all behind her."

"Hm." I puffed on the last of my pipe. "Does she realize there are people still sweeping up after her?"

"Well, that's my fault, isn't it?" Viv was hopping up and down to keep warm, reminding me of Kelsey. "She didn't ask me to take up her cause. In fact I think she has been pissed and scared, wishing she had never told me."

"But she hadn't told you who her rapist actually was, right? It was because of her reaction when she saw Joker again."

"Yeah, exactly. And now she really doesn't want to think about it any more. Anyway, I'm still glad I took action. I don't regret what I did at all. Not a bit. So, she couldn't stand up for herself. I did it for her. I don't care." Her voice rose fiercely, "I've been thinking I'll transfer—well, except for Cooper. I'd go back for Coop."

I tapped the dregs of my pipe out on the stone corner post of the garden fence, Hecate jumping up beside me. "No guarantee that Cooper will be there, you know. She only had a contract for a year. It has to be renewed—I mean, she's assuming it will come through. There has to be a stronger pull than that, say, good courses by other profs., some decent friends?"

She shrugged. "Oh yeah, but nothing is as strong a pull."

"So, what made you go to McKee in the first place?"

"My Mom went there…before…when it was still an independent women's college. And it was affordable.

"That's it? Not because it has a good Women's Studies department? Not because it might be a good place to be out?"

She smiled wanly. "My mother didn't think about that when she pushed me to apply, but I kinda got the picture when I went to visit."

"Yeah, a supportive place. Why do you think Cooper likes being there? But she isn't into love affairs, I'll say that much. And a relationship, well, I can't help but think you've heard her philosophy right in class. Piece things together…she doesn't believe in marriage either. Maybe I shouldn't wish her on you. She's thinking about other things—like her career, for one. And maybe you don't want to hear about the age thing, but there is an age thing. Someone turning forty is going to feel different about her sexuality, her body, her needs, than someone turning twenty. How we look at time changes, how we use it. No, I prefer to think of time kind of like air or water, a dimension we live in—gets more compressed, maybe, more under pressure. Harder to breathe! Treasuring it as it grows scarcer!"

"You want to discourage me! But you can't. I can't help feeling what I feel!" She turned away and began walking across the lawn. And for the first time, I caught her pain like a whiff on the air. Even at her distance in the dark, I could tell she was crying, or trying not to. I walked up behind her and for the first time it felt right—I wrapped my arms around her.

I wanted to spill the truth about Gem and me, but I just could not. I felt no matter what I said she'd take it as some sort of betrayal. Or was I being protective of myself? I was attempting to muster words if not my own courage. I was afraid of saying exactly the wrong thing. It was true—I had found Gem enough of a challenge, even though we always talked things through and I trusted her deeply, to wish her on anyone else.

Then Viv demanded abruptly, "Don't you ever get lonely?"

"Ah!" I said pulling back, my eyebrows charging up my forehead in surprise. "You did get plunked out here in the middle of nowhere all of a sudden, didn't you? Loneliness…" I half-snorted. "What was it Rune always used to say?—'I'm just off being cool by myself somewhere.' It's a matter of attitude, isn't it?"

* * *

An attitude I had worked on a long time without much success. How could I tell her about that? When I first got up to the farm, Solitude was the Angel I fought with furiously. So afraid to have to count on it. So mad. Working on my fear, working out my fear. Having to trust myself as my own companion. Again and again. But over time it became more like the barn cats having a spat, lots of hissing and spitting and ass fluff flying.

During just such a spat after an early March blizzard—about two feet of snow—I was shoveling around the barn in the morning. Everything still like it is after the snow has finished falling. Sun bright and painful. And I was feeling isolated. So damn isolated. I was even scoffing at myself, singing, "Hardy-har. Poor isolated Ida," when I heard a snowmobile coming over the hill there beyond the first hay field. Buzz, buzz, buzz. Then I saw it coming across the field, then whizzing on up the track through the woods, right on up to the barn. Now, I admit it, I do disdain snowmobiles though why, surely I shouldn't say, because don't I like the trails they leave so I can ski? But I was pissed at this thing coming at me Now there's a contradiction, all isolated and getting pissed because someone's invading it.

The snowmobile made a swift, quick stop on a u-turn, spraying snow up in my face. The driver climbed off, a big guy with a stained one-piece, black snowmobile suit, bright green neon stripes, a matching helmet also grungy as hell. He whipped off his helmet and out tumbled this thick mane of dark hair. (Elsa would've loved it.) It was a woman! And she gave me this wide smile, big gap between those front teeth, her face crinkling up. I guessed her to be close to fifty. Someone who had worked hard, knew a thing or two.

"Whee-ahh. Haven't had enough snow to come over here in so long. Lorraine here?" she said in a deep, husky voice.

"Nope." I leaned on my shovel.

"Hm, didn't think so except I saw someone was living here permanent this winter, saw the truck out front a lot. Thought it was one of her boys."

"Just me. I'm helping her out. My name's Ida."

"Pepper," she introduced herself with a nod, pronouncing it more like 'peppa.' "Listen, would you tell her next time she's up that I'm going to set some traps over there on her side of the hill. I saw a lot of fisher tracks today. Maybe set some in the ravine and catch me a coyote or two."

"Sure, if it's something you do."

"Oh yeah, yeah. Lorraine lets me as long as I don't get one of the barn cats. The she'd skin me alive for sure, heh-heh." She gave this shrug and a chuckle. "Usually have the traps outta there before the cats really get to roaming. Known Lorraine since we were kids, you know. My Dad and I used to trap together. Don't do so much now. No money in it, really. Say, wanna get on and take a spin?"

Taken aback I agreed. After all, I had been thinking of taking a ski but felt too tired from all the shoveling.

"I don't have a helmet...wait, I could use one of the riding helmets."

"Sure!" she said. And I fetched the one in the grain room—the extra one with the neat rip in its back velvet. So I came out of the barn, adjusting the chin strap. So cool. Climbed on the back, hugged around her, and she was a big, strong woman, couldn't see a thing behind her, unless I peered around her side. Away we went. Whee-ahh! Just like she said. She took me for a spin over the hay fields. What a rush. How the snow sprayed up in my face. I was saying, "Not too fast!"

She yelled, "What, you want to *crawl?*"

She took me over the hill and showed me her place, a trailer there, was taking care of her very sick mother at the time. Her folks had had a dairy farm which her mother sold after her dad died, just across the road from where they were now. They could still see the barn. Like a lot of Vermonters, they kept a bit of land for themselves and put a trailer on it. All the money went into taking care of her mother.

Now Pepper, she is the real separatist. Self-sufficient. Or as they say up here, she's independent. No phone, just a radio scanner. A hound dog chained up in the yard, would go hunting in the fall, worked as a milker for many years, a school bus driver. On the rescue squad—but that's volunteer. Hey, even I knew she was the girls' basketball and track coach just from reading the town report come March every year. (Lorraine told me how Pepper was a star basketball player before girls had competitive high school teams. She was allowed to practice with the boys she was so highly regarded…for a girl.) And she's a backhoe operator! Now that I that I think is quite handy. She has helped me a few times with moving rocks, borrowing equipment on a weekend, if and when no one else wants it. Usually in November just before the deep freeze!

So she was what the Angel of Solitude sent to my rescue that day. Then about a year later, hadn't seen her except in passing, she comes to find me again. Late February. A different kind of messenger this time—in her truck, nothing but icy patches all around. No good for snowmobiling.

"Say," she greets me, but sober-like. "Will you come with me to get the box for my mother? I could do it myself but it would be better with two."

So of course I went with her. I didn't know what she meant at first, but then as we were driving along, she tells me her mother died early that morning. Yeah, I knew she could do it alone, but, I thought, wow, she came to get me to help! Didn't quite know what we were doing. So, we go over to the funeral home in Lewiston and sure enough, we get a particle board box—six feet three inches—put it in her truck and drive to her house, she kinda cussing under her breath about how small her mother is now for such a damn big old box.

"You seen a dead person?" she asks me.

"No." Thinking how I had never seen Rune like that.

"I can cover her up but I was just letting her get used to the idea of leaving. We have to wait for the medical examiner."

So we sat together with her mother who was still in bed. And she showed me a photo album so I could see what her mother had really looked like when she was well, when she was big and strong too. The examiner came, someone she obviously knew—someone who knew the family from way back. We got the certificate, went to the town clerk, got a permit to transport the body, went back and together we carried her mother, all stiff as a board, and laid her carefully in the box in the back of the truck. I thought, wow, where have I been all this time?—to know you can still do this in Vermont. But I found out later when we talked to the man at the crematorium that not too many folks do it at all.

"I don't have flowers," she says, then goes into the house awhile and I'm sitting on the tailgate of her truck, just waiting with her mother in the box. She comes back with a small, ratty old teddy bear. "She can have my teddy, don't you think? She gave it to me when I was little, seems right."

"Absolutely." Then a silence as she screws the top on the box and we just sit on the tailgate. "Were you with your father too when he died?"

"Nah, he went into the hospital. Farmer's lung. Might have been okay if he coulda kept himself out of the barn. Old barn, you know. Silo full of molds you can never quite clean away. But he couldn't keep out and then his lungs just gave in. That's why I told mother she must come home from the hospital when it was time. On the farm you always see the animals being born and die. I told her we made the dying cows comfortable all the time, why not ourselves?"

A chill runs through me then on that February day, a season too reminiscent of Rune's death—so different, so deathly cold. I look at the woman near me already used to her solitude, and clasp her hands for the warmth. Then swear I not to indulge in loneliness again.

Fifteen

When we arrived at Kite's on Tuesday, we noticed that Mel's car was missing—didn't look like she was seeing clients after all. I drove my pickup directly around the house—the garage end. I could see tire tracks on the lawn going that way and knew it would be okay to do it too, careful not to run over any perennial beds, what with my special rocks I had brought to add to Kite's wall. She had wanted a vertical stripe at each end made from white quartz. And that's exactly what I brought for her, five large chunks from the quarry.

All excited to present them to her like they were a dozen red roses, I jumped out of the truck, expecting Kite to be hard at work. Her pick and shovel were there sticking up at odd angles from the ground.

"I'm in here," a plaintive voice called through the sliding screen door from the living room.

Viv and I barreled on in there, my boots thudding heavily, to find Kite groaning on the couch.

"Fine fix to find me in." She smiled wanly.

I went to sit on the coffee table beside her. "What, what?"

"Oh damn it." She flung a pillow across the room for emphasis. "I'm a complete idiot. I broke the cardinal rule of any stone worker and wrenched my back." She grimaced with pain and chagrin.

I took her hand. "Lifting something too heavy? No. You didn't cover the stones and they were wet? You slipped?"

"I think I was just too tense and pissed off over everything and getting ahead of myself. I know, I know, I should've waited for you—"

"I wasn't going to say that at all," I protested. "How bad is it? And where? "

She winced as she tried to show us. "My lower back. Gone into spa...sm. Muscle."

"You taken anything for it yet? What about a heating pad?"

"I took...a couple of Ibuprofen. I'll just lie here till it passes..."

"Where's the heating pad?"

"In the bedroom clo—" (she grimaced through a spasm) "—set, top shelf."

I motioned for Viv to go find it and she nodded over her shoulder. "On my way!"

"Damn, damn," Kite moaned. "I don't believe I did this, and now of all times. I don't e...ven have Mel around to massage it. Ain't that the breaks, huh?"

"Want me to call her? Where is she anyway? I thought she was seeing clients today."

She lifted her head slightly, incredulous, then let it fall back. "You kidding? Call her now? To come over and help me out? 'Oh Mel, I need you, I just wrenched my...back!' It's too late for all that."

"Why too late? She'd come right over."

"You don't understand! It's over. She took her portable table—I told her it was too much having her see clients here. If she wasn't going to be with me and Kelsey, she should go completely, quit screwing me around. The whole damn relationship is over. She'd just think I created some sort of crisis to make her come over and have another scene. We've had enough, believe me. She'd be peeved, and hardly offer real sympathy. And as she always says, you need real sympathy in your hands when you massage or you won't do any good. I mean, what timing, huh? Never, ne...ver, I never do anything to my body, have never asked her for massages. And in fact, rarely got them, only if she were in an extremely generous mood, which has been less and less, I can tell you. And so now I fucking well go and do some real harm to myself." Her smile was comically sad.

"Well, we could always call Sadie," I offered with a shrug, smiling slyly.

"The *competition?!*" She almost laughed but thought better of it as it obviously hurt to; slapped her thigh instead. "Ha...wouldn't that be the ultimate! She hates Sadie's guts, though why, I don't know. She should be grateful. After all, that's why she started to take on men clients. I'm the one who should hate Sadie's guts. There was always this teasing threat Mel had—'you ever so much as go near Sadie for a massage and I leave.' I'd say, 'Is that a threat?' And she'd say, 'No, it's a statement.' I kept my end of the bargain, didn't I? A lot of good it did me."

"Sorry I mentioned it," I said lamely.

"Ah nah, it doesn't matter." She waved a hand in dismissal just as Viv arrived with the heating pad.

I sat on the coffee table holding out the pad, an ugly green and black plaid number while Viv plugged it in beyond Kite's head at the end of the couch, then helped Kite roll onto her side slightly so I could tuck it behind her.

"Oh goddess...oh...oh yes that's good."

Now I swear up and down I'm not one who mixes pleasure and pain, but wow, she sounded erotic in a way I'd never ever had the luxury to hear (from her, that is). And such classic words!—I mean,

I've read that in books so it must be true.

She sighed as she began to feel the pad heat up. "I'm sorry, guys, this is so stupid."

"You've been going through a lot," I said reassuringly. "Viv and I can still put some hours in here, and we'll be around. We'll put on some music, and you can just lie back for awhile."

She wailed. (I can't remember when I'd ever seen her so pitiful—once when she had a bad bout of flu, yeah, but she had been very quiet then.) "I'm supposed to pick up Kelsey."

"When?"

"Three-thirty sharp or I'll get a late fee."

"No problem, Viv and I will pick her up." I had always thought it very wise of them to put me on the official pick-up list. Part of the family. Day care, ah, such a great buffer zone. Leave your kid off in the morning with kindly, fun teachers and have your estranged spouse meet child at end of day. No fuss, no muss. "You have her for the night?"

"Yeah."

"I could stay here and help out," Viv volunteered cheerfully. And well she could because I had chores to take care of.

"See?" I carried on the hopeful note. "All taken care of."

Kite reached out to hold my hand, tilted her head forward as much as she could and said meaningfully "Why do I feel like you and I are all that's left of Blue Corn?"

I commiserated with a nod. "Two husks."

What I didn't say but wanted to was: because it all boils down to a couple thing, Kite. Always. And we just never did get that together. Jeez, we could have made Blue Corn into our last name and all, coz you and me, kiddo, we're the ones who wanted that dream-scheme to work for much longer than it did. And all this is almost more than I can stand. *Now!*—why the hell did I give Mel a break back then just coz she got to you first? That kind of thing has not stopped other people from moving in on the one they want. I just kept on hoping you'd see me. Soo polite and repressed of me. Fuck Mel, I hate her guts.

Kite lay back with a groan. "Huskies."

"Huskies," I snorted, "Rah, rah for the home team."

And I saw Viv eyeing me there from her perch on the arm of the couch, some little gleam of realization going on behind those bright eyes. I looked away.

Overwrought.

"Oh goddess," Kite sighed. "Remember when we did that inventory on all the tools…shit, Rune was already packing by then. Wasn't she the one who said, hey I want my own tools back or trade or get bought out? Yeah, yeah that was it. And we came into the kitchen all through the day slamming stuff down on the kitchen table, and Willa was making the list of who had bought what when, and we all argued over the screwdrivers. And…and Kristy literally driving that damned phillips right into the table!"

I shook my head laughing at how dreadful it had been, how shocked we all were—that we had that kind power with each other—Kristy!

And Viv was looking intrigued, left out.

And Kite chirped à la Kristy, "'All right then, this is the fucking collective screwdriver!'"

Ruined. And so, by the way was our kitchen table.

Because there we all were after the most bountiful harvest we had ever had (no dope), the farm in mint shape, a veritable showpiece (except for the house), taxes paid (!) and Rune was packing to leave, only because of her mother, of course. Meanwhile Kristy and Elsa were barely speaking to each other, and Kite's great uncle had taken a turn for the worse at the nursing home. So much so, that Kite's aunt had had a little chat with her about how if (not when) he died, the farm would most likely be sold to developers because of his expenses. Out the window with dreams of a long-term lease that Kite had been working on for years with her relatives. 'Better start thinking where you and the gals can move to next. There are plenty of outlying towns with lower taxes and neglected farms. You know we can get top dollar subdividing that land, being where it is,' she was told.

I hung my head in pain over the memory. "Let's not think about it."

"The begin…ning of the end. Why can't I ever see it coming? You're right, Husky. It's too awful. Let's not think about…it."

Hey, was the room reeking of self pity or what? I knew I had to burn some incense or something. So I jumped up and made for the CD rack—yes, yes, they had gone CD except for their old collection of tapes that we had all made from Willa and Spence's albums—things like Garthwaite and Alive!, later on Lauper and solo Slick. Yeah, we all did like them—good parties to that. But I didn't want to stir up old stuff, so I looked to the new. The Roches; that had to be Kite's choice (Mel was more like k.d.lang on the sultry side).

And so we muddled through, Kite to dozing, Viv and I to moving the white rocks into place with a bit of the good ol' oof and urk. I was too sad to even tell Kite about what I had brought for her. She'd see it sometime. It was one of those things and seemed to happen to us over and over; things she did for me too.

Like the time she fixed my old truck for me, took it in to her cousin to get some holes patched after Spence had promised and promised to weld it, and winter was coming on. It was supposed to be a trade between Spence and me since I'd already brought her old copper piping I'd salvaged for her to sculpt with.

So, yet again on a warmish sunny day in late October I left my truck for Spence to work on and went off to pick apples with Elsa, Kristy and Willa, part of our collective's seasonal deal with the local orchard. Another contact through Kite, of course, because she knew farmers in the area since childhood. I think it was Rune's turn to clean house and she was grumpy because she didn't want to be around Spence who always interfered with one's choice of music. I remember I said I'd trade with Rune, let her go pick apples but Kite—and Mel too—said: absolutely no way, Rune always managed to get out of cleaning. They were quite adamant about our policy of keeping to the duty roster that particular day.

At the end of a long day in the orchards with bushels of apples to process, what do I find but my truck looking all spruced up with the red paint even matching—well, almost, but you had to look closely. I noticed Spence was oddly subdued, accepted my thanks with a nod and a vague look. But Spence was like that sometimes—especially if she was stoned.

I didn't learn the damn truth for months. I don't know if Kite ever knew I knew. But that's how it has always been with us. Of course Rune told me—I think the day she packed to leave, and I'm sure it was because she had no desire to give Spence any more credit than she deserved. No, not a fraction.

"Spence didn't fix your frigging truck that day," she said with a sneer. "It was Kite. That's why she wouldn't let you switch with me. She took your truck down to Roy's. Spence, nah, she slept late and sat out in the sun and got stoned. And Mel and Kite came back from dropping the truck off and she let Spence have it. She said, 'I don't know why, but I'm covering your ass. And next time if you have a fucking block against doing something, have the decency to say so.' And Spence said something like, 'I was getting to it, I was getting to it—I just came out here and the truck was gone.'"

Rune mimicked her to a T so that I could even see Spence drowsy and her hair spiked up at odd angles from sleeping on it. "'Bullshit and you know it,' Kite was yelling at her, 'and you're going to split all that wood today instead of me.'…And Spence going all haughty, 'Oh, is *that* my punishment, heh heh,' you know. Kite stormed into the house, Jesus, for a minute I thought it was *the* white tornado…and pointed at me and told me I'd better just 'keep my lips sealed on this too.'"

Dear, dear Kite. I took it as a sign of her deep, covert love for me. Well, that's why I was bringing her white quartz, wasn't it? We had found our way to communicate. Deep code. Gem's right, Gem's right about all that.

"So what is there to eat for dinner?" I asked as I stomped in the French door, but then removed my boots. It was almost time to go fetch Kelsey. "Want me to stop at the store for you or anything?"

Kite roused up from her drugged dozing. "Oh no, there's stuff in the freezer I'm working on finishing up. Just pick a container. You'll probably have to put it in a bowl of hot water to help get it thawed out in time."

I opened the freezer as Viv came to get a glass of water at the sink. Finding the first unidentifiable container, I plunked it dutifully in a bowl of warm water and worked off the top.

"Oh no," I gasped in disgust. "This isn't what I think it is, is it? Not Mel's black bean stew!"

"Is it black?" Kite muttered.

"Yeah. With little bits of what looks like corn cob in it."

"Then that's what it is."

"I swear I thought I'd seen the last of that stuff *for good*."

"You are," Kite said dully, and yet didn't I detect a slight note of sentimentality?—Over Mel's black bean stew, for chrissake. That did it.

"This stuff is going out, woman, out." In more of a fury than I'd been willing to admit, I stomped out the back door and thumped the contents of the tub onto the compost pile down by the garden. Deed done, I turned around to find Viv following in hot pursuit.

"She says, no, don't!" Viv cried horrified.

"Too late. It's buried in the compost," I said without looking back over my shoulder.

"What is it about Mel's black bean stew?" She was at my side, arms flapping.

"We all took turns cooking, see. Sometimes we'd get in patterns—or ruts. Tofu, well, we all cooked tofu in one form or another, tofu and garlic, tofu and onions, tofu and tomato paste, hot and spicy tofu. That came in the late seventies when a new enterprise really got going with the stuff and we bought it by the tub-full at the local co-op. But we always had the dry beans to fall back on. Now, I'd make pinto beans with cumin, believe me I got sick of it myself. And Elsa made dahl because she had been to Nepal and knew about some good spices. But Mel's black bean stew—I don't know what the hell she put in it, but I hated the stuff. Everyone else would eat it dutifully the first night—and the beans wouldn't have been soaked long enough, still hard. Anyway the stuff would sit around, and we'd keep opening the fridge and there it would be staring us down day after day. Mel would eat it out of a bowl with chopsticks, a big dollop of yogurt on the top." I had stopped in the middle of the lawn at this point, describing the stuff with my hands so that I may as well have been demonstrating an ice-cream sundae. "And after days she'd complain that we weren't helping to finish it up. Then Willa would carefully take it out because somehow it was okay if Willa did it—a personal dynamic thing. So, in effect, what I just did was a Willa-thing. Dutifully ridding the household of Mel's black bean stew. Do you see? I've *had* it with rice and beans anyway."

"I don't know if Kite will see." Viv shrugged as we headed indoors.

I made a grand entrance, bowing at Kite's feet and waving the empty container. "Don't give me grief. I've purged your house. And you didn't really expect me to serve that up to Kelsey, did you?"

She smiled weakly, sighing. "No she won't touch it."

"The kid has sense!"

"She likes macaroni and cheese. There's a box of it in the cabinet." She waved her hand.

Viv was already in the kitchen, following the directive, and came out with a natural brand box of the stuff. "Oh, yeah, great! I learned to cook for myself by making this."

Appalled, I said, "You make Kelsey macaroni and cheese out of a box?"

"She can almost cook it herself. She likes to help. You still have to boil water and put the elbows in. It isn't instant," Kite explained defensively.

"Microwave instructions." Viv tapped the box with her finger. "That's how I did it."

"Well, thank goddess, you don't have a microwave." I slumped onto the coffee table next to Kite. "So, why can't you have a good time and eat macaroni and cheese too?"

"Not enough in one box."

"Viv, see if there's a box of pasta in the cabinet. I'll buy some sauce if you don't have any. No more black bean stew for you, ever. Doctor's orders."

Kite clasped my knee. "Thanks, pal."

With arched eyebrow: "That's Husky to you."

And with that, Viv and I had to bound out of the house with Kite yelling after us, "Don't forget you have to pick up her car seat with her—it should be above her cubby!"

My watch said three twenty-nine when I dashed into Kelsey's room which was in the Sunday school wing of a Unitarian church. Even though there were no pictures of Jesus in halos on the walls, it definitely still held that ambiance. I glanced at Viv and could see she had picked up on it instantly like a dog catching a too familiar scent. True, there were pictures of shepherds all around, high above the kid's art. Shepherds from around the world, photos, posters; and from different times: 17th century English, 20th century Middle

East, late 19th century Navajo.

"Just like the one my mother runs," Viv whispered.

We had no more time for chit-chat. Kelsey was skipping towards us, having dutifully put her book away, her teacher bidding us all a cheerful goodbye, making sure Kelsey had her lunchbox and artwork of the day. And what a productive day she'd had by the pile. As usual, lots of horses and rainbows, except I am proud to say, ever since she had been a regular visitor to the farm and known some real horse personalities, her works were always pictorial stories of what Hepp, Juniper and the others were doing. Fortissima, of course, always had a wild mane, head tossed high. Indeed, today, she had a special one for me (since we had phoned earlier to notify her) of me feeding Mosey an apple. Big apple. More like a red pumpkin. I loved it. Arms straight out holding up this big apple and my hair all standing on end as if I'd seen something real scary, say, a bowl of Mel's black bean stew with a dollop of yogurt on top. Oh, and a rainbow in the sky.

Viv received the unicorn.

"Hm, what does that say about you?" I whispered as we headed to the cubbyroom. "All I see is an old mare."

She dug me in the ribs with a fist as I squirmed out of the way.

Kelsey was all business, sorting out her cubby, dancing from one foot to the other. She stopped suddenly and gazed up at the two of us, saying shyly, "Are you two sisters?"

"No," I said.

"Kite said you weren't." She went back to gathering her stock.

"But why do you think we are?"

"Coz you look alike," she said with a flounce.

"Wait a minute. For one thing, she wears her hat backwards." I crouched down, Viv leaning over behind me. "I want to understand something here because we've been told that before. And now you say it too. In what way do we look alike?"

"The way you look," she said with finality.

I had to think about that for a bit. Then, "You mean the way we look at you?"

"Uh huh." Back to dancing, all her work stuffed into her backpack. "Get my car seat."

"Sure, sure."

What did it mean—that I had the same piercing, intense gaze, pointed, inquisitive, earnest? No, I didn't like that. Or did I? Wasn't that something Willa had told me to cultivate—power in the eyes. Is that why all dykes looked alike? Because their eyes were more direct? It was one theory I'd have to ponder. But then Kite would look like us too.

All I know is I drove back to Kite's with my sunglasses on. Maid in the Shades. All of us squeezed into the cab, Kelsey secure in her throne of honor and Viv leaning against me to keep out of the way of the stick shift. In our haste to fetch Kelsey I hadn't thought about the ramifications of the car seat.

Upon arrival, as Kelsey wriggled free from her seat to the door I'd opened, she revealed the truth at last, poking gently at my face just above my sunglasses. "Dark-bushy eyebrows."

* * *

Leaving a warm home scene with some regret because I knew it would be a good place to be that evening, I drove home to the horses who greeted me eagerly along with all the cats rushing from the barn. Hepp was especially eager because she knew I was going to walk her on a lead around the meadow. Routine was what I had to maintain, and why I couldn't just bag coming home and hang out over at Kite's.

Besides, I was relieved to find myself alone at home for a change since I was so used to solitude, but also because I got a call from Gem that night. A call of my very own, no, she didn't want to talk to Viv about anything. Here we were, as instant as macaroni and cheese in a box. But my baby was very troubled. I didn't like it at all. Threatening notes coming to her through campus mail. Always computer typed and printed. Anonymous of course. Sometimes two or three a day.

"Do you want to fax me one to look at?" I said.

She sighed, "No, they're too awful. And mostly they're the same, well, maybe some minor changes. Obscenities and threats, matching what Viv got before she left. Thank goddess she's out of here."

"Did you turn them over to the police?"

"Yes, I have. Seems whoever was bothering Viv may have decided to hassle me now."

"Why don't you come up with Lorraine this weekend? Get away from there—"

"I can't!" Her voice was strained. "I'm in the *middle* of giving finals and grading papers! Just two more weeks after this. I'll try and wrap everything up fast and catch a ride up with Lorraine Friday the twenty-seventh then. That would be good. I'm telling you I can't wait to get out of here."

"Nor can I. Listen, you've got to be careful. Have you told Natalie?"

"Absolutely."

"Oh. Well good, good."

"Ye...es," she said long and drawn out. "And just about everybody else I bump into around here. I'm making a damn fuss about

128

it to the department chair, McKee provost, the dean, the president. I'm not taking this without making a stink." Her voice turned pragmatic then as though she had composed herself. I like to think it was because of my steady voice calming her. "Look, I can take care of myself, and I'll go and stay with Nat if I need to. She offered."

"Good. You do that." I was surprised how practical I was sounding in return, that usual little Nat-o-meter of mine hardly registering at all—I mean, the needle was staying steady in the black this time, not even budging over the line into red. Was I going to grow out of my jealousy at last?

But she took it all wrong, my Gem. She was so ready for a reaction from me, she read my tone all wrong. Didn't I say I was being practical? Wouldn't I want my baby to be safe with Natalie rather than on her own, alone in her apartment at a time like this?

"Now don't get all huffy, Ida. That's not what I need right now," she snapped, exasperated.

"I'm not, I'm not," I protested. Not this time. "I want you to be with someone. Obviously I thought of Nat first, for chrissake. Go stay with her. Look, let me send you a letter. There are things we need to discuss. I'll even get help faxing it—"

"What things?"

"Look, I'll fax it tomorrow. Maybe it'll clear some things up."

"Clear what things up?" Tone getting real defensive.

"Cool it. Like I said, the letter will explain—about why I think of Nat as a solid friend and good resource at a time like this. Give me a break."

I could just see her shaking her shoulders the way she does when irritated, that silky hair flying back to the jerk of her head. "Look, I don't have time for this now. I'm sick of it, I'm sick of your jealousy. Do you realize what a strain I'm under right now? Not just trying to get finals over with and out of here, but this other stuff is a real downer, let me tell you. I can't process right now. I don't need you starting up about Nat."

"You sure are under strain coz you're not hearing me," I spat. "You're taking me all wrong when for once I'm doing right. What's going on here? Read my letter I'm sending tomorrow. It'll definitely be a change from the other mail you seem to be getting now. You know what, this phone thing between us isn't good at all. We never argue in letters, well, not like this, over nothing. Let's stick to that."

She sounded very tired. "You're right. Let's stick to that. I'll wait for your letter. Let's hang up, this is ridiculous."

And so we did. Not a code word of passion.

We had never had such a terrible exchange. How disorienting. Even after I had walked around outside smoking my pipe, I could not shake it. How could we have such tension? How could she think

I was giving her a hard time when she *knows* I know she's having it tough?

I rummaged in the fridge for something to eat but the sight of that black bean stew had done in my appetite. Or maybe I was just falling into a depression. I think I ended up having bread, butter and honey comb. With a glass of milk. Sure cure.

And I wrote Gem a letter explaining about Viv's amorous revelation, asked for advice. Assured her we'd make it whether she had a job or not. Then because I realized I didn't have the faintest idea how to fax something, I went as usual and put the letter in the box at the end of the driveway, raising the little red flag.

Believe it or not, the next day was taken up with work, as usual. Without Viv around I actually felt more productive. A lot to do in the garden, preparing beds for lettuce, spinach, mustard greens, arugula. Sure, Lorraine and I were no longer market gardeners but we still took the garden by storm. I never felt right unless I had the freezer full, plenty of tomato sauce, and a well-stocked root cellar.

I had also promised I'd replace all the broken or rotten planks in the horse paddock behind the barn, and have the place painted with pitch against cribbing. And I said I'd make sure the driving cart would be in order along with the harness for Lorraine's work with Cloud. And I had to handle Hepp every day—Curley's Ledge Hepzibah, the first of Lorraine's stable, her pride and joy. Not to forget Fortissima and any signs of heat.

It wouldn't do for a farm girl to go off and get too distracted by lovers' tiffs or old flames, now would it?

Sixteen

"You never told me about the Purple Book! I can't believe it," Viv exclaimed after we had at last climbed into my pickup, waving good-bye to Kite who was up and hobbling about. I had already taken Kelsey to day care to be picked up on the other end by Mel. Perhaps it was a bad time to leave Kite but she claimed she wanted to be on her own. She had all her accounts to catch up on.

"The Little Purple Book—L.P.B. Funny, but I haven't thought about it in a long time. I think I lost mine someplace," I answered noncommittally, slipping a dubbed Etheridge tape, care of Viv, into the tape-player. I rather think that I'd tucked the memory of that L.P.B. away out of embarrassment.

"See, that's why I really should talk to others in the collective, get different viewpoints."

"True. To be honest, I'd much rather show you the lesbian farmer's lunar almanac we made or our recipe for corn relish, by far more interesting—"

"Important! It was your manifesto! Kite said it was your creed, a very concrete set of statements you all wanted to live by. But she doesn't know where hers is either. She said she had one in the back of the photo album, but it wasn't there! She made me bring boxes out of her closet and we looked through them, her papers and Blue Corn farm log—she let me make notes from those. Weather, weather, weather. I was really hoping you'd have yours. I've got to see it. This could be the key to my paper!" Viv was insistent, those piercing eyes on me so that I winced.

"Kite exaggerates. No listen, it was a joke. A joke! Even Kite knows that."

"She didn't talk about it like it was a joke. And she was surprised you had forgotten about it."

I coughed into my hand. "Oh yes, well, we were serious at the time, sure. Too....A manifesto. Just the thing for a lesbian separatist group, eh? We were bouncing statements around, playing, entertaining ourselves. You must understand, we didn't have TV spoiling our visions! We relied on self-entertainment. Anyway, Willa wrote our statements down and then typed it up on ditto masters and I ran it off on a borrowed ditto machine. This was way before personal computers and printers or even cost-effective photocopying! Light years before, like by about ten," I laughed. "And you and your friends at school make instant 'zines!"

"Yeah, and I want this manifesto to take back." Viv was itching. "I'll do a new edition."

"Okay, but you have to print four pages up, fold the sheets into quarters, cut and collate. It is a small book, remember. One statement to each page."

"Yes, see..." Viv leafed through the pages of her notebook hurriedly. "We did find this scrap folded up in her log with a grocery list on the back. Part of it is faded, must have been a ditto sheet that didn't get all the ink. Here, the first four statements. See! Number One—" And Viv, waving the unfolded paper, read, "'We, the womyn of this lesbian separatist collective will never espouse—'"

"Yeah, note that word 'espouse'," I interrupted, jabbing at the sheet with my forefinger as I steered with one hand.

"—'and vow to reject all patriarchal forms of religion, dogma, political systems, even revolutionary, as negative and destructive to the very core of our existence.' Now that is true, absolutely true, as is Number Two: 'In every great upheaval, womyn are spoils of war, used and abused solely for perpetuating male systems through the control of mind and spirit, and ultimately, forced breeding. Unless married, ie. property of the male, womyn are seen as whores or witches to be raped, burned or forced into menial, slave labor as political and religious whims dictate. The victimization of womyn never changes.' Now, you can't say that was written as a joke, because it's true, none of that has changed."

I sighed. "No, none of that has changed. Except that being a wife doesn't exempt you either. We didn't quite get that right."

"Number Three: 'Therefore, we vow to nurture and foster only the female in all that we do, think and speak, working with our bodies and souls to bear fruit from the land to share with our own, not in mere defiance of patriarchal systems, but towards our own evolution, towards our own boundless survival and freedom as womyn.'"

"Oh yes, I remember, and Number Four is about individual will within the collective whole. That's where we started to bog down. We gave up after four more statements." I leaned forward over my steering wheel. "But let me tell you, Viv, I suppose the L.P.B. wasn't something I hung onto because, in my view, couldn't we just live what we thought was true? Such as, spoken agreements that evolve and change as we evolve and change? But Spence wanted to find a printer, all this talk of hundreds of copies which we could even put in with our baggies of dope. I mean, come on. I only printed it up for ourselves, something for ourselves, not something to use as propaganda."

"What did others think? Rune, for instance?"

"Rune? She didn't want to put it in with the dope. And Elsa agreed that if it empowered us to do it, and if it was a useful tool for others, she was behind it. Kristy thought we should just tack it up on the wall, and any woman who came to visit our land and help out—which happened often—could have a copy if she wanted. Then we thought we'd send it to *Lesbian Connection*, still the ultimate 'zine, you know. The manifesto itself, now that it was a real entity, became this thing, this issue between us all. I think we buzzed on and on about it for months until the energy dissipated. There was some link in there though that started us arguing about race and class. Maybe Willa got fed up with us at one point—I seem to remember her saying something about how it was all just a 'white girl' thing anyway to want to do a dumb manifesto. Elitism—that was it. That started a wild fire, because then Rune started saying, 'Don't tell me it's white ass stuff because it's the working class that is always forced to eat that manifesto shit, it's a rich girl thing.' Direct slap at Spence, right? It had nothing to do with any of that. We were all just itching for some kind of fight to ruin our shangri-la. The honeymoon was over. We were becoming *family*. Talking behind each other's backs, yelling at each other during meals. And we were all starting to argue."

Viv folded the sheet back up and stuck it in her notebook pensively.

I urged, "So don't make too big a deal over our Little Purple Book." A pain echoed through me. "You see, it opened a can of worms for us. Pandora's box, okay? We were never the same after that, the initial innocence gone. It seems that Elsa and Kristy fought more after that, or fought more openly. Things were more abrasive: Rune and Spence's open hostility towards each other, Kite's growing frustration—which I thought I shared some—at our inability to really come together over major jobs, such as planting or harvesting, things you have to do when the weather is right, not put off. Or getting all the wood in before November. And I know I was feeling more blue because of my passion for her. I thought Mel was wishy-washy—and Kite could only adore her. Total bummer."

I must've got the truck home on the fuel of my words alone because just as I finished, there we were in the dooryard; I was turning off the ignition. Etheridge's voice died with the engine; what had I even heard of her the whole time? I was thirsty…maybe because she was singing about needing water. We both got out heavily. Cats poured from the barn; a horse nickered.

"Kite said she stuck by Mel for so long because she was an incest survivor." Viv slammed her door matter-of-factly but the sound hit my brain like a hammer.

My own door thudded shut with its perpetual squeal and shudder. "Who? Who was the incest survivor?"

"Mel."

"No kidding?" I think I just stood there dumbly for a few minutes. "See...some things we never did get around to for all the *issues*. Damn. They never told us." It hit me as some kind of deep betrayal, and yet, now things made sense. So simple. I couldn't ever fathom how deep the shame was that Mel must have lived with...never to tell *even us?* I looked at Viv, dazed. "How come you the fuck know?"

"Kite got to talking last night. She said it didn't matter anymore. She had sworn to stick by Mel for as long as Mel needed her. It was a promise she had made. Now, she guesses, Mel doesn't need her anymore."

"Bullshit." A great anger welled up inside, one I didn't try and justify. "Kite is still there for her. She just said that coz she's down and feels abandoned. Mel will return to her and use her up again. I wish Kite would make the break."

"I can't believe Mel never told you all!"

"Incest survivor issues came up only in the eighties—coming out about it, I mean. It was a hard thing to do. Certainly we discussed the matter—she had plenty of opportunity to tell us. She always projected this totally sheltered upbringing! Her parents were musicians, on the road a lot. She stayed with her grandparents...and uncles. Sheesh, I remember her talking about how they would come home from the factory, her father's two younger brothers who never left home, and expect dinner on the table at six sharp. And how she'd have to wait on them. Shit. That was all she ever said. I always thought she was more sexually naive than I even was. If she never told us, it must simply have been too godawful, and something she hadn't worked through."

"Yeah. Kite says it's because they're both Catholic that somehow it seemed so hugely bad. And they couldn't explain that...the way it felt."

I gave a helpless look as we headed indoors. "Mel wasn't the *only* one there assaulted, manhandled or raped. And so now you see, Viv, exactly what bothers me about Mel. I'm sorry, I'm sorry but it's true. There's a—"

"But maybe that's part of the damage she sustained," Viv countered. "You see it as a character flaw when maybe it was a wound. And maybe Kite understood that."

"I'll say, she paid. Look, I have to tend to the horses," I said spent, turning away into needed solitude. "Would you feed the cats?"

"By the way," Viv said, handing me a scrap of paper, "I found this in Kite's journal. There were more stuck between the pages—

like markers. This one was on the page dated March 1983."

I looked at the scrap written in my hand: 'K—Find the 500 pounds of lime in the shed, gone up to Bartlett's to get spreader, I.'

"Is it a love letter?" Viv tossed at me as she strode away.

Why did my hand tremble? "Yes, yes—mine were."

* * *

Later that night, I remembered that maybe I knew where a copy of the L.P.B. might be. In Rune's boxes of personal papers—journals, photos, letters. I had only given the boxes a surface going-over before because I had found it unbearable. But I thought I could open it with Viv and let her sift through. So I found them among my things up in the loft of my cabin, brought them down. It was one way Viv could get some of Rune's point of view. In the first box we found papers dating from the late seventies and early eighties. We opened one or two of her journals, written in her neat block printed letters. Short entries of Blue Corn Days. We even found a pressed tip of a marijuana plant—with seeds.

"I think we should plant them," Viv suggested.

"Heirloom seeds...no, it's not the time or place. But I think we should smoke this Blue Corn dope, only fair you should have some." And I put the little bit in my pipe offering it to her. I'd had enough in my day, hadn't I? And there among Rune's things we found an actual, four by five inch copy of the L.P.B. You'd have thought she'd found the Holy Grail. "It's all yours, Viv. Be careful."

She read all eight statements aloud. All things boiling down to keeping the 'tribal thang' going. And I'm sorry but I laughed and laughed, especially at the part about common, shared property and being totally independent and self-sufficient as a collective. Right. It was Kite who fronted for us, being a native of the area—taking such comments as: 'Kathy (how she was known locally) I hear you got some sort of commune up there on Bertie's land,' made all the contacts so we could bask in the backyard and gloat how we didn't need the system. And the only reason we didn't get into free exchange of bed partners and open relationships is because we didn't dare bring it up. Goddess beloved, I guess I was stoned on second-hand smoke. And I needed to laugh real bad.

* * *

In front of the stoked up Torrid Zone which warmed my cabin on that chilly, drizzly evening, Viv read to me from Rune's journals. I listened while rubbing saddle soap into Cloud's harness and going over which seeds I would plant. Hearing her read the entries aloud made it sound almost like poetry. My diaries, when I kept any were always rambling and untidy. Why didn't I think to write like Rune, terse, succinct?

Oct 6, 1979—Geese flew over. Balmy. Split and stacked three cords wood.

Oct 7, 1979—Raw, cold wind. Dug up potatoes. Hauled wood.

Oct 8, 1979—Split wood. Brought in and covered pumpkins.

Oct 10, 1979—Put plastic around foundation. Caulked storms windows. Hauled wood.

Oct 11, 1979—Hauled wood. Foliage at peak.

Oct 12, 1979—Hauled wood. Clutch went on tractor again. Two hours to fix. Saw three deer.

Oct 13, 1979—Wood ready for splitter. Began to rain. Covered everything.

Oct 14, 1979—Split and stacked three cords.'" Viv took a deep breath. "What—she do this all by herself?"

"No, she is leaving out the 'we.' That was in the early years. We were still culling the woods around the place. Kite's cousin had come in and logged a stand of maples. All kinds of trees got cut in the process so we got those for firewood. Went into the woods with the tractor and chains, dragged four or five logs back at a time. Kite would chain saw them into stove-lengths to split. She wouldn't let anyone else run the chain saw. So when Rune says the wood's ready for splitting, she means that Kite had finished sawing it up. The following day we'd rent a motorized splitter for a day. Pretty quick and deafening. Took fourteen cords to keep us through a winter. Later on we had logs brought in by the truckload, again by Kite's cousin." I chuckled. "Whenever he'd bring a load, we'd retreat into the house, leaving Kite to deal with him. Years later I met him once over at her new place. Of course he didn't know me from beans, and he went on and on how he never believed anyone else was there coz he'd never seen us. That's separatism for you—shoulda gone out there and learned something from him instead of acting like some hidden harem."

Half-listening, Viv was leafing through pages. "Wait a minute, here's a reference to the L.P.B!—'Nov. 20, 1979. All this manifesto stuff is beginning to get on my nerves. We've been so dizzy with it you'd think we'd made it to the TZ...' What's that?"

I laughed, "Why the 'Torrid Zone,' of course. Rune made up the term. It means we thought we were *hot shit*, you know, that we'd arrived at utopia."

"'...but it's beginning to be a drag. We're arguing.' That's the only mention...no, wait a minute. What's this—Isis?"

"Isis? What's it say?"

"Isis contradicts herself. I don't know who she's really agreeing with, me or Vashti.'"

"Go on. Any other names?"

She flipped through more pages. "'Astarte and Luna not talking.' Lots more on chop wood, tote water. Freezing rain. Ah, 'Maya and I got high…' uh, 'chimney fire. Luna always closes stove down too much. Maya and I cleaned chimney again.'"

"Maya—that must be me. I remember climbing on the roof one damn cold day. When was it, December? Luna can only be Kristy—she did close the stove down too much, always scared. We always had to check. I think we made a policy after that not to let her deal with the stove, but she'd do it anyway. I think that was the time we discovered, to be fair, that we hadn't cleaned the chimney that summer. No one else wanted to go on the roof except for Kite and Rune. Interesting though—I never knew she gave us all code names. Vashti must be Spence, and Isis—Willa. It's true, Willa always played devil's advocate. You'd think she had one point of view and then suddenly she had another, half the time siding with whatever Spence thought was cool. Sometimes needling her much to Rune's delight, then switching again. Find any more names?"

"Castora and Polluxa."

"What! Now that's a gender switch. Must be Kite and Mel. She always thought they were joined at the hip."

"Then who's Ceres? 'Axle on Ceres van broke.'"

"Kite had the van. So…she made up different names at different times."

More page flipping. "Yeah, here: 'Read Caliope's copy of *Lady-Unique-Inclination-of-the-Night*.' Here's another: 'Cut Athena's hair.'"

"She could cut hair very well. I don't know who Caliope is in that case. What's the date?"

"March third."

"Well, she had a house full of goddesses. What a gas, so TZ, huh?"

"What did she think?—that she'd confuse anyone trying for a sneak look at her journal? Now, wait a minute, listen to this: 'Why Isis has to have a show now beats me. Moving canvases in zero degrees. And no snow yet.' Doesn't she mean Elsa?"

"I remember that—the winter we didn't have snow. And Elsa had her first real show and she was so uptight about her canvases in the cold. So…she used names interchangeably! Who is Isis indeed! What a laugh. Isis could be any one of us or any one else for that matter. Some young dyke she met in her town. And she did it simply to keep our lives private!" I dropped the harness, suddenly. "Oh Rune, how I miss you." I wiped my eyes. "She's the one I miss, you see. She's the one I miss. Don't read me any more, okay?"

"I don't mind if you cry."

"Thanks a bunch." Then I spoke quickly to regain my composure, "You can research the diaries all you want, but you'll find that Kite was the real guru, the unrecognized kind, because she didn't even acknowledge the power she had herself. Wouldn't have thought of it. Just kept things ticking. Never mind the L.P.B—that's why I call it a joke. We were absolutely dependent on her—her vision, her sense of management. She could have had us all under her spell if she'd thought of acting that way. Well, certainly I was, but that was my own doing. Do you see?"

* * *

Whenever I think of Kite, I can still see her on the old faded blue Ford tractor her great uncle had left to our cause—meaning he'd left it in the barn when he went into the nursing home. 'Ran when I parked it,' he told her.

I see her roaring up and down the field, plowing for the corn crop, left hand on the steering, right hand on the huge rear fender as she turned that way to watch her progress, her face shaded by her Beacon Feed cap. Dressed in worn out hiking boots, cut-offs and one of her faded T-shirts tight over her muscular shoulders, so sporting a real farmer's tan, I could watch her bare leg muscles flex on the reluctant clutch and brake pedals.

Do I have to come right out and say this was sexy, or what? Do I? Kite on a tractor, hm mmm. How I leaned on my garden fork and lusted.

Meanwhile Kite taught me about farming. It has to do with one's sense of time, the way you set a pace, the way you take on a task and stick to it until its done. Kite was not one to be hurried or distracted. Once she had taken on a job, she finished it, even if the weather changed or the sun set, or dinner was served. Sometimes it was maddening. But over time I came to respect and understand how she ticked.

She showed us on the land how it wasn't the clock that dictated to us, but the weather, for instance, the moment the soil temperature was right. Other things we thought were more demanding were put aside. If it was time to plant corn, we planted corn. And the fact of how many hours we were supposed to put in towards the common endeavor became moot.

Now Elsa had the same kind of devotion, that is, to her painting. If she had worked five hours in the field, she'd stop, put her equipment away and go to her studio. Kristy would just as likely follow her indoors, mostly to lie around. And Mel had a thing about getting to the kitchen to cook, even if it wasn't her turn, if she thought we were taking too long about some project.

But Kite would just keep steady on, even if the rest of us drifted away to do nothing better than put on records, get stoned, *pretend* we were artists or have idle conversation. She'd kid us: 'In your *spare* time, how about getting that wood stacked?' or 'Oh by the way, when you have a little *time off* would you prepare the chain-saw fuel mix?'

I didn't get it for the longest time. After all, my five or six hours were done—did I have an obligation to go on?

But Kite had come from farming and it was in her blood. She came from a stock of people that the Industrial Revolution and time-cards hadn't quite dashed yet. I began to understand that farming didn't just mean producing food from the land, but came with a completely different view of time. She was adsorbed into it, much as Elsa was into painting a canvas. No task but the one of the moment could be as compelling or as inspirational. If she were plowing the field or strumming her guitar in the evening, (say, singing the Ferron song 'If it's Snowin' in Brooklyn,' except substituting the words Blue Corn,) it was all part of a continuum, one activity balancing out another.

I wanted that too. I thought we'd discovered something really radical—wimmin's time, *yeah*.

Didn't I have anything that could be such a vocation, nothing else to distract me from my purpose? I wanted to stop thinking about an hour as representing at least five dollars, when I knew she was beyond thinking whether her hours even amounted to fifty cents.

I thought that if I was able to find this way of being in myself, then surely I'd find enlightenment.

I suppose I have found it to some degree, but I still find myself too easily distracted, fragmented, interrupted. I'm still too frantic, too impatient. Except when I'm working with stones the way I do because you have to move slowly and carefully with them, some of which weigh much more than you do. You have to think about lifting and moving them using leverage, and not damage yourself. I have to think of the consequences all the time—if you put your hand here, is it possible that instead of the rock going that way, it may slip and crush your fingers?

When I work with stones, I'm thinking how all those walls along old pastures were made only as one part of a larger whole, that of turning forest into field. Piling all that heavy rock around was so one could hitch the horses and plow. At any rate, now I can say, well, I got five hundred dollars for that wall, figured at about fifty hours of work when I really spent more like sixty or seventy. I could be satisfied it was a reasonable endeavor because I lost myself in the task while I was doing it, fitting stone to stone. And enjoy my cold beer at the end of each work day. Yet through all the millennia of people moving rock around, that's still a tellingly modern approach to time and money. I still need to get to the point where I can put a stone in the place I think it fits and feel the way people did on say, Easter

Island, or the Orkneys—something that just had to be done because that's where the rock belonged. A greater purpose—that's what I like to feel when I build a wall.

Because that's the way Kite farmed.

And that's why it was so awful that she lost Blue Corn.

And that's why I think of her as an unsung guru. Either that, or she's part of a dying breed. If it is the former, then it's about time I sang about her; if it's the latter, I'm singing before it's too late.

Seventeen

Lorraine came up for her weekend and the major task was to fit Cloud's harness on. A matter of seeing whether our maturing mare had outgrown it or whether she could use it one more season. Cloud loved the attention, first the currying, then the brushing, the soft brush over her face and ears, the stiff brushes through her mane and tail, next the piece by piece fitting as though she were getting measured for a party dress. She trembled to the touch.

Viv who was working on her lap-top in the living room came bounding out to give me a message.

"From Flo," she said. "She's all in a state. The bank is going to remove the painting. And she proposed buying it! She has until Monday to come up with the money—ten thousand dollars!"

"Ten?" I stopped in mid-buckle, astounded on all fronts, not only that the painting might disappear from view but also at how the price had gone up. "Elsa sold it to the bank for two thousand!"

"Yeah, and Flo wasn't kidding when she said it was more than her severance pay—"

"They're laying her off?—shit."

"She says she can put up about half the money short term but needs others to buy in too, at least until she can find another buyer who'll take it. She says she's on the phone like crazy and if there's any way we can help out to let her know. She wants you to call her back soon as you can, wants to see if you could help move it."

But I wasn't even hearing her. My heart was in my throat. Fierce despair throttled me, that no matter how I hurried all I'd get to on time was the funeral.

"Well, what do you think?" Lorraine's steady voice broke through to me as she always could. Maybe she saw me pale. "I think I could put up, say, two thousand, Ida. I could do that. Can you match that? And unless Flo has a place, we could always keep it here."

I gulped. "Here?" Mentally calculating what I had in savings. Two thousand would pretty much wipe out any spring to my cushion. Wipe out my Olivia cruise once and for all, my trip to Machu Pichu.

"Sure," Lorraine expanded, "it's the safest place. If people break in up here they do it for liquor and guns, not art. No one has ever bothered Taylor's Matisse in the bedroom."

"Matisse? You mean that brush and ink painting of the boy over by the bureau?"

"That's the one."

"I never knew that was a Matisse."

"See."

"Wow," said Viv, dancing from one foot to the other. "Think of that? And we could have Elsa's painting here! Matisse and Matthau—major art gallery at Curley's Ledge."

I turned to her. "I thought you didn't even like it."

Viv shrugged. "Maybe it's growing on me."

"We can store it. I don't know if we can display it." Lorraine spoke as she caressed Cloud, beginning to take the harness off again which she would hand to me piece by piece to put in a box. "There there, Cloud, yes, we're taking it all off for now. I know you don't like the blinders. Looks like we're down to the last buckle holes but it'll do. No, I'm sorry we can't go out till the cart's ready. Soon, I promise. Next week."

I began undoing the harness where I stood on the near side of the horse. "The only wall space we have big enough is down in my cabin. Hm, I wonder if we could get the Women's Museum to take it since they have another in her series already. Look Lorraine, this girth-strap is about cracked through here."

"Mm, I'll have to replace that."

Viv snapped her fingers. "No! I have just the place. McKee Institute! They manage to find funds all the time for archival material. I know because I had a work-study job in the office and they talked about that a lot—acquisitions. Every year they have to use up the allotted funds or lose the amount altogether by July. Just before I left they still had ten thousand bucks. So they're into it. I bet if I said it was because of this paper I was doing and all, and we got Cooper behind it, we'd be golden."

"We would?" I gawked at her.

"Yeah!" She squeaked with sheer pleasure.

Lorraine looked at me quizzically over Cloud's rump as she loosened the crupper.

Viv rolled her eyes at me. "Don't you see? For a student to make such a find! What a coup. And do I ever have one here! It'll put a neat feather in Coop's cap too, a push along the tenure track there. She'll get the real credit. And if I don't get an A-plus-plus for this paper with Exhibit A! Can we go phone Coop now?"

"Hold on, hold on. Let me talk to Flo first, okay?"

"And Elsa too, right?"

All this as Lorraine snapped the lead onto Cloud's harness and I took off the cross-ties.

"Can I take her out?" Viv put out her hand for the lead, taking the mare off to join Juniper.

Lorraine watched her for a moment then turned to me. "Looks like she thrives when she has a cause, that one."

"Don't let her fool you. The real cause in this case, is Gem," I said tersely as I hoisted the box up to my hip, to take indoors.

"Really? Oh dear." Then she burst out laughing, stopping short when she saw my sour expression. "What? Gem didn't warn you?"

"Only to tell me to take the picture down of her. Sheesh, I think Viv sleeps with it when I'm not looking. I don't quite get it that she didn't really tell me...maybe she hoped it would go away. Or something. I'm waiting for a reply to my letter about it. But if you ask me, Gem seems, well, distracted...all the school stuff, the anonymous threats, but...but she got so uptight about things when I said I thought it would be a great idea for her to stay at Natalie's—you know, her lawyer friend."

As we headed towards the house, Lorraine leaned into me with an elbow. "Don't be silly. You've said Gem would be up front with you if anything changed."

I just growled as Viv jogged up to join us.

* * *

"Okay, Flo, so what's our plan of action here? Yeah, Lorraine and I can put up four thousand. Who else?...oh, that's good. All right! Make the checks out to you...okay...you're writing just one check for them, got it. Five hundred short still? Don't worry about it. We'll scrounge it up somehow by tomorrow, squeeze some more out of myself and Lorraine. Kite? I don't know. She's recovering from a back problem. I hope she can. No, no, I really doubt she can come up with any money. She's always overextended what with the house and business. Mel? Nah, forget it. Mel's off having an affair. Oh you heard? Hm, news travels fast."

"What's she saying?" Viv whispered emphatically in my other ear as I paced the living room with the phone. "Tell her about McKee—"

I waved her away impatiently. "Elsa? No, I can't say I have, but I have her phone number somewhere. Yeah yeah, I'll give her a call, for sure. The others? Look, Flo, I haven't talked to them in ages. I don't even know where Spence is these days. Never mind about that. First things first. I can get Kite. Yeah, I'll be there. Like I said, we can move it up here. Let's see...I'll have to scrounge for cardboard and tape, oh...crated? Excellent. That's excellent. Let's just hope it doesn't rain. Well, of course I'll bring a tarp. Okay. Fine. Yeah—"

"Hrrrr," came Viv's stifled scream of frustration, arms flapping as she trailed me, another U-turn at the end of the sofa.

"Okay. Nine o'clock. See you then." I clicked off the receiver, exasperated. "I can't conduct business with you buzzing in my other ear, Viv. If you can't contain yourself while I call Gem, you'll have to go outside."

She shook her curls out at that one with a look of mild disbelief.

First I hunted for one of Elsa's invitations which I knew I had somewhere in the cluttered drawer of my desk. Ah yes, there it was. *Landscape with City Block*. Manhattan Island, I think, how it used to look a few hundred years ago…with some modern all-glass sky-scraper plunked in the middle, reflecting it back. Oddest thing I'd seen her do. Can't say I was into her new stuff much.

What did I think, that I'd find her at my disposal in the middle of the day, paintbrush in hand? Of course I got her voice-mail or the offer of a fax.

Too breathlessly I said, "Elsa, here's a blast from the past. It's me, Ida, and I'm helping buy *Women in the Field* from the bank here. We want to find a real home for it but meanwhile I hope to bring it to my place on the farm with Kite's help, I—" Her machine cut me off there.

Viv was very good, didn't say a thing, slouched attentively on the couch while I swore at the phone. I began to dial Gem, then stopped, aware of my sudden nervousness. Nervous with Gem? Sheesh. Why? Very conveniently due to the absence of a safe distance we kept by writing letters, huh? Besides, our last phone call still left a bad bit of fuzz at the back of my mouth.

"Yeah well, so I'll get her answering machine anyway," I said aloud as I did.

"Send a fax!" offered Viv, ready to serve as she clicked on her lap-top. "We'll whip out a letter with all the particulars, then she has a little time to think about it. Not on the spot, you know. Go head, dictate."

"You my secretary now?"

"I'll delete anything I don't like," she sniffed. "Here, we want to say how much McKee Institute needs this painting and if there are still funds ready to use up, hey, presto, we can deliver the painting right away. Why don't I modify it slightly while I'm at it here, and send one to Henrietta Lester—she's the Archivist."

"I admire your enthusiasm, Viv, but don't get ahead of yourself here."

"Ahead? I mean, you don't understand, Ida, the gallery is head-to-toe with paintings, photographs, lithographs, even films of women in the workplace. I mean, you think Cooper didn't know why she was sending me? Damnit, they even have a photo of my mother when she was ordained. Of course, it's, you know, not on display and also, she was an alum, right? But hey, they had a whole show on women in religion when I was still a junior in high school and didn't give a shit. My mom dragged me up there to see it anyway. But you know, for McKee to have a Matthau, and come to find out she worked out here in a real wimmin's land collective."

I had to snort. "You didn't know squat about Matthau—listen to me!—I mean Elsa, before you got here!"

"But now I do. See, that's the point. What a discovery. Jeezee Peezee I could even make it into the alum magazine if this all works out. That would make a story!

"You're a scream, Viv, a real scream."

"Yes! Here, listen to this—I made it formal-like: 'Dear Professor Gem Cooper, semi-colon.'"

"Don't put Gem, for godsake, put Geramie."

"Really? Oh. Okay. Just being…isn't that's what you call her?"

"Yeah, it's what I call her, get it?"

"I didn't know that. So personal. Thanks, that's really important for me to—"

My head sank into my hands, "Oh goddess, spare me."

"That's Hatshepsut to you. Okay, here we go: 'A truly exciting opportunity has presented itself to me and my research scholar'— that's you and me, see, now hold on, wait—'who has been studying the woman's land collective, Blue Corn, 1977 to 1987, where the now renowned'—no, do you think I should say respected?—'respected painter, Elsa Matthau, made a series of landscapes which depicted the women at work on their land. One of the series is now part of the permanent exhibition in the Women's Museum, Washington D.C., another exhibited by a prominent law firm. A third has recently come up for sale and local Matthau friends have rallied to save the painting from certain storage or art dealers by putting forward the quickly collected price. But no one can keep this large'—how big is it, again?"

"Ten by six feet," I said peering over her shoulder at the screen.

"Okay. '—nor are these benefactors in a position to bear the burden of the cost. We would very much like to propose offering this painting for acquisition by McKee Institute Archives, and would be happy to meet at your earliest convenience. The price of Elsa Matthau's masterpiece, *Women in the Field*, is ten thousand'—"

"Oh, it's a masterpiece now, is it!" I slapped my thigh.

"Well, you know, hey I'm selling an idea here. Signed, Ida— what's your last name?"

"Muret."

"Yeah. That's right."

"Sheesh, you're really on a roll, aren't you?"

"Okay, we'll just print this baby out, and then I'll address one to

Ms. H. Lester, to be consistent. And see, I'll put my initials in lower case like a real secretary—vl—Vivian Lovejoy. My last name is Brewster actually, but I dropped it. Lovejoy is my middle name from my Mom's side."

"Now what?" I asked watching the neat sheet of paper coming out of her small printer. Wow, to be in school again and have these kind of gadgets. Not even to need white-out "There's a typo in 'Field.'"

"Damn. Okay, well, we can keep that as a draft. This next one— we fax it."

"Right, put it on your research account, okay?" I sighed at the prospects of high phone bills which I so carefully avoided.

"No, problem, we'll add that to our commission fee."

I think I rolled my eyes at her but obviously it didn't bother her as she whipped the sheet out and set up the fax for transmission.

"Sign here...Done," she announced. "Now for the next."

"Well, hey, it's been swell, Viv, but don't go getting your hopes up," I said staring at the draft in my lap, and I had to admit it looked good there on paper, even with the typo.

"Oh you," she pouted. "Why don't you think things can work out? You're so ready for defeat. Why try?"

"Oh yeah? Am I or am I not going to get Matthau's masterpiece tomorrow?"

"Sure, but what I mean is, and don't take me wrong, puh-lease, but like when Rune was killed, you kinda threw up your hands and just let it happen to you too. The collective scattered and you just let it go, not because you wanted to, just coz you're...you're...you're a defeatist. And here's your big chance to pull it all back together. Make Elsa help you get ahold of Spence. Get ahold of Willa...Kristy too, even if she is on the West Coast. And, and even Mel, like it or not. And if she won't come, screw her. That's how real families are. You just get everyone you can together. What a great thing to do for Rune. You know she'd be into it."

"Out of the mouths of babes." I sat stunned, looking at her.

"That's me, dyke babe!" And she pressed the fax button. "Presto. Hey, let's send a copy to Elsa while we're at it!"

"True. Rune did always call me the most passive-resistant person she knew. I just thought it was because I was stoned. But to be fair," I waggled a forefinger in the air, "if there was a row to hoe, I was out there doing it. And I was the one who picked up the pieces after everyone split. Pff, why am I defending myself to you!"

She knelt on the carpet, leaning with her elbows across the coffee table so that her lap-top slid to one side, and waited for Elsa's copy to print out. "Duh, I'm not asking you to, okay? There, now Elsa can find that. And now, we've gotta call Kite. Here's the phone."

"Right. O...kay. Let's see if she's up off that couch yet. Yoho, Kite! Yes, I can't tell ya how happy I am I didn't get your machine. Yeah, yeah, of course Kelsey's bit is cute, but—yeah, yeah, she's definitely the next Ellen and Leah rolled into one, but—You up and about? Good, good. No no! I just really wanted a real person. Look, here's the scoop—"

Lorraine called into the room, "Hello folks. You done yet? Remember we were going to groom the horses and take a ride?"

Viv jumped up. "Oh shit, totally forgot. We'll be right there!"

That, after all, was the real task of the day. With Lorraine on Fortissima, Viv on Juniper and me on Mosey, we were all to take our first jaunt of the season. It was to set us up so that Viv and I could at least work with our two mounts, Lorraine not wanting Viv to take out Fortissima on her own yet, except to groom and longe her. And hey, if we were going to enjoy the luxury of faxing everybody, we certainly had no business forgetting to earn our bread.

Horses still barefoot, we did eventually set off through the old logging trails in the woods, taking Fortissima through brambly places and Juniper through wet spots, things they liked to get all worked up about. Mosey would just go through anything; all I had to do was hang on. And wouldn't you know it we found a pink lady slipper right in the middle of the trail; stepped so prettily over it.

* * *

I got a cryptic fax over the weekend—she wasn't even risking a live voice on this end, I tell you: *Got your letter about Matthau painting. Will get the idea rolling. Awfully busy and cranky right now though, so don't call, please. Here's a list of other people at McKee you could send the letter to, but give more bio. on artist, list of recent shows etc. Will check with you Mon. or Tues.—Geramie.*

Hm, couldn't decode that piece no matter how hard I tried. But I can read tone.

"Here, Viv." I tore off the note at the top, crumpling it, and handed her the list. "More fun and games for you."

"What she say? What she say?"

I didn't want to be emotional, but I did feel stung, the kind of sting where you don't really realize it at first because of the numbing sensation. "Oh, she's too busy to respond...later..."

* * *

"What an awkward size," complained Kite where we stood in the lowest level of the bank watching Flo walk toward us in the corridor. She supported one side of a tall and slender crate which in turn, rolled on a dolly beside her. The other side was propped up by one of the bank's maintenance crew.

147

"No, no, I'd rather have it this way—it's ready to install, see, as soon as McKee decides to buy it," I insisted. "You just follow right behind me on the trip home."

"Trust me, I'll be the very one to rear-end you." Kite clutched her forehead. "Oh god, remember all those times we rented moving vans for this shit?"

"Hey, wait a minute, I've got twenty-two hundred at stake in this shit, and you can't just order a new part if you make a dent, okay?"

Viv, beside me, ogled the crate with too much interest to partake in nervous chit-chat.

"Well, grrrls," greeted Flo, looking both harried and relieved. "It's all ours. We'll have to carry it up the steps from here—won't fit in the elevator. It's going to be cumbersome but light."

Didn't seem right, I have to say, to see her on a workday dressed in those designer jeans and sweatshirt, clear evidence of her fresh dismissal.

Kite and I didn't react to her comment, just went at the box as we had so many times before, instructing Viv and Flo to walk on either side, just for security while we each took an end. Luckily the strapping the bank shippers had put on, helped with our grip. Otherwise it was as big a pain as hauling a mattress. A light one, sure. Yet I saw Kite grimace even with the back brace her logging cousin had loaned her.

My truck waited at the loading dock, ready with two-by-fours at an angle towards the right-hand side so that we could set the painting in and then tilt it down. With my six-foot bed plus the open tailgate, the two and a half foot overhang wasn't as bad as Kite made out it would be. We bound the crate in with my ropes and tested for any play. I added a red kerchief to the rear for good measure.

"Come on, Flo, can't I change your mind and have you come up to the farm with us? It won't be the same without you," I begged her one more time, all previous attempts met with her usual business-like 'I'd really love to but I can't'.

She seemed to be biting her lip in thought one last time, then with a more light-hearted shrug, "Why not? I don't have a job as of today, right grrrls? A whole Monday free for adventure."

"All right!" Viv jumped up and down.

Indeed, why not? A more beautiful May day could not have been ordered. The trees were crowning out with an intoxicating green. And I had a Matthau on my truck bed.

Off we went—I took Flo with me and left Viv to follow up with Kite. Too bad Kelsey wasn't along but it was a Mel day—and there seemed to be no more flexibility to parenting in that family these days. Hey, don't even get me started. Now the fights are over scheduling and how to share the kid, Mel insisting that Kite had to be up and fit first. Of course, Kite was up and fit, but Mel's argument was that Kite couldn't lift Kelsey and this was some parental necessity, that is, what if there were some life and death emergency? 'Then I'd damn well carry her, wouldn't I?' Kite had relayed to me. No, no, Mel thought it important to have Kelsey close during this time of upheaval, that she needed to bond with her new home a bit too.

Well, you know whose side I'm on. And there are sides now, believe me. As things look stickier, I keep saying to Kite, "Hold on— say yeah, yeah sure, honey, because Mel is in the middle of a whole new romance and she's going to be pushing Kelsey off on you like you won't believe. Just wait. Resist her, and she'll tug at you so hard, give you such grief, you could lose Kelsey—don't think I can't see that threat. The pain of it is in your eyes. Look, it's not like I haven't seen a thing or two down the years. If you watch so many tug-o'-wars a couple has on any number of issues, you get the hang of how they play the rules. Frankly, Mel—she's all bluff, a fierce self-righteous wall of bluff. But you've been the backbone all this time, Kite baby. Say: As you wish, honeybunch."

Of course Kite doesn't want to believe me, even though she knows perfectly well. I have to remind Kite of every time she butted and crashed right into that hard bluff. She doesn't remember! Where did it get her? Day One at Blue Corn, it started, Mel insisting she wanted the big upstairs room for them while Kite wanted the downstairs—the old parlor. Mel carrying on like a diva and I had hardly stepped in the door, Rune's eyes just bugging out, and Willa and Spence not quite knowing where they were suppose to settle in, so they went to the back room which ended up being Elsa's room later, of course. The minute Kite said, 'Okay, honey, but I have to leave the four poster bed downstairs then since there's no room for the headboard upstairs. We'll just use the box spring and mattress…', even carried the stuff up, oof, urk, with help from Rune and me—and what happened? Aha, Kite started chatting upstairs at night with Rune and yours truly, oh sure, smoking joints on the landing, talking about Kite's farm plans, lingering, not quite wanting to go off to bed yet. She was into it and we were avid listeners.

One evening Mel's crashing around their room and thundering down the stairs with things under her arms. Kite looks at her, huh, what's going on here? Pretty soon, down goes the mattress and box springs, urk, oof, to their proper bed frame. You bet—Rune and me doing the grunt work.

I know I know, I digress but that's what I was stewing about in the space of half a minute as we all opened vehicle doors and started off for the farm with Elsa's *Women in the Field*.

"Hells bells!" Flo yelled, rolling down her window, giving the bank the finger. "What a way to go, eh? What a way." And she rummaged in the brown bag she found at her feet. "What's this, Ida? Champagne?"

"Ah, that!" I said with a triumphant smile. "Heh heh heh. That is a bottle of hard cider Kite made with her cousin last fall."

"Alcoholic?"

"Well yeah, it has a bit of a buzz—"

"I thought you guys never drank at Blue Corn."

"What makes you think that? Oh I know, that's because often we didn't have money, or maybe just enough for a couple of six-packs on Saturdays, right? Spence and Willa usually split a bottle at a time so they usually had at least one and a half apiece. And Rune and I found we could play that game too. And then there was always a guest or two. But that was pretty much it."

"Na uh. Not when I was ever there. I thought all you had was mint tea and tofu around there." She was serious.

I scoffed gently, "We only had tofu because it was cheap." And then I remembered, of course, Flo used to be an alcoholic. "We don't have to open that today, Flo."

She looked over her shoulder to check on our cargo. "Listen, I almost forget I'm an alcoholic. Almost. I'm so good. I just became a workaholic instead. And now I'm thinking that this is so good for me...I can think a whole new line of action here. Did you know I have two condos? Well, like a true capitalist I had one paying rent for both, well almost. So, I can sell my condo, keep the other as a rental for cash flow, as a back up. I can free up some cash to keep me going for awhile, find somewhere else to live, maybe share a house with someone. My ex even invited me to stay with her, but I don't know if I'd like that on weekends...but see, I could do things, say...work for gay rights, pro-choice, stuff like that, stuff that I just pay the twenty-five buck membership fee for once a year and forget. But you know what, Ida? I was in my element as a workaholic, people, people all day. No time to be lonely, long hours overtime. Money! No real time for lovers. They come, they go. Hell, I could even have a relationship with someone now."

I couldn't quite tell if she was sincere or sarcastic. Her tone kept changing to the point of wistful in the end.

"And I guess I'll even get my hair cut locally instead of going to Boston."

"Woah."

"Yeah, I know, I know. Whenever I went down on company business I'd get my hair done."

"Goodness, I thought we were pretty well serviced around here. We have cellular phones now, helicopter medical service, can plug into the Internet, get fresh bagels, hey, and we got you to keep us in touch with all the gourmet trends."

Meanwhile I went up Route 7, the byway, so I wouldn't feel pressured to go more than fifty, keeping Kite in my rearview mirror. I liked that. I don't know if I ever had Kite in my rearview before, had I? Surely I wouldn't forget something like that. If I took my eyes off the road just long enough, I could see her grinning and laughing with Viv.

I wanted to be in that truck with her.

No I didn't.

I liked her right there in my rearview mirror.

"Look, Flo, that's the wall I'm working on, coming up on our left. Stintson's. That installation will bring me close to two thousand bucks by the time I'm done. What a steal, huh?" I boasted.

"Very nice." She gave a careful, appraising nod. "Just don't ask me to load it in your truck."

Eighteen

"So, where do we put it?" Kite stretched herself out where we all stood in the dooryard. I began undoing knots in the ropes. Flo stripped off her sweatshirt to reveal a T-shirt with the image of a three dollar bill. At my quick double-take, she winked.

"I'll just run in and see if there're any faxes!" And Vi was off.

Crossing my arms I took to leaning against my truck. "I dunno. Thought we'd store it in the small loft over the horse stalls."

"Won't that be a pain to get up there?"

By now Flo was cradling Hecate, talking kitty to kitty. "Aren't you displaying it, Ida? C'mon, what about in your living room?"

I snorted, "My living room."

"Well yeah," Kite took up. "We want to be able to see it. Perfect wall. Isn't it a good twelve feet?"

"The loft cuts into some of that. And my couch is barely eight feet from it. Talk about close up. Besides, we'd have to crate it all up again—"

"Ida, c'mon." She leaned against the truck on a muscular arm, brushing her hair back eloquently with the other.

There was no way I could say no to Kite. It had never been one of my strong points.

"Get a load o' this!" Viv came running out with a wide paper streamer behind her. Breathless. She had stripped down to her baggy boxer shorts and halter, revealing her body with a freedom I certainly didn't express at nineteen when I covered myself in long sleeved work shirts, and I didn't think that I could get away with flaunting a perfect belly button above my waistband nowadays like that. It just had to be better for young women now. "Wait a minute, wait a minute. Bad news or good news first?"

"Bad news?"

She took my question as a request, tearing the streamer apart. "Okay. Here, a letter from Riétta Lester saying we need to fill out some formal questionnaire, some information sheet which will come in the mail sometime soon. Procedure, you know. They'll have to take it up at the next board meetin', da-da-da... Screw that! The next board meeting in July!—my ass. I know they have money they must spend in the next thirty days. Flo, you look at this. How can we jump on them?"

Just as I was about to take a look at the fax it slipped on through my fingers and off to Flo who studied it with Kite looking over her shoulder.

"Here," Viv shoved the next paper at me like a consolation prize.

While Viv explained the McKee idea, I read: *Ida, how extraordinary and wonderful to hear from you. Sorry not to get to talk to you. All I get is your machine. So this. Yes! I'm thrilled about the developments with Field. You are my Hera. Let me know what the next step is. If your first plan doesn't go, here's another idea—see if the local gallery wants to take it on commission—they were always terrifically supportive of me. Maybe I could do a show, bring some of my new stuff up. Listed below are galleries and dealers who have done well for me, and who also do appraisals. You should pass those on to your contacts. Talk to you soon. Love to Kite and Mel.—Elsa.*

"Hm, not a bad idea. Plan B. Here, Flo, wanna be the official Matthau broker?"

"Okay, this is good, this is good," was all Flo replied.

"No way! It's gotta go to McKee!" Viv insisted with a stubborn lower lip. "But this might give us some leverage—nothing like a bit of competition. I could write a letter, goes like this—gallery excited about taking Matthau's painting so don't miss your big chance to bid on this painting extraordinaire."

"You have your broker!" Flo declared. "That's the spirit. We need to take a photograph. People always like that kind of treatment."

"You're right." I pointed my finger at her. "Wait a minute. I think Lorraine has a camera—she takes pictures of the horses all the time. Let me go see. Hope it has film in it. We need really optimum lighting. Where?"

"I think right against the natural grey siding of your cabin," Kite suggested, taking in the sun's position. "That's where we're heading with this thing, anyway."

Flo added excitedly, "I'll take the film with me and get it developed in town right away. Viv, get a letter ready. We'll send a slick promotional package out tomorrow to the highest bidder."

"McKee," Viv insisted.

"But we haven't talked to the local gallery!" said naive little old me.

Both Viv and Flo just looked at me—"Eh."—in unison.

* * *

Having fortified ourselves with sandwiches we managed to unload the crate at my cabin with ease, gently setting it up against the siding. With Flo and Kite holding it in place, just in case, I set up

Lorraine's tripod and camera. We had three shots left on the film—she sure liked to take pictures of her horses, that Lorraine. I motioned for them to take their fingers away. Photos done, we slid the painting through the wide doorway once I had pushed the wooden door back. While the girls hung the canvas I even put in my screen door for the summer. The sunshine and the breeze made us all feel euphoric.

"Ain't it somethin'?" Kite said with a click of her tongue and a shake of her head, cider bottle wedged between her knees where she sat on the end of my futon couch with Viv leaning on her.

Flo sat squarely between Viv and myself taking up the other end. She nursed a seltzer with a twist of lemon, thanks to Lorraine's refrigerator, "Mm hmm, yeah."

I just sat dreamily gazing at my one and only real wall, now a bonafide mural. "And to think I had great plans of putting a window there."

"Don't know about that nude though," Viv clucked, to goad me. "She's gotta go."

"Think?" Kite looked at her askance.

"Yeah, I think the real focus of the picture is the tractor, you three around the tractor. Why should that be a background motif? It should be the tractor and then these workers beyond in the field, one bending, one rising."

Kite protested, "But Kristy represents the earth goddess, fertility. The rich loam is the real subject of the painting…see, the hair in contrast…and that women are the farmers. I mean, that's where Elsa was coming from."

I sat in silence, thinking that I'd let them have it out.

"Viv has a point though, now that I think about it," said Flo. "So why do you want McKee to have it?"

Viv gave her an exasperated look, making me relieved that I wasn't the only person to get the treatment. "Because it's art, it's illustrating history—image! It could be the very key to my paper!" Then she paused. "I want to do it for Blue Corn. I want to do it for Rune."

"Woah." That made Kite sit up and take notice.

Yeah, right, I thought. You want it for your own purposes, Viv. Get back in the good graces of McKee, get in good with your favorite prof. Then I shrugged. Hey, whatever works, kiddo. I like your pluck.

If I had such pluck I'd offer to install a visionary stone wall and terrace, using marble blocks. Say a curved wall like a crescent moon, each block cut and fitted to the circle, an arch on the horizontal, creating a terrace, each block marked with a rune, and in the middle three steps gently sculpted, so that the center of each looked worn by the feet of priestesses in procession to their now vanished temple. One for the maiden, one for the matron, one for the crone. That's how it came to me, my vision, a moment of pure bliss thinking of Rune as the four of us sat there, the other three still discussing the canvas. And some plantings—Kite would know what to suggest, but definitely apple trees and a …beehive. Not the modern box kind Rune used and which I now had tucked on the far side of the barn, but something conical like ancient ones. Out of clay. Willa would know how to do that. Or have a spring, a fountain with something like the Gorgon Knot left by Spence, and which I now used as the overflow spigot into a horse trough.

"I think I need to get going back to town." Flo's voice cut through my daydream. "You ready, Kite?"

Kite stood up and stretched out, handing me the cider bottle for recycling. "Last swig's for you."

"Yeah, got to get back to my stone wall job," I rallied, taking the gulp and wiping my lips with the back of my hand. For it was certainly going to be useless speculating on the cost of marble at this point until I got paid for a job completed. There, for the first time in about twenty years, I was dreaming about marble again, but with a real spark of passion this time, no thoughts of hacking away at it to find some hidden form. I would simply build with it. Not with rocks the way I found them this time, but sculpting each piece to fit in its place.

My dreaming was like a fever. Maybe we were all feeling something in that spring sunshine, heady like the sparkling cider as we bounded outdoors and up the track to Kite's truck.

"Does McKee ever have artists-in-residence?" I asked as Viv and I waved the truck away.

"Yeah. If they're having a show and can get the artist. But usually for short stints, a week or two. Say—?"

I knew she was thinking I meant Elsa, and I let her for the time being. I wanted something bigger. Blue Corn artists no longer pretending to be pretenders.

* * *

When I got home at the end of the day, I found Viv sitting on the patio with her lap-top, notes clamped down under each foot against the breeze. Hm, looked like she was writing up a storm, eyes glued to the screen.

"Fax in there for you," she stated without greeting.

So I sat on the low wall, slowly untying my work boots before pulling them off and sauntering into the house barefoot, first grabbing a beer from the fridge.

The fax was not yet torn off the machine. Odd, I thought. Viv was so good at it.

I ripped it off and went to sit in the coolness of the living room.

Ida — news about Elsa's painting is really and truly a terrific idea. I've done my best to talk it up and get some action. Don't know if funds are still floating for acquisitions this year but did urge Riétta to take request seriously. I wish it could be better timed for me personally that is, and not while trying to wrap things up, worrying about whether I'll be here next year and all the other tiresome hassles.

Then I get your letter. And all I can say is shit. I can't deal with this. Yes, I know I should have warned you about Viv…I guess I thought it would just go away, or it seemed insignificant in light of the other issues at the time. I didn't know you'd get some grand confession.

I was hoping we could talk this summer when we had time, face to face. But things have gotten so out of hand and I have been emotionally wrenched lately. I'm afraid I have to be frank and I'm afraid to be frank. Letters are the best, really. They have always been a good way for us.

I always told you I would let you know if things changed between us, if my loyalty shifted or should I say, expanded? Lately, I have really counted on Natalie. You will probably think I have too much, when it should be you. But it seems as if it has all been part of this whirlwind I'm sucked up into. And she is there, yes, at the quiet, calm center. Life is like that. I know you know. But she is THERE. She is what is happening to me, with me right now. This possibility has always been there since we met, and I have always kept it at a distance. And I know you have felt it acutely from the first time you were in the same room together. Her desire, her jealousy, your desire, your jealousy. And me cringing in the middle on this see-saw of emotion, because I see her when I'm here, not you. And then when you come, your strength dazzles me.

But the point is that I'm here. And she's here. And yes, I've allowed myself to be caught up it this. My choice. I own up to my responsibility in my actions. I know I can't make sense of them for you, only that it makes sense for me right now. Not sure what that will mean. I have not altered my plans about coming up to you this summer. But I know it's not simply my choice, but hinges on you, of course. I have not changed my plans for her. Perhaps this will clarify why our last conversation was so awful, because you were saying, go to her. And I already had.

I'm sending this immediately, as is, before I chicken out. Reply when and how you see fit. Yours, Geramie.

This from my Gem?

I read the letter again. Again. Our secret love code was completely missing. I asked myself, But am I stupid or am I stupid? She's saying she *slept* with her somewhere in there, isn't she? Well, isn't she? She means sex.

Sex?

Was that ever a loaded scrap of a word, or what? My girl was having sex with another girl. Did that mean someone else wanted her as much as I did? And she wanted her? Got turned on and all?

What a scream.

I sauntered out onto the sunny terrace, going to sit on the wall, letter still in my hand as I took a long gulp of beer. The sweat of my afternoon had dried away to a chill.

"So," I said, my jaw shivering, waving the fax, "I got this…and you won't tell me you didn't read it, will you?"

Viv didn't look at me but watched a sheet of paper coming out of her printer. "I was getting this package ready. Flo's coming by this evening so we can put it together. I said she could stay overnight. I hope that's okay."

"Of course."

"Do you want to proof it?"

"Sure. But not right now."

We sat in silence as she pulled the sheet clean and laid it on the small summer table beside her lap-top.

"I didn't know it was going to turn out to be a private letter," she said by way of explanation.

"Of course not. Gem should've known better." I waved the letter across my face, adding with acerbity, "Maybe she assumes you're out in her tent."

She snorted. "Oh yeah."

Another long silence.

She sighed, "I knew she was with Natalie. I knew. I didn't know she was with you. I shoulda—"

"It doesn't matter, really. Not now, I mean, what you did or did not—"

"Damn her!"

"Damn her?"

"Yeah, damn her for treating you like this. Aren't you ripping?"

"Oh, that." I might have laughed some other time, the sweet way she came to my defense out of her own wound. With one knee up I rested my outstretched arm, letter dangling along my shin. "You know, I always think of Gem as so reasonable. Our agreement of loyalty and that we would talk to each other before making changes. She never denied her attraction to Natalie. She just said it wasn't something she allowed, that she had no need 'to explore it further.' She was with me. I really believed she would discuss what it would mean to us before she became…before she…well…and then she couldn't do that, it seems. She made the step already. It kinda changes the discussion we must have, I think."

"'I didn't know you'd get some *grand confession.*' Fuck that!" Was the response I got, one I rightly deserved since I was talking

157

aloud to myself too.

I snorted, "I think I understand why she wanted me to keep quiet about her while you were here. Speculation about her love life is one thing to deal with, but wouldn't do for word to get around that she had two lovers, now would it? I don't think she trusted you to keep from yapping to your friends."

My Gem, choosing someone else before talking to me. The awfulness hit me as I dipped my forehead to my knee. Bump. Bump. The paper crumpled up in my hand. But I didn't rip it up into little shreds. I don't know why. Later I stuck it in my journal. After all it was a significant piece of my day. "I need to put the horses out. Want to come?"

"Sure." She closed her lap-top with a look of disgust, heaped all her things together and went to drop them on the couch as was her habit now.

We walked together to the stables going through the routine, speaking tenderly to the horses, feeding them carrots. And at the time I thought how wonderfully calm I was. Calm because part of me had predicted this outcome some time ago; I just thought I'd get advance warning, enough so I could make a good stink about it.

"It can't be as good with *her*," Viv growled fiercely as we closed the gate behind Cloud, Juniper and Hepp.

"Can't count on it, kiddo. And I don't want to think about it. It isn't helpful." I made my way to clean out stalls, she taking a manure fork to share the chore.

"Sorry, Capt'n."

My Gem. Damn.

Well, better throw out that possessive pronoun with the manure, honeybunch. Heave ho.

And I thought how stupid I was that day talking with Kite and telling her how we could make Mel go on a purge.

I wasn't hungry that evening, no, I was in this great state of calm—that's how my fury is—smoking my pipe on the wall outside while I heard Viv banging around in the kitchen.

At long last she came out, saying grumpily, "I'm making some nachos for when Flo gets here. Shit. Why don't you act pissed or something. I don't get it! I'm throwing things around I'm so pissed and I never even ever slept with her! You are so...so fatalistic or something."

And only then did it occur to me what I needed to tell her as Flo pulled in the dooryard. "Viv, haven't you ever been in shock?"

"Shock—" she actually flared her nostrils at me like Fortissima. Then with a turkey waggle, "If it's shock you're in, why not use it and, like, make waves?"

* * *

"Plan of action here, grrrls? Look, I've brought some very nice folders with really nice plastic sheet covers inside. Used them all the time for presentations at the bank. That one for the photo—did we do a good job, or what, Ida? Look, I did them up eight-by-ten glossy. Four color jobby." Nachos and pleasantries aside, we sat at the large kitchen table, oohing over the photographs Flo had brought of *Women in the Field*. "All computer enhanced now, you know. I took the shots over to a friend of mine and we played around a bit this afternoon. Monkeyed with the colors just a little…got that real texture to the loam. I think this one works best. Pretty, hey?"

Viv leaned on her elbows. "*Too* cool."

"Excellent." I nodded, pushing over all the printed drafts of information and biography Viv had composed on Elsa from lists I had given her. Not only that, she had actually drafted an outline of her paper on Blue Corn, promising a lacework of interviews and the discussion of Elsa Matthau's work, followed by a bibliography citing works on the Shakers and the Oneida Community, to the Nearings, and articles about women on the land gathered from alternative periodicals. A complete list of the books on my shelf, if you ask me. Her working title read: *Post-modern Women's Land Movement, One Portrait 1977-1987.*

"Oh well, you worked this up real good, Viv. Real good. A-plus on this paper," Flo remarked.

Viv beamed.

I skewed up my face. "Post-modern. What the hell does post-modern mean? 'Modern' means that of the present. And weren't we pre-post-modern anyway?"

Viv took a deep breath, bracing herself against me, I could tell. "It's just a handle, okay? Don't get all bent out of shape."

"I'm not—!"

"Are too. It has to do with art, right? Tying it into Elsa's paintings. What was it you said anyway—the 'art of surviving'?"

"Yeah, well by that I do mean post-modern—as in the after-life."

Flo, carefully preparing two folders, talked right over us, "Priority mail ought to do it. I think, anyway. Any word on how things are going with the acquisition funds? Gem going to pull strings?"

"Oh yeah. Believe me, she'll do all she can to get funds for it. If she doesn't go to bat out of ambition to get tenure, then she'll do it out of guilt." I laughed but it didn't sound as robust as I intended.

"Guilt. Oh dear," said Flo tapping the photograph so it would lie flat as she pressed down the plastic sheet.

"Yeah, coz she's having an affair!" Viv blurted.

"An affair?" Flo bowed her chin, lifting her eyebrows. "Oh dear."

"I don't think what she is having is an affair," I corrected. "I think Gem would be the first to defend herself on that point. Gem doesn't have affairs. That is, shall we say, an archaic term. Let's say she has expanded her loyalties."

"My, my, this is an unpleasant little turn, isn't it?" Flo shook her head sharply. "I think it demands our presence at this McKee place sooner than later. Maybe we should go deliver this painting and sit on the doorstep until we get paid, make Gem feel so guilty."

"Yeah! Big crowd of us!" Viv chimed.

"I don't think I'm quite ready for that. I don't even think I want to see Gem. Look this is very raw news. Very raw. I haven't even composed a reply yet."

"Want me to help draw one up?"

"Viv, no. No, no! Please, let's deal with the painting, okay? That's what's important here. Gem would be the first to agree that the painting is what's truly going on. This, this preoccupation we have as a culture with romance, with sexual liaison and scandal— you know, it just comes out of being bored, comes out of a need for stimulants, sensation because in this *post-modern* era people don't have enough meaningful work to do. If you are involved with your-self as a *whole being* integrated with your environment, things like this take their proper *perspective*. And pray may romantic intrigue be the least of it."

Even while I was talking away, Viv was tearing off a scrap of paper and scribbling madly.

"What the hell are you doing?" I snapped at her.

"Writing that down. I think I remember Gem, I mean, Professor Cooper saying almost exactly that."

I kicked my chair aside as I stood up. "Damnit, of course you do. Where do you think she gets half her fucking ideas. It's from shit we talked about. Want another soda, Flo?"

"Ida!" Viv's face was positively aglow. "You're making waves!"

"You bet I'm making waves. I mean what did Gem and I talk about all this time, why did our relationship work at all?—it's because it was based on the premise that we each had our own important thing to do, and neither of us would compromise the other on that point. The very premise we built on! Go back to the L.P.B., Viv—the statements about keeping work and play in the proper perspective. Keeping sexuality in the proper perspective. Even keeping language matriarchal. Back to the land! Oh yeah. Work to feed ourselves, keep ourselves clothed and warm so we could each do our art. Each! Not just Elsa! Avoid, above all, messing in each other's lives. You know, I think we pulled it off pretty well, come to think of it. Coz when it got messy, like a safety button going off, we split apart. If we're going to take this painting down to

McKee and you want to get us all together, then it's gotta be a Blue Corn show. All of us. And Rune's needlepoint screens too.

"Your outline is incomplete, Viv. I mean, your paper is your paper, I know. But we need to include the kind of personal work we each did, and why. And we will go down there and we will propose all this. And tomorrow I want to go start pricing marble.

"Viv, you say you want to do this for Blue Corn, for Rune. Well, I finally know what I'm supposed to do. Now it'll be terrific if McKee comes through on Elsa, but I have something too. It should really be a permanent installation, no way to know if they'd go for that—well, and if it wouldn't work out at McKee, then some other place. I'll make an initial working piece here...out back. Out of stones, but ultimately in marble.

"Meanwhile let's get this packet ready. If we mail it out tomorrow first thing, we could all go down there, leaving early on Thursday. We'll leave the horses out so we don't have to worry about them. Come back at the end of the day?"

They were both looking at me attentively.

"Wait a minute," Viv said at last. "I'm not supposed to go on campus."

"It's just a day trip, you, Flo and me, and Kite if she can. Just to see Riétta. Joker won't even know you're in town, especially if you go low-profile, know what I mean? And we'll all stick together. The point is, can you deal with it?"

"Well, I don't want to stay here alone!"

"Let's get to it then," said Flo with a pragmatic slap to the table.

Nineteen

The next morning while Viv groomed and longed Fortissima, I began to scout out my work site. Flo left early to mail the letters after we had also sent a preliminary fax stating our plans.

The three steps I wanted to lay had to rise to a vanishing point so the bank behind the house wasn't ideal but the incline was right. My only other choice would be to call Pepper in and create a mound of dirt somewhere. And that would involve money which I so recently didn't have.

Besides it didn't have to be permanent. If anything I had learned that stonework wasn't necessarily so.

With stakes and string I began to measure out the piece, pacing it out. I was a big one for pacing things out. Making doodles in my notebook as I went. There were sumacs I was going to have to dig out, and it was awfully close to the compost pile we had for when we cleaned up the garden. No matter.

The thing was to keep working because I sure didn't want to think about Gem, and also, to be careful so I wouldn't wrench my back or something and be confined to a couch having to think about Gem. Besides I knew I was having a real hard time with the thought of still being erotically involved with someone who had become lovers with someone else. I just couldn't handle it. As basic as a reptile not being able to move about unless it had the warmth of the sunshine.

She should have talked to me first, I kept muttering to myself. Except in my heart of hearts I knew that wasn't the issue. Warned me? I had had plenty of warning really, just by the repulsive negative charge Natalie and I always gave each other. And whether I wanted to or not I had to respect the fact that what she was going through made a lot of sense to her at the moment—spring, the intense end of school term, not knowing whether she had a contract or not, being harassed by threatening notes. And I wasn't there on the spot to support her.

Hadn't we talked about how a true feminist would never subsume another in a relationship?—no Gertrude-and-Alice B. for us. Especially when I had a strong urge to devote myself to someone, never believing it might be at my expense. No bondage. Lesbianism at its best needed to be wary of what patterns it imitated. How did she put it?—in it's purist form lesbianism had to cultivate the erotic attachment of two equally wild and free spirits in mutual admiration? As far as Gem went, I knew perfectly well I had to stand on my own and be cool by myself.

Whether I liked it or not.

I took my shovel and began to dig and cut away at the bank, working with such deliberation that soon I was engrossed in the task as I created the earthen shape for my wall, steps and terrace. Time once and for all to cure myself of the ghost sickness that had clung about me these many years, my loss of soul.

I wanted to hear Rune's laughter quickening inside me again, because I couldn't remember. I didn't hear it with my inner ear, like a tune I couldn't quite recall. Spence would know. Spence would be able to imitate this lost laughter.

While I dreamed and worked, I also thought about an estimate. I had this beautiful opportunity for a wall which would separate a lawn and garden from woods and creek. But I was definitely going to need Pepper's help at least one day to dig and prepare a level course. I had to come up with a reasonable figure in terms of unit hours for the job even though I knew I'd always end up short. As long as I had my beer at the end of the day, right?

"You busy?" Suddenly I heard Viv's question though I hadn't heard her come, had long ago dismissed her from my mind especially since she had settled in the living room with her work and music. "You look like you could use some lemonade. I have some on the patio."

Her tone was odd, I took note, as I set aside my tools and went willingly for refreshment, "What's up, Viv?"

"Say I found Isis?" She said it as a question, pulled a chair next to me and sat down, plunking a book in front of me on the stone wall. "This is from the box you packed up in Rune's room back home. I thought just her books were in there but it's her last journal, the one that ends two days before she died. Here, the first mention is November 6th: 'Ran into Isis today on the street. Could not believe it. I think the last time I saw her was the day she told me she was joining the army. And I was heading off to college. She sure has changed since that skinny kid she was in sixth grade, that time she stood on her head and we gave her water to drink to prove you could do it upside down. I can still see those knobby knees against the wall. How we used to practice kissing in the girl's room, charging lunch money at the door for anyone who dared to watch. Just for practice, of course—French kissing. Now she looks strung-out, kind of jaundiced look, yellow in her eyes. Alcohol, drugs, something.'

"Next mention is here, November 14th: 'Went for a beer with

Isis—turned out to be two whiskeys with a beer chaser and she let me pick up the tab. I said how about coffee next time. She laughed and said not before four in the afternoon. Talked about the old days a bit but she couldn't seem to remember much, foggy, scattered. Her clothes look expensive but not warm, even the leather jacket. Has her head shaved on one side and dyed red on the long half. Seems to have a lot of time on her hands. Wanted me to get high with her, said she had the most powerful stuff, but I just laughed and said all I did was computers now.'

"Then here, a week later again: 'Went for a coffee with Isis. Took me to a bar and had liquor in hers. She looks ten years older than I am. Runs with a tough crowd from the sounds of it. I worry. Told me she got a dishonorable discharge because of a drug conviction. Wanted to know if I could lend her fifty bucks. Too weird what ghosts you run into when you go back to your hometown.'"

I peered at the entries for a long moment myself. "Hm, no. In all the time I knew Rune, she never mentioned this 'Isis' that I can recall. I remember her talking about a couple of girls from school, girls she had crushes on. That kind of thing. She never talked about her best friend in sixth grade." I fell silent, trying to think.

"Why do you think she chose the name Isis for her?"

I shrugged. "First thing that came to mind?"

Viv read on, her tone insistent. "'November 30th: Isis asked me to meet her after I had my visit with Ma at the hospital. I really had nothing better to do though I've seen a poster at the health food store for women's pick-up basketball. Thank goddess that will start next weekend and I can do that after visiting hours. She doesn't seem to have a permanent address, not one she'll tell me about anyway. Says her boyfriend works at night. Dealer or pimp is more like it. So we walked the streets downtown. Talk about a wasteland. Said she needed money for her kid who lives with her mother. I don't know if she has a kid or not since she couldn't keep the pronouns straight. Wanted two hundred to pay the doctor's bill, just till the weekend, then she'd pay me back. Very convincing but I said I couldn't help with that kind of money, even if she were being on the level which I'm sure she isn't. She was always good at talking a good line. Asked her about AA and all that, where she could get the help she needs. She just laughed and said she'd been through them all.' Then there are pages and pages of her mother's treatments, stuff she's fixing on the house…oh yeah, here—just before Christmas. 'When I got out of seeing Ma after her treatments who was there but Kali right in the waiting room.' Look, Ida, she's switched names."

"Uh oh. The blessing into a curse."

"'Desperate for money. Owed someone a lot of money. I

thought it was bad enough she came around at work looking for a hand-out. She had a fit, said she needed at least five hundred. She got really belligerent in the parking lot. Just till the weekend. I said no, gave her a twenty I had on me. I really didn't think I wanted to see her anymore. Was I too hard? I just don't know who this is. Yeah she was always a fiery, street-smart kid, but this is scary. I wonder if she was high on something.'" Viv finished and when I looked up it was directly into those fierce, probing eyes. "Here's another at New Year. 'A call from Kali. Real friendly, up. Wanted to apologize, invited me to go out. Told her I didn't want to go to an all night bar. No, thanks, no way. Not for me. At midnight she called, getting me out of a sound sleep. She was higher than a kite and carrying on. Told me to have a happy New Year, that things were looking real good, laughed uproariously, hung up.'

"Some more, undated, 'A whole week of peace without Kali showing up at work or the hospital. Honestly, I dread running into her.' An entry after that about the septic backing up and having to call the plumber."

"Here, let me see that…yeah, that's right. It's the plumber who called her uncle at work to find out where she was because she was supposed to meet him and let him into the house on her lunch-hour, and meanwhile she hadn't shown up for work."

She flipped the page. "Last entry: 'Maybe I was wrong about Isis. She's frantic because she's in deep shit. Truly deep shit.'"

"Viv, this is too heavy. Do you know, I was just feeling a shift today, out there working on my piece for her. Finally, finally something dislodging. And then you find this. It's too uncanny."

"So, are you wondering what I'm wondering?"

"It's kinda hard not to, isn't it?—but let's not just jump to conclusions here. For one thing her family could have told the police about Isis seeing her often. Just because I don't know anything about her doesn't mean she wasn't up there on the Short List along with Spence. And what if she was just like Spence, getting heat for nothing." I hoped my gaze was just as fierce as hers.

"But Rune mentions her over and over with a definite concern. I don't see journal entries like that about Spence. Over and over, she's being nice to her. She senses something…Look here, by Christmas Isis-Kali is waiting in the hospital for her. Wasn't she killed after evening visiting hours with her mother? Remember you said she was really good about getting vibes, wouldn't hang around people she didn't feel right about? Well, she isn't feeling right about her. If Isis stopped at the rest area to help her…hey, she could have caused the flat by doing something to her tire back at the hospital parking lot…she could have been *waiting* for her, wanting money and things got out of hand. She could have driven the car to the rest stop *after*…punctured the tire *there*."

I shrugged, trying my best not to let her see how her words made my skin crawl. "Okay, so it's possible Isis killed her. From the little we know, that is. But this isn't Clue, Viv, for chrissake."

I felt like a load of bricks was falling on me, and there she was perched over some kind of gameboard.

"She had a motive—money!" Her voice rose a pitch, "Don't you want to follow it up? If Rune were my friend, I'd sure as hell want to at least ask about this woman."

"What? Are you the budding P.I. now? Would you have wanted to question Spence too?"

She slammed the journal shut. "Shit. I don't believe it! Can't you at least call her mother up and ask her whether Isis was questioned? Can you remember her at the funeral? Wouldn't she have been at the funeral?"

I cradled my head in my hands. "Oh Viv, I was so out of it at that funeral. A swirl of faces around me and I was so distraught by the way she was being buried like that. If I was in shock and dismay, I mean, her family was in just as bad a state too. I think we would have noticed if she had been there, especially when we were tracked down. And really, Viv, if the detectives were on our tail, they had to have ruled this Isis out at some point too."

"How could they if they didn't know her real name? The only information they had was Rune's date book. And they didn't get far with that."

"You want me to go to the police with this? You must be kidding? Next thing they'd say I was withholding evidence."

"You'd feel better about Rune if you knew who did it," she said flatly, but her eyes held a gleam of triumph.

"Oh yeah? Like justice will be done by it? It won't bring Rune back, will it?"

"Yeah, but it will clear Blue Corn."

I hissed, "We are in the clear."

"Yeah, so maybe they didn't ever chase you all down and charge you, but what about in your heart? All this time the killing remains unsolved—it's like something hanging over all of you." Her blue eyes blazed. Her eyes were blue! All this time her eyes had been blue and I had never quite gotten to seeing their color.

I sat back in the garden chair and looked back at her for a long moment, spoke slowly, "Look, Viv. You have to understand something. What happened, happened a good seven years ago. You know how there is a law about if a spouse is missing and presumed dead for seven years, you can legitimately remarry? And I think that's the time frame for Statutes of Limitation, and for common-law marriages to legalize themselves."

She leaned with her elbows on the wall. "So, what's your point? Statute of Limitation gonna apply to this?"

"No, not that. I don't think it does in murder…no what I'm driving at is those seven years—why that's the number chosen. And I'm thinking it's because that's how long it takes to heal or to get on with things, get a life going again. Doesn't one's body completely replace all cells over seven years? Do you see? I think that's how long it has taken me. I have a life again now. A good life. And maybe the others do too."

"Maybe," Viv retorted. "But you still have scars. Being suspected. Talk about being thrown a curve. You want to be cleared. If I could make that happen…"

"You are a budding P.I., aren't you?"

"Why not? I think it's going to be part of my activism. We dykes have to wear all hats, don't we?" This while she patted herself on the head, my old Beacon cap as firmly plunked there as ever. "Who is going to represent us better than ourselves?"

"You're right," I nodded, thinking how she was definitely gung-ho about research.

"Then you could have a reunion. This cloud is what's holding you apart. Especially Spence.

"You want to vindicate Spence, huh?" I sat back in my chair.

"Yeah…I kinda like her."

"Kinda?" Did I detect a hint of a new infatuation? "You're right to. Some of us were like a calming herbal brew—Elsa, Kristy, Mel, Kite and me, for sure. But Willa, Rune and Spence—they were the spice. Especially Spence. She was—"

"Like cayenne?" Viv looked at me wickedly.

"Flaming hot."

Hey, Spence is an unsung guru too. No, more like an icon, keeping in tune with the times, snapping her fingers to the right beat at the perfect moment, fingers on the pulse. She should have had real power and money, that girl. She could have made dyke culture the Happening Thing all on her own.

Go for it, Viv, I thought. Go and vindicate Spence. Of course she was relying on me to help.

* * *

I didn't feel safe. Again I was in the Blue Corn house. A dead house, all emptied out. Just the husk.

I was sleeping downstairs in the front room for some reason—Kite and Mel's room, woke up to my aloneness and the dim light of night. I walked in the ruins. Yes, ruins. I kept asking why had the demolition been done while I slept without anyone asking? Why didn't I hear them? The floors were littered with debris, the windows gone, the house exposed to the elements. The wind.

And someone was there. Lurking. Waiting. Ready to break the door down the minute I fell asleep. Coming for us and I was the only one left.

At last I woke up for real, sat on the edge of my bed and looked out the window into the morning sunshine. The long back pasture where we put the horses in to rest after shows and where I had chosen to dig, was alive with dandelions and also trout lilies down in the wet places.

"Good morning, Ida," I said to myself too cheerfully. "There is no one. See. The police still haven't come for you."

So, shouldn't I stop dreaming this now?

I had to find Detective Daniels' card. I'm sure it was burning a hole in a box of books or tapes and letters somewhere. It disturbed me so much now that I couldn't even do chores properly. Odd thing, when I climbed into my barn loft, it was as though I had no more searching to do. One of two boxes had to have it among stuff I'd piled in there when I was moving out of Blue Corn and never looked at again. Maybe in an old almanac.

As simple as that. I found it—Dee Daniels—and raced to the phone. At the same time, panicked. Like Hepp when the vet comes. Was I really going to do this? Would I even get ahold of her? Would she even remember the case after all this time? Was she even 'in the business' anymore. I mis-dialed on the first try. Again. Then I managed. My voice cracked as I asked for her. Took awhile and then I was given another number. I didn't think I could dial another.

Viv who was working on her lap-top, nudged over to me when I was put on hold, but she didn't say anything.

Daniels *remembered*, in fact her words were, "I was wondering when you would call me. It is not a case I could possibly forget."

I asked, "Why did you think I'd call?"

"Something you remembered. Something that came up. Sometimes it happens." Her nasal twang was pronounced. "That's why I gave you my card. Where are you?"

"In Vermont."

"Ah, of course. Too bad. I was hoping, by chance, you were more local. Then I'd be offering to meet you."

"Why's that?"

"Easier to talk," she said slowly as if it were a loaded phrase I should understand. "But this will have to do."

"Yeah, I don't think I'll be back there any too soon."

"Sorry to hear that. Maybe I can change your opinion. What do you want to know? Maybe I can help."

So I explained too breathlessly and ass-backwards. I read her all the entries, and asked her what else they had found out.

"Nothing conclusive, nothing for a conviction. There are a

range of possibilities. How unfortunate you didn't find that journal *then*."

"I was pretty driven to distraction at the time, in case you forget!"

"It's just that trails grow cold, you know. You must understand, immediately after a crime this is an extremely pressured job. You have to grab every lead hoping something will take you to the end of the trail as quickly as possible. I'll see what I can find out. Sometimes you just go on gut feeling—hear what I'm sayin'? Sometimes you just hope the evidence you gather proves you out. Sometimes it does. But sometimes you have to lean a little on people, make them uncomfortable, trip them up. Do you understand?" From her tone I could almost figure she was apologizing for our ordeal so long ago.

"Even when they don't know a fucking thing, weren't anywhere near the crime and might be completely in shock that they lost someone they loved!?" I said, enraged.

"Everyone protests innocence, even the murderer of the most premeditated crime! We can't know till we've sifted through what we find. And in Renata's case, we really couldn't even tell for certain whether there was more than one perp or not."

"Perp? How about killer? Call a damn ice pick an ice pick." I yelled into the phone, "You guys wanted it to be us so bad! Tell me, what was so suspicious? That we were dykes?"

"Look, don't shout at me," she interrupted, sounding just like she did when she went woman to woman with Spence at the rest area, then sank into a weariness. "Obviously, no one is going to go to bat for me on this one, so I'm going to have to *tell you myself*, hear what I'm sayin'? I stuck out my neck for you guys back then to make sure it wasn't pursued further, exactly for that reason. Hang on a minute—" Her voice was gone for a few moments. I heard a door shut, and then she was back, "There was a strong element around here that wanted to run you into the ground."

"You mean Findley."

"For starters. And I mean into the ground. He had his reasons...uh...he was convinced. We had two pieces of evidence that could have been worked up by the prosecutor. One, we had the fact that Renata was going straight and had left the commune, causing deep a rift—"

"Straight? What the hell do you mean by straight?"

"That was from her brother."

I gasped, "*Tom?* Hell. Rune wasn't going *straight* except in the sense of computers and a back account! And she left with the intention of coming back!"

She plowed on, "And that cult members were either going to

extort money from her or force her to go back. Something went wrong, perhaps she resisted—"

"We're a *cult* now?"

"Look, I'm just telling you what was going on here. We had the vehicle, we had the motive. We even had a description that fit one of you. They were ready to do a line-up! I had to go out and find conclusive evidence to make it clear you could not have been in two states at once."

"You did?"

"All I needed to do was point out that one and one doesn't equal three. Pretend to gather evidence for the prosecution that would clear you instead. Wasn't hard to prove that you were stuck in a snowstorm and that I90 all the way to Albany was closed on the twenty-eighth and that not only were many flights cancelled, but there was no way Joan Spencer could fly from New York and back in the time frame she had. Not according to the coroner's report which put time of death between eleven and midnight. Until then, the prosecutor had three witnesses who could report seeing a woman who fit Joan Spencer's description during the month before the murder. The *theory* was that one member was sent to deal with Rune, I mean Renata," she finished hastily. "The point is that a case could have been made against you, counting on the fact that you had no resources for a good defense or even an appeal. Especially if it was put into motion quickly. There were complications to that. For starters, we had let you go at the time, thank God, and you were in another state."

"Good thing you saved them the time and money," I snarled. "They underestimated the friends and neighbors we had around here. I have no doubt we could have come up with a good lawyer."

"Believe me, I had an inkling, especially since you had been arrested at Seabrook." She sounded as if she were about to laugh, then held back. "But still, it would have been dreadful. We would have all gone through the wringer. No one wants a messy procedure and to lose too. Aside from the politics in the department and all, I did get promoted eventually, in part because I spared the prosecuting attorney a possibly very serious headache. He even thanked me, off the record of course." Then as if enough chit-chat was enough, she was back to business, "Listen, I'll see what I can find on this sixth grade friend, okay? Hold on to that journal—it could be important. How can I reach you?"

I suddenly choked, afraid of a hook. After all, I still lived in fear and dread of the police swooping in. "I'm not easy to get ahold of. I don't deal with phones. Wait, I'll give you a fax number."

"Good. Believe me, there's nothing I'd like better than to see this particular case solved."

"Why's that?"

She hesitated. "Because...I don't like to see *family* get the shaft, hear what I'm sayin'? I'll be in touch."

As I hung up I shook my head. If that wasn't code, what was it? "I don't know, Viv, but I think we may just have a dyke detective on our hands."

Twenty

"They actually want to buy the painting!? I don't believe it. I simply don't believe it. Let me see that," I exclaimed to a very smug Viv who handed me the fax from Riétta. There it was in writing. I read aloud just to be sure: *Upon expert advice we are pleased to announce that the McKee Archive would very much like to purchase Elsa Matthau's* Women in the Field. *At this time we do not have the funds for the complete price and commission fee of eleven thousand which you out-lined in your letter, however we would propose a down-payment of five thousand, the balance to be paid in installments which we would like to negotiate with your broker. Upon receipt of your aforementioned packet in the mail we will be happy to discuss your additional proposal for some future date. Please contact us at your earliest convenience, yours sincerely, Riétta Lester.*

"Sheesh, Viv, we did it! Thanks to you."

"And Flo," Viv quickly added. "We must call her. As the broker I don't think she's going to like this installment idea. They should be able to borrow against some other budget or a bank for chrissake."

"She'll tell us what to do. Meanwhile we're going to have to crate that baby all up again. We won't have to go down there tomor-row empty-handed! What a buzz."

She laughed, "C'mon let's call Flo, let's call Elsa and Kite too."

We did, we did. And Flo said she was so thrilled and nervous she'd have to call in sick, but oh shit, she just remembered she was out of work.

"No, no you're not. You're the broker!" Viv and I chimed. "And we need you to make them buy it flat out." In any case she was going to come right up and be part of the party. She'd bring a sticky date pudding, all the rage nowadays.

"Really? What happened to your tiramisù cake? I kinda like that."

"Passé. Leave it to me, I'll call Riétta from here about arrange-ments."

We called Kite. She said she didn't see how she could come because it was a Kelsey day until noon and no way would Mel agree to an extension, never mind letting her take Kelsey across state lines.

Mel had informed her that she was planning to get married. Married! Not new news to Mel, apparently, but something in the works for months already—they had just been waiting for his divorce to be finalized. Kite was reeling. And Mel wanted a lawyer to handle their custody agreement, until then any liberties with the routine they already had with Kelsey would jeopardize future negotiation, especially since Mel was, after all, the biological mother.

"You could fight it, Kite, you could fight it in court," I restrained myself from screaming. "There's precedent in Vermont now."

"I will if I have to, Ida," Kite said. "But right now I'm not going to rock this little boat and give her one iota to use against me. When she has a bee in her bonnet like this I have to let it buzz until it flies out by itself. If I put up any resistance she'd use it to push on. I'm not going to settle for less than equally shared custody, let me tell you, but I'll wait till she gets pregnant—which she will, you wait and see—and we'll see how much she wants me to take Kelsey then."

What! Had Kite come to at last? "What about the house?"

"Well, it was my inheritance that got most of it going. But like with Kelsey we have never signed legal agreements. Didn't think we had to, did we? Outlaw marriage. And as far as Kelsey's college fund goes, I'm the one who keeps it going. So I'm not without leverage, am I? Look, Kelsey and I will come up and celebrate after you get back—on Friday or Saturday, okay?"

"Kite, it won't seem right without you since you were really the catalyst for this to begin with, cluing us into the painting at a critical point."

"I really can't."

"Hey, it's okay kiddo."

"Know what, Ida? I'm strangely relieved over all this, that it's finally clear…now I feel like I can take a step forward for myself."

I had to sit in the sunshine with another cup of coffee after that one, before gathering myself enough to call Elsa.

And she was home. To hear her voice after so long…oh, I had forgotten, or had her New York accent become more enhanced now that she lived there again? She wanted to know where to meet us, where was this McKee place anyway? I let Viv give her the directions as I paced the patio in a mix of emotion.

Afterwards Viv came out. "What about Gem? Are we calling her?"

"Fax her, Madame Secretary. Tell her that our presence will be brief—leave any mention of your name out for safety's sake. Just say Flo and I are bringing the painting down tomorrow and we know how busy she is. We'll understand how difficult it will be for her to make time, and so we accept her excuses in advance."

"Wow, that's it?"

"That's it, and don't take liberties with rewording the message.

Oh, and add that we'll bring her car down and leave the keys with Riétta. You and Flo and I can squeeze in the truck for the drive home, can't we?"

"Aren't you, like, going to talk to her, give her some kind of answer?"

"That is my answer. Oh, you can say I'll leave a note in the car under her seat, but this way she has the leeway she may need. I'm off to get the stalls ready. Come and help bring them in when you're done?"

She shook her head as she went in. "Sure thing, Capt'n."

* * *

On Thursday rain was predicted to arrive later in the day but we didn't care because we would have unloaded the painting by then. All packed up and setting off well before nine for the three hour drive, I let Flo and Viv follow me in the Honda, Flo doing the driving there. When we reached Connecticut, Viv would join me and navigate.

"Off with that cap, kiddo," I said plunking it on my own head. "Low profile, remember? And you're to stay in the gallery."

When had I felt such excitement? I pretended Rune was beside me and that I told her to pick the tunes. I thought, what would she like nowadays? She'd always go for Bonnie Raitt. So that's what I played.

It was a beautiful building, that McKee gallery with it's spacious rotunda, windows in the domed ceiling. We took a tour, walking slowly around, our footsteps muffled on the carpeting as we waited for Elsa to arrive, having already unloaded the painting which was being stored in a closed, side-gallery.

Leaving a restless Viv with Flo for a bit, I went to put all Viv's due assignments in campus mail, then thought I'd duck into the bookstore across the way, really well-stocked with non-fiction by women authors. Great place to pick up periodicals or journals which I would never subscribe to. I lost myself in browsing for awhile and then I heard two students talking at the cashier's desk.

"Yeah, did you see that? McArthur got tenure and Cooper's now Assistant Professor."

That shook me awake. I gathered the news was posted on a corridor bulletin board where I surreptitiously went after paying for my goods. Indeed, her name was posted there under a big 'Congratulations' heading. Suddenly I felt panicky, itchy around the neck. Here I was on Gem's turf not even daring to see her, dreading even a chance meeting, and I was hearing news about her. News that on the one hand I wanted to greet with jubilation, running to catch her up in a celebratory hug. News which meant she had signed a three year contract, tenure track, news which meant security, news which also meant that she would be staying here with Natalie large and looming in the picture. Aargh. Too much. When I went to the rest room to recover and was washing my hands, someone bounced into the room, crying, "Viv—Maid in the Shades! Shit, didn't think you'd really come. Don't you know that he—?"

"Know what?" I turned quickly and looked at the young woman who was approaching me ready with a high-five slap to mine which didn't arrive.

"Oh sorry, I thought you were—" And she turned, beelining out the door.

"Wait!" I hurried after her, hands still dripping with water just as two women bumped in, swinging the door in my face. When I finally got around them there was no sign of her.

Damn. I had turned too soon in my surprise as if I was supposed to be privy to anything about Viv. Whatever she was going to say she wasn't going to say to me. Yanking off the cap, I stuck it in my back pocket.

I hastened back to the gallery, immediately distracted by Elsa greeting Flo and Viv. Ah, to be caught up against that large embrace! Meanwhile I could tell Viv was antsy to talk to her. I was ansty to talk to Viv.

"I have a surprise for you," Elsa winked. "Should be coming through the door right about—"

"Spence!"

"*Too* cool."

There she was, head-to-toe in leather, stud in her left nostril. Short hair dyed jet black and shaved up and over the ears. I gathered her in my arms as we thumped each other on the back.

With a quick hand she cradled me under one of my breasts, whispering, "How're them melons?"

I just laughed. "Sinking, they're so ripe. And you're as wicked as ever."

"Yeah...I like to keep my hand in it." She winked, and I knew she'd accepted the compliment.

As Flo hugged Spence I turned to Elsa with an inquisitive gesture, "So how did you find her?"

Elsa chuckled. "She found me! Came to one of my shows last year and now we do lunch, what—every month or so? We're planning to rent a huge studio space, even live there together. I don't know, Spence—think we'll be able to get along?"

"As long as you stay on your side of the line," Spence kidded back.

"Yeah—and we were planning to collaborate on a show this fall even before your message."

I could feel Viv nudging me from behind as she hopped about. "Oh, of course—this is Viv who started this whole thing by coming up to ask about Blue Corn. I think she'd very much like to have some time to talk to you."

"Oh, right!" Spence pointed at me with a limp wrist. "Your lover teaches here, Elsa says. When do we get to meet her?" And I could see her scanning around.

"Not so fast, Spence! Actually, I don't think she can get away today. Finals…you know…" This as Viv literally hung on to me. She had never done that before, like a kid hanging onto skirts or something. Couldn't shake her off. I was surprised at her shyness.

"Then maybe we can catch her this summer. I've really been wanting to come up and paint in the country again. I've been feeling at a dead end with my mirror series," Elsa spoke as we all slowly wandered again, waiting until our appointment with Riétta and other members of the Acquisitions Board. "I find I'm still using sketches I made back at the farm. Even Spence. Tell them, Spence."

Spence spoke in the halting way she used whenever she talked about personal things. "Yeah…you know…just doing these sound sculptures. Remember how the kitchen floor was so creaky? Well, I have this set-up, looks like a platform really…but it's this creaky floor. Wide floorboards, of course. Each board gives a different tone by being wired to the synthesizer. So when you step from board to board or even one end as opposed to the other, you get different sounds. You can just walk across if you want for slow, deep tones or you can dance a bit or whatever. By the way, I read the copy of the proposal you sent to Elsa, and I see you're working on something. I like it. I like it, Ida, I really do. I'd like to contribute too."

Let me tell you, those last words of hers were *loaded*. I saw this acceptance in her eyes about what I wanted to do for Rune.

"Then laugh for me like she did. I can't remember…inside, you know, gurgling inside."

Her look of surprise only lasted a half-second, and then she burst into laughter like a song. Just like Rune used to.

"That's it," I said with deep satisfaction. "Viv, hear that?" I still hadn't been able to shake her off.

Spence gave a sharp jerk, a twitch to her head, directing her words to Viv, "Well…I mean she's probably told you…Rune and I never got on that great. I mean it's not that we didn't get along. What the fuck was it, Ida? It was like two household *felines* that just never get along and there they are living together and eating from the same fucking dish. I used to think it was this, uh, dominance thing, you know, or like certain things just don't mix well…or something."

Spence laughed, her own singular 'heh heh heh' that I'd picked

176

up from her and kept as my own. She was in a good mood, not the way she was the last few years at Blue Corn when she walked around with this little black fog hanging low around her eyebrows. Indeed she had really stuck it out there much longer than was right for her. That was clear. She looked so tall today, shoulders back but relaxed, definitely a sexy thrust to her slender hips in those tight pants. Yeah, she looked good. Now, Elsa looked good too, but tired around the eyes, a bit heavier.

We went outside for the last of the sunshine as clouds gathered in, to sit on the stone steps of the art building and snack on blue corn chips which Flo had brought in her clever way, making us exclaim and laugh, as well as some salsa, and ginger ale to drink. Content, the lot of us. Well, except for Viv who was acting nervous, not eating, sitting close to me, head hung down.

"What's the matter with you?" I whispered.

"Just want to get this over with," she said sullenly. "Maybe I shouldn't have come down."

"Someone expecting you?" I mentioned her friend in the rest room.

She looked at me wide-eyed, "No."

Then why did I have this feeling she was lying?

I didn't have time to pursue it because just then the secretary told us that the committee had convened and were ready to meet with us. After that the appointment didn't take long, niceties all around, Flo taking care of the business, followed by the promise of some future discussion for perhaps, an early fall show date. I knew we were riding in on Elsa's ticket, and that was fine. It became clear, even without discussion, that I was going to have to think of Rune's memorial as a temporarily installed sculpture and would have to make my plans around that. Not a bad idea, really. In fact, if it was going to be an indoor thing, then I could really polish up the marble, give it the appearance of something brought in from an archeological site—just a piece, a glimpse, a fragment.

By the time we emerged from the building the skies had opened. For a time we lingered in the doorway discussing where we could all get a bite together before hitting the road, Viv over-eager to ride with Spence and Elsa in their rented Buick. I gave her a quick warning not to talk about Rune with Spence or Elsa yet—it wasn't the time or place. Her nod was exaggerated as she sped through the rain with them. I have to admit I was glad to get her out of there as I did not like her nervousness. Meanwhile I dashed out to Gem's car to retrieve Flo's rain gear and to put my letter under her seat so I could leave the keys with Riétta.

My note went something like this (I kept only the draft, the more infantile parts scribbled out):

177

Dear Gem, here is your car so you can pick the right if and when to come and see me. We always talked about our emotions, our limits as we tried to define our relationship. I thought it was working out pretty well. I always had a good time with you. And it was also because I knew I was your One and Only. I liked being that. I don't think I can handle something else. And we never promised Forever. Our here-and-now take on love was just fine. Maybe you can handle Expanded Loyalties on a sexual level. I'm not comfortable with it. I would feel too restrained, on guard. And with a lover I need to feel all my chakras wide open, full tilt boogie. An intimacy of secrets that stays between the bed sheets because both lovers really thrive on that with each other. I can't tell you what you must thrive on. I fully support that you do what you must, but if it is to involve simultaneous lovers, I can't be part of it. My own limitations, perhaps. All I know is what I can't manage, that I need to call it quits. In friendship, Ida.

I added a hasty, scribbled postscript in the car: *Heard that you got your promotion. Congratulations! Check out Elsa's painting. We uncrated it so Elsa could inspect it, but it's not hung yet. A fall date for a Blue Corn show is in the works which will be a culmination of Viv's work too. You were right to send her. She has taken good care of me. And she is relieved about your promotion too—for academic reasons, I'm sure.*

Even as I drove off with Flo alongside me in my truck, I could not quite believe that I hadn't seen Gem, that she hadn't appeared at the last minute to claim me.

"Eehah!" cried Flo, waving the envelope with a check for eleven thousand. "We did it! No messing around. I pay everyone back and we split the commission fee."

"You and Viv split it," I said. "As long as I get money back so I can start buying marble. Just make sure my phone bill's covered. Seriously, don't look at me like that. You two brokered this deal."

(It was only much later we found out that Elsa's appraiser in New York had told Riétta the painting was worth a good fifteen thousand, and that it would more than likely double in five or ten years. But them's city prices, right?)

Over dinner outside of town Viv seemed to be much calmer, relieved not to be on campus, I thought. She kept nudging me. I knew she wanted to tell Spence and Elsa what we knew. That task was perhaps harder than what I had done all day, even the letters to Gem. But we managed. And I gave them the diary pages we had photocopied which I had planned to give Elsa anyway. When Spence began to thank me—really unraveled I could tell—I turned her around towards Viv. We'd still be sitting in the dark if it weren't for Viv.

By the time we had seen them off, I had such a splitting headache—all the excitement, all the tension of not seeing Gem, all the emotion around Spence—that I asked Flo to drive us home to

Curley's Ledge. As the windshield wipers slapped back and forth, Viv, sitting in the middle, kept us in music and conversation while I half-dozed against her shoulder.

What a day.

A fax was waiting for me when we got home: *Ida, thanks for my car and the letter. I do want to talk to you, not leave things like this. And I respect your space. I would never have encroached on it now except on another matter entirely. But I thought I should let you know I was shocked you brought Viv with you. If I had any idea you would be so foolish, I would have stopped you. This guy has been harassing students to find out where she is. How did he know she was going to be in town today? Or is it coincidence? Did she tell anyone she was coming? Find out. I was relieved that apparently you had no confrontation or anything with him. Then come to pick up my car I find all four tires are slashed. Please, please call me, Gem.*

I showed Viv the letter, quizzing her severely. "Did you tell any of your friends you were coming down today? Someone who could have told him? Today of all days when everyone is leaving? You wanted to say goodbye to someone?"

She paled, "No. No. No way!"

"Come on, Viv. This is serious. You did tell *someone*."

She shrugged, relenting. "Just some friends."

"Who?"

"Just some of the Maids, so I could find out what was going on, you know."

"You mean, about Joker."

"Yeah, but they didn't show. I thought I could see them after the meeting but it was raining, and we all left anyway."

"What, you called them up?"

"I faxed a note."

"Shit, Viv. So how come Joker found out then? He must've for this to have happened!" I waved the fax paper at her. "Give me a break here."

She yelled, "I don't know! They were going to give him a message from me, okay? Through his ex-girlfriend. She's one of the Maids now. She must have told him."

"What kind of message, damnit?"

"Oh, I don't know. That maybe we could talk. He can't graduate this weekend with his class and he's real sore about it."

"I guess! What did you think you could do? It's way out of your hands now."

"It was supposed to be a Maids in the Shades action, okay? A bunch of them were supposed to show up, and we could talk or something. Make amends so we could all move on with our lives. He's supposed to apologize to Serena—which he did already—and to me."

179

"How do you know that?"

She shrugged."I've been keeping in touch with some friends...Of course he wouldn't get his diploma yet, because of his court date but he could walk with his class anyway. Because we'd demand it from the Dean. Except they didn't show. I thought there'd be a message for me about it."

"Maybe because they knew it was out of hand! Viv, I thought you had more savvy than that! The law is involved here now. We're talking an unstable boy."

"We were taking care of it just fine."

"Oh right, what about Serena's rape? Are you forgetting the real issue here? What about his potshot at your car. You took that to the police!"

"I know! And that was a mistake. You should know!"

"What?" I asked icily.

"That police are a big mistake."

"Jesus Christ. We're just damn lucky he didn't confront us, you know?"

"I wish he had! Don't you think I want this behind me too? How can I go home this summer if he's still mad. He can track me down there easy. It has to be between him and me—we have to make the peace."

"Look, I'm going to do this call. Would you remember this is a safe-house and that the whole idea is not to be contacting even friends?" For the call I took the phone upstairs, stomping up each one in fury. I think Gem and I both started sniffling at the same time on hearing each other. Where to begin? With each other or with the problem?

"We're safe, baby, we're safely home. What about you?" My tenderness came out of emotional exhaustion.

"I'm...I'm staying with Nat...of course. We've been with the police. All kinds of questions. Would he have known my car? At what time did you leave it there? Could it be an unrelated incident? You know students do that all the time at the end of the year. All that..."

I racked my brains over details. I had backed my truck to unload it up close to the front door. Flo had parked the car in one of the few open spots across the parking lot from me. That was around noon. Viv had been with me upon arrival. Viv and Flo had stayed firmly put at the gallery while I had made a quick trip to the store.

When we came out to snack on the the steps later, we had gone to get the food from the Honda. If for some reason Joker had spotted us then, he would have thought that was our car. He may well have slashed the tires while we were at the meeting. There was a lot of coming and going of cars and people. We certainly had never spotted him, nor had he approached us and also, it had started to pour while we were inside. When we had left for the diner the rain was really coming down, the kind of rain that makes you duck quickly into your car and which reduces visibility. If he had spotted us, maybe he didn't want to fool with five women all at once as we had laughed and enjoyed ourselves for a good hour, mostly talking about the projected show, and how they would get in touch with Willa and Kristy to let them know.

Meanwhile, Gem reported, the police had gone off to locate Joker who was apparently living in a tent at a nearby campground, though doubted they'd find him in a tent on a night like this.

Gem had not been telling me everything, she admitted, about the threats this guy had been making in various ways. How she knew Serena was the rape victim now, only because Serena had called her saying that Joker had phoned one time right in the middle of dinner to say his fraternity demanded he pay five hundred dollars in restitution to her, and oh by the way, he was supposed to apologize to Viv too—did she happen to know how to get ahold of her? Luckily Serena said she did not, called Gem up because she was afraid. Upon inquiry the fraternity denied any such discussion with him.

Yeah, so don't count on getting any money, Serena.

"I was going to tell you all this, it's just you had this painting deal you were busy with, and I knew Viv was okay," she concluded.

"Well," I mumbled, "obviously we should have known he was still on the prowl, because yes, I would never have brought her down."

After all that, we were back around to staring at each other, as it were, and not knowing what else to say. So we stumbled over each other in lukewarm apologies and promises to catch up—perhaps as early as the weekend, knowing full well we had no reason to chat that soon.

Reporting to a sober duo downstairs, Viv took the news with glazed eyes, saying, "I've read that stalking victims often feel fated…after a while…sucked in to something beyond their control. I feel like that. Like a gravitational pull. Do you think Rune felt that?"

My impulse was to say, "Don't be silly." Instead I said, "I don't know. Just hold your own course, kiddo. After all nothing happened, well, except to Gem's tires. Thank goddess we weren't driving the Honda home."

I went to bed miserable and with a headache while Flo and Viv took to curing themselves with videos, crashing on the living room floor in their sleeping bags.

Twenty-one

"Ida, wake up—there's a fax from that detective!" Viv was shaking me awake. I sat up, eyes out of focus. "Check it out!"

You would think by her prancing around my room that today was a new day or something and we didn't have to worry about our yesterdays no more, no more.

I steadied the page in front of me: *Please call me. I have news.* Talk about cryptic.

So I hobbled off to the phone yet again.

Daniels had tracked down Rune's sixth grade friend who was named Shari Hoyle. She was arrested two months after Rune's death in a drug sweep. Before being brought in she must have popped some pills, a suicide dose—methadone.

"Know what that stuff does to you, Ida? Blows your mind, causing erratic and violent behavior. Very possibly she was trying to hide evidence." Daniels went on to explain, "Shari suffered a critical overdose while in custody and had to receive emergency treatment. She was unable to stand trial due to severe mental impairment. Confirmed by psychiatrists, she had no memory beyond 1985, a good bit before she even met Rune again. But more to the point, I found a match to the thumb print on the car."

What thumb print? Indeed. We'd never known about it, that was for sure.

Daniels was saying, "A thumb print was left on the inside lip of the trunk. It matched the fingerprints of Shari's dealer, pimp, boyfriend or whatever he was who was shot to death in the sweep. When he was taking off the rear license plate, he must have had to take his glove off to get a screw out and left a set of prints on the yet open trunk in the process. Only the thumb print hadn't been smudged. That print was the only other thing conclusive I had going against the grain, as it were."

Then she said more emphatically, "It was the left-over 'one' that would add up to three. Of course, none of your prints matched it. And I wasn't going to let that bit fall through any convenient cracks.When I saw that Shari was connected to the drug bust, I checked on this guy who had served prison time before, and bingo, the match. Now you must understand, we still have no way of really knowing what happened that night, whether Rune was helping

182

Shari get away and he caught up with them, or whether it was just a ruse to rob Rune, whether he hit Rune or whether Shari did. The point is, Shari is unable to be of any help to clear that up, hear what I'm sayin'?

"I also found out that she's in a state-run mental institution, very placid, likes to sing along to music and with no recent memory, lives very much in the present moment somewhere before 1985. Still thinks she's serving time in a Texas penitentiary which she did in the eighties. Talk about a living hell."

"Thanks, Dee." As I hung up I gave the receiver a second glance. Pff—you'd have thought we could even be friends under different circumstances.

Absorbing the news over breakfast with me, Flo then took off— she had cats to get back to. I sent Viv off to do chores and see to her laundry, not ready to be as giddy as she, while I went down to check the mailbox, already thinking about writing to Elsa and Spence and Willa with this news, wanting to pull the weight off all of us, make peace, begin a new cycle. There, as I stood taking in the cleared skies, listening to the return of the thrushes in the woods, and thinking now I could make my peace, I came across exactly what I like about rural living—a driver with horse and cart coming down the dirt road. Pleasure driving, of course. As I suspected, it turned out to be Carole, a friend of Lorraine, and her Morgan gelding, Pierrot. He was a fine creature, coal black with the arched, thick neck and shoulders that distinguishes male Morgans. Lorraine had been sad to learn he had been gelded—she had so hoped to breed one of the mares to him. She could've even ridden the mare to his farm, instead of going through all the trailering hoopla. I don't think she ever quite forgave Carole.

Anyway there was Carole enjoying the beautiful morning with Pierrot.

"Say, is Lorraine here then?" She halloo-ed as she drew him to a halt in front of me, and pulled her leather apron away from her boots. She always wore such an apron on training drives because she wore long skirts when she drove in a show.

"No, no, later today—not till evening. Why?"

"Evening. Oh, well wasn't that Taylor's car over at the sugarhouse? Figured they must have come up early. But I can catch her another—"

"Taylor isn't up yet. What car?"

"Car? Let's see—a red sporty number. New model. Mustang, I think. Thought he must have traded in his—"

"Mustang? Vermont plates?"

"Plates? No, no, out of state…blue. That's why I thought he was up."

"Taylor has New York plates—you mean Massachusetts or Connecticut?"

"Connecticut. So they were!"

I could feel my scalp prickling as though my body feared what my mind had not already quite added up—and couldn't because the fact was impossible. Come on. Red Mustang? I spoke quickly, "Well, I'll have to go check. Must be a photographer or something after quaint, decrepit structures."

Or something.

"Must be," she agreed cheerfully. "What a relief. For a minute there I thought he must be going through some late mid-life crisis or other—buying a red car!" And then with a touch of the whip to Pierrot's rump, she waved. "We're off then. Give Lorraine my best. Tell her I'd like to do the loop with her any time."

"Sure thing!" I waved.

Then dove into the big house kitchen, clawing madly for the phone and the piece of cardboard which listed all emergency numbers. My fingers felt thick and numb as I punched the buttons on the portable, craning my neck to look out the back parlor window towards my cabin where Viv had gone to put away her laundry. "For chrissake, Viv, stay put. C'mon Elwyn. Answer your damn walkie-talkie there."

He answered on the third ring. "El-wyn here."

My voice was on edge; I choked out, "Elwyn, it's Ida. I need you to come up right away. This guy…I think…I think his car's over at Taylor's sugarhouse. We could have a problem. He could be around here somewhere already."

"Say no more. I'm on my way. Don't hang up. That's the sheer beauty of this cellu-lar. Can talk as I drive. Now, if he was over at the sugarhouse, and on foot, he'd follow the power line. Look out there, do you see anyone? Anyone along the edge of the woods?"

Damn it. "No."

Uh-oh. "Elwyn, the horses do. The horses see something. He must be along the woods of the low pasture. They're looking that way. Stock still."

"Where's your sis-tah?"

"Down to my cabin—just a bit ago. I don't know if he saw that or not."

Shit. If I had been driving would I have noticed a red Mustang following us last night? Would I know what they looked like these days? It was raining steadily the whole way back, dark enough that Flo had the headlights on. Would I have? And how long had he been watching us—all through dinner, waiting outside the diner? Following us all the way. Where had he been all night in the downpour? On the old couch in Taylor's sugarhouse? I shivered.

184

A diversion, that's what I needed. Something to draw him to the big house. It was then that I saw Viv's green plaid, and very baggy, boxer shorts still draped over the couch, even though I had reminded her to clear her things out of the living room. Now, in a flash, I saw the great rationale for not tidying up. I set the phone down long enough to pull them over my jeans. Beside the couch were even her purple sneakers—I jumped into them. Sockless. They fit with a pinch. Then I remembered the broom closet. Dashing there, I flung open the door and grabbed the lavender cap from Viv's first day— still safely hanging on its hook. Yep, the word 'dyke' was still emblazoned above the visor.

I can't believe I'm wearing a baseball cap backwards, I fussed as I yanked it on, and picking up the phone, dashed for the back patio door off the hallway by my room. I stopped as I pulled open the door. The idea was to look casual, relaxed. Yakking on the phone. I sauntered out into full view from the pastures.

"Elwyn, I have walked out onto the patio—"

"Don't do that." His voice registered alarm. "What if he has a high-power rifle?"

"I have to make him come up here to the house," I said, putting one foot up onto Taylor's chaise-longue, and pretending to stare at my toe while I looked out the corner of my eye at the horses. "I mean I don't know if he saw her go down there or not, but I have to distract him."

"Yeah, well keep talking if it makes you happy. Now, I thought you said he wasn't her boyfriend."

"He isn't. But he does have some sort of grudge." I didn't like the panic I heard in my voice.

"Yeah? How does he know where she is—unless she called him?"

"She didn't call him. But she did tell some of her friends we would be on an errand down to her school yesterday. Just a day trip. A bunch of us. I don't know how he could have known we were there or where to look for us. I mean, Viv was specifically confined to the art gallery. We were very careful not to wander around campus or town or anything. Somehow…"

The horses hadn't moved, all five of them, even in separate pastures. They knew there was a bear in the woods.

"There, I see him, Elwyn." I was surprised at my calm. "He's walking just inside the woods, just beyond the hot tape. I think he sees me here. I hope he does mistake me for Viv." I shifted and paced the patio slowly, imitating her little half-steps, her natural inclination to encourage a draft under her arches.

"Do you see anything that looks like a rifle?"

"No. I don't. He doesn't look like he has anything. Looks like he has a sweatshirt on. He has his hands in his pockets." I walked into the house again so I could peek from a window and not be seen. "He looks like he's trying to find a way around the pasture." I could hear a truck chugging up the hill—like it needed a new muffler—and already I felt better. If anyone could diffuse trouble it was Elwyn.

Then as I glanced out the parlor window, what do I see but Viv *climbing out* my high kitchen window—since I didn't have a back door. And she was wearing my clothes!—my old denim work jacket, its brown corduroy collar up, my barn boots—my comparatively tight fitting jeans, even my old, beaten straw hat that I used to wear at Blue Corn. Was she thinking, or what?! Yikes, watch out for the horse trough, kiddo! I knew I'd lose sight of her soon below the crest of the pasture between the big house and my cabin. What was she up to? She'd have to cut across Fortissima's pasture, not a sane prospect no matter the time or urgency. But then again if anyone could, Viv could. Was she going to cut up along the narrow end by the woods where I had been putting up fence when she first came? She could come that way to the house, yes. Up by my dig.

Now I could see her, first the top of her head. She carried my bow saw—I hadn't seen that. Maybe she had put it down to get out of the window. She sauntered unhurriedly. Her whole body moved differently, shoulders slightly hunched, hands in jean pockets, the saw hanging from her left shoulder. And her walk!—heavy footed, trudge-trudge, as if she had some solid lower back pain. Wahl, ain't that a gas—she was imitating me, I think. Was that really how I walked? Hatshepsut forbid.

She arrived easily and safely to my relief, but when I glanced out the window—no sign of the boy. And the horses had shifted to graze, maybe reassured by Viv trudging. I didn't like it.

"Look at you. You look like me!—are we in sync," Viv greeted me as she dipped at the knees. Down, up, down, up.

"Do I really walk like that?" I screwed up my face.

"I think it's the boots."

I was trembling, livid that she had brought danger right into *my space*, nightmares of that empty Blue Corn house haunting me in broad daylight. My jaw shivering, I said too calmly, "Hm. Look out the window. I can't see him."

As she looked out, I noticed how pinched her face was, and how she huddled with her arms folded about her. She shook her head, "He's hiding."

"So you recognize him, then?"

She nodded.

At that point Elwyn pulled in. Over the phone which I quickly put to my ear he said, "I'm in your dooryard."

"We've lost sight of him, Elwyn. Keep a lookout, Viv. I'm going out to see Elwyn. He's come to help."

"Don't leave me in here alone!" She gasped breathlessly, looking around wildly.

"I'll be right at the back door. It'll be open. Just stay put," I said over my shoulder, and marched out to see Elwyn who had climbed out of his truck giving the door a good slam as he tipped his hat slightly in greeting.

"You look like your sis-tah."

I stuck my hands in the big pockets of the plaid shorts. "Decoy. I was hoping to make him come up to the house. But we can't see him anymore."

He scratched under the brim of his greasy hat. "Could be he went back to his car now that he's spotted you. Not really much I can do unless he comes to the house."

"Wait him out?"

"I could go over and see if he comes to his car, tell him he's trespassing. Not much else I can do except to chat him up a bit. But he can just keep coming back. If there's no restraining order on him...not much I can do. How's the sis-tah?"

"She made it indoors here. She's scared."

"Wahl." He just rubbed his chin for a minute, adjusted his hat. "I think maybe I ought to check that car out. If I meet him, maybe what I should do is invite him over."

I gasped, "Think we can?"

He shrugged, "Gotta talk to him. What's his name again?"

"Joker Atwell."

"If he knows we're aware of him, might be a good thing. I can ask him why he thinks he's going to do any good by hanging around and whether he really wants to see the girl."

We couldn't see down to the woods from where we stood talking in the dooryard, nor could we be seen. The immediate scare had evaporated. I understood that he really couldn't do anything for us, and that we were just standing about. Joker's visibility had shocked me, now his invisibility was scary, hanging over the coming summer like a specter. If we didn't force his hand today, we'd be stuck with him for who knows how long. No way was I going to allow this to interfere with the farm peace.

"You're right, we have to try and talk to him. Shall we keep the phone line open? You could bring him over, or we could come to the sugarhouse. Whatever's best. Could be he was wary of trying to get past the horses."

Elwyn nodded, and turned back to his truck.

"What if he's armed?" I blurted.

"Kind of figuring he is." Elwyn pushed his hat up a touch. "Likely he's been drinking too. Give me your number there."

He reversed into the road dialing me, and we kept an open line. Meanwhile I strode back into the kitchen, and of all things, began preparing coffee, handing the phone to Viv who still huddled by the windows, peering out with one eye.

I explained where Elwyn was off to as she paled, those eyes of hers looking all the bigger.

Then, calmly, as I put coffee in the filter, "You are not fated to his craziness, okay? Right now, you need to keep thinking as actively as you did when you climbed out the window. His craziness is his. Whatever he's doing he brought upon himself. You must not cave in."

"I was dumb to go down there yesterday."

"No, you were dumb to let even one friend know, and me missing a bit of information or I wouldn't have let you. "

She shifted, rubbing her hands up and down her upper arms. Shook her head firmly, then blurted, "Look, I had reason to think I could work something out, okay? That's how I was brought up, and you want to *talk* to him now! I wanted to stop the energy—it had all gone on too long and far between us."

"What? Why?"

"Because I *know* him. It's a long story…I took his girlfriend away from him. We were all kinda in the same crowd. Saying we were all bi and whatever…then he went back to form in a hurry after his girlfriend left him for me. He was really pissed. He thought I'd seduced her or something just to make her a lesbian. Even though we only slept together a few times, she dumped him for good, became one of the Maids and all. She's the one who stole my vibrator. He lured Serena to rape her just to get back at me. Serena wasn't even a lesbian, much less interested in the Maids in the Shades stuff. But he thought Serena and I must be lovers just because we were roommates…"

I leaned into the doorjamb. I felt numb, defeated. "I can't deal with this," I said, and in my confusion, I began to rattle around in the kitchen, getting out the bread bowl, the yeast, the warm water from the kettle. Beginning to make bread. I stopped in mid-action, "Listen, pal, I've spilled my blood and guts to you. I can't believe how awful I felt when you were blabbing on about Gem—that I had not *told* you before. Meanwhile you're sitting on a powder keg *in my home* and not levelling with me. It sucks, okay? Fuck you."

The phone still on but mute, except for obvious sounds of his car, we both stood there dumbly. I didn't know if Elwyn had heard all that or not. I didn't care. No underwear he hadn't seen. Leaving the bowl I went to stare out the windows, my hands in those big pockets of the shorts, getting used to being there. I could make the shorts flare out sideways with my arms. Sure was a lot of material.

Then I saw Hecate sidle up to the cabin door and claw at the door post to be let in. To no avail. She then sat on the step with her ears back before bounding off in alarm, tail like a bottle brush.

"Did you see that, Viv? Did you see Hecate?"

"Yeah." Her voice was stone cold. "He went in there, didn't he? He's in your cabin. How did we miss that?"

"The gall! That's my house," I stated hotly, grabbing the phone back. My sense of violation had been instant and complete.

"I knew I had to get up here. I knew it." Viv was hopping up and down, the boots slinging dry mud onto the floor.

"Viv, take *off* the boots." Then to Elwyn, I said, "Did you get that? Yeah, invited himself into my cabin across the way. We didn't see—"

Elwyn said dryly, "That's called 'have-a-heart' trapping. Good. I'm turning around. You can hang up."

I did. "We know where he is now."

We know where he is! Shit. At least he wasn't the bogey man any more, but he was still faceless, to me at any rate. What was on his mind? Did he think one of us would blithely walk in there and be blindsided. A blow to the back of the head. That was my own private nightmare. Was he going to take potshots at us?

I heard Elwyn arrive again, and when he hallooed as he opened the back door, I called for him to come in. "Help yourself to some coffee. It's fresh."

"Don't mind if I do." He took off his hat and hung it on the back of a kitchen chair. And then with a steaming mug he joined me at what had become our official look-out. We stared out at my cabin for awhile. Elwyn rubbed his finger around the rim of his mug before taking a few sips. "So what would you be up to now if things were normal."

"Bringing the horses in. Lorraine wants them in their stalls during the day, to be let out for night pasturing."

"And if you bring the horses in, I can drive down the track there through the pasture to your house?"

"You could."

"Let's bring the horses in then."

"I don't know. I kind of like the fact that Fortissima's in the pasture there. And I'm pretty sure she's coming into heat by the way she bombed out of her stall the last time."

"Wahl now, you wouldn't want the horse getting caught in crossfire."

"No, no I wouldn't. You don't really mean—" I didn't bother to finish. "Shit. Viv, you can stay in here if you want. You're me after all. I'm the one wearing this darned cap."

I couldn't tell if Elwyn was smiling or not. Off we went to the barn to prepare the stalls, then to get halters and pockets full of dried corncob bits. Except for Fortissima who would only come for apple. A real Vermonter.

As we prepared to fetch Mosey and Fortissima, Elwyn nodded at the cap. "That Viv there's last name?"

"What?—Oh, Dyke?"

"Dyke." He nodded in satisfaction. "Went to school with a fellow named Dyke. Leonard, was it?...Lenny Dyke."

I took off the cap and looked at it as if I'd never seen it before. "Hm, must've gotten it at a family reunion." Stuck it back on and whistled at the barnyard gate—which was really just an insulated wire about chest high. "No, actually, you don't want to go to my place and ask that Joker if he knows Viv Dyke. Maybe Viv, The Dyke. It's...it's a political thing—"

"Just pulling your leg." His face crinkled up all smiles at me. I hope I smiled as big back. "Wanted you to relax a bit."

The horses came trotting up, Elwyn taking Mosey. It should have been a simple task. Except for Fortissima who wouldn't take the apple piece, what with her ears back and teeth bared. She reeled around sticking her tail towards me so that I ducked back through the gate. "Come on, girl. You pissed coz you didn't get here first? Or coz I left you out yesterday?" But she wouldn't turn around to me. Her gaze was fixed in the opposite direction. Okay, okay. She had a fix on my cabin. She was a smart girl.

I decided to bring in the others and see if she'd calm down. But she didn't. Everyone else came in prettily to their hay and goodies. Then again I went back for her and she came up sweetly. I held out an apple tidbit in my right hand, halter ready to slip over her head in my left. Damn if she didn't get her apple, toss her head high and reel around again. A kick for good measure. But I had ducked back under the wire in time.

"You got quite a number there." Elwyn came to lean on the post next to me. "Maybe she's trying to tell you something."

"I don't doubt it at all. She doesn't want to be left out of this plan, seems to me."

"Want to give her a little hay here so's I can drive through the gates?"

"I'm coming with you."

"Are you now?" It wasn't a challenge; he was interested.

"The guy is in my house. If I have to meet him, I'd rather just go for it or I'll never find peace in there again."

"I see what you mean. Damn nerve he has entering. Too bad you didn't lock it. I could arrest him on the spot for breaking and entering. You leave your door unlocked—it's like leaving out the 'welcome' mat."

"I don't even have a lock on the door."

"Good, then at least we know he can't lock himself in. Let's go." And face the music. I was shivering in the sunshine.

"The best thing to do," he said as we walked to his truck, "is to be going about our business. Now is there anything we can deliver down to your place, something you need?"

"I need to take some bales of hay down to the paddock as we will be closing horses in there from time to time."

"I'll bring my truck up—where?"

"Right below the loft window will do. He'll be able to see what we're doing."

"Good."

We also had to let Viv know what we were up to, telling her to stand by with the phone.

"You see trouble, I mean real trouble, you call the state troopers. Here's the number. Just tell 'em Elwyn needs backup. That's Quarry Road all the way to the top. Don't worry—I'll have the CB going too," he directed her. Then he turned to me. "Maybe you should go in your own get-up, ey?"

"Right." I went to strip off the shorts and tossed the cap to Viv, but stubbornly kept on the sneakers. "Stick it on the chair by the window…or something. Hand me my shirt you're wearing."

"Or you know, Viv," Elwyn said slowly, finger to his lower lip, "you can leave quite safely right now. Is there some place we could send her?"

"Why don't you take my truck and go directly to Kite's? Do you remember the way?" I asked dryly—simply because I had no saliva in my mouth.

She nodded. "Yes, yes, but I can't leave. I mean, he's here because of me. I'm not running."

Elwyn paced to the windows. He motioned with an out-stretched arm, his stubby fingers waving at me. "Come on, Ida, we've got our own call to make. Now you leave anytime if you need to. I mean it."

"I'll stay here by the phone," Viv answered firmly.

"Say, got some sodas we could take along?"

"Sure thing. Seltzer?"

Back at the barn I swung up into the hayloft and opened the door, heaved three bales down to him in the back of the truck. Then we were off—I opened the first gate, closed it after him then hopped in with the bales. In four-wheel-drive we bumped over the rutted track. Same maneuver with the second gate. Fortissima watched us, but seemed to be sticking with her hay, foraging in the pile for the apples I had hidden there.

Elwyn leaned out the cab as I shut the second gate. "Climb in the cab, why don't you. That way if you need to duck real quick you got some place to hide. If you need to get out of the situation real fast— if something happens to me, that is, you get in my seat and reverse the hell out of there, got that? You may have to bust through your fences there, you know.

I simply nodded and climbed in beside him.

"Just remember, I'm going to treat this as though he belongs here, that the house is his. That he has a right to be there." He grinned at me reassuringly. "If he's a complete idiot he'll shoot as I step out of the truck. If he has a grain of sense, I can get him to come out."

Twenty-two

"Say!" Elwyn called loudly, head sticking out the rolled down window as we pulled up to my cabin. Slowly he climbed out of the truck, the door his only security. Taking the bottles of seltzer and reaching through the window, he set them on the hood of his truck. I noticed how he placed both his hands on the door, left hand near the top, right hand on the window sill. "Mr. Atwell now we aren't gonna pre-tend that we don't know you've taken up residen-cy in this here hunting camp."

My home. This hunting camp. I winced.

Elwyn continued, "Any chance you'd come out and have a drink here on the porch, say, and have us a chat?" His pushed his hat up his forehead a bit with his left hand which then went back to rest on the door. "Now, my name is Elwyn, and I'm the town dog catcher and constable in that order. It's my job to talk to folks, help out as I can. Now, we're trying to get on with the farm work here, and we sure would appreciate talking things out with you so as we can get on with our work."

Silence from the hunting camp. As I sat in the cab, my sweaty hands rubbing back and forth along my thighs, I was in what you'd call an agitated readiness to duck.

The wooden inset door of the camp opened slowly. I knew that creak too well, always forgetting to oil it. A young man emerged gingerly. Wearing mud-splattered jeans and a faded red sweatshirt, his hands stayed firmly in the big front pocket. So, he wasn't a complete idiot.

"Uh...listen," he said, his hands coming out in an open gesture, shaking his head, "this isn't what you think...uh...I came to see Viv. I was just looking around, you know."

"So it would seem," Elwyn droned, "but why not come right to the door like a gentleman."

"Look, I lost my nerve, okay?" His hands wide in an apologetic gesture again. "Then I saw this place. I thought it was a barn, you know? I needed to get myself together."

"Want a soda? A selt-zer? Can I bring drinks to the porch so we could sit down?"

This Joker gave a disarmingly puzzled look. "Sure, why not?"

Elwyn nodded in my direction. "This is Ida. She runs the farm

193

here. You mind if she joins in? That is her house, after all."

"Why not? Why wouldn't she come too? I mean, why would she sit in the truck? This is her house, right?" Again the open, flailing gesture.

I felt glued to the seat. I couldn't help noticing the shape of something in that big pocket—a weight in it like a rock. Yeah, just like a rock. He'd better not have lifted any of my blasted rocks was all I could think as I heeded Elwyn's quiet encouragement in my direction. Yeah, one of my rocks in his pocket. Or in his head.

I couldn't believe it, even as we all sat down on the porch.

Elwyn motioned for me to take the top step offering Joker the huge, splitting-stump to one side while he took an up-ended cinder block for himself. I was going to have to do something someday about my porch furniture.

"Did you notice my collection of rocks?" I asked politely. "I build stone walls and those rocks in there are each significant and arranged in special order, representing different places I've been, you know, different samples of rock. You wouldn't believe how old some of those chunks are."

He looked at me as though I were out of it. Well, I was out of it. I thought he had one of my rocks in his pocket and so sure, I was feeling quite put out.

"Sure, yeah, I noticed the rocks," he said. "Very nice. Look, I didn't touch them." He twisted the cap off his bottle and took a sip. I could see sweat on his upper lip, or was that his mustache? Goddess, he was young. This was the bogey man, this kid? Big strapping kid, sure—but soft around the edges. Fatty. If that wasn't one of my rocks in his belly pocket then maybe it was beer paunch.

"Have you come to apologize to Viv…you know, like you did to Serena?" I asked in the same tone as I had used talking about my rocks. I wonder if I batted my eyelashes. I thought he was going to spit out his seltzer.

"How do you know that?"

"Well, I know about what's going on down at school. And she's told me now how she wanted to work things out…down at school yesterday."

He nodded. In agreement, I guess.

"I also know you don't want to go on being banished from your fraternity for very long."

His surprise didn't veil the fact that he didn't like me knowing so much.

Elwyn cut in fast, but ever so gently, "Do you want to apologize to Viv?"

He nodded, "Sure thing. Sure I do." He wiped his forehead with the cold bottle. "That's why I came. But I couldn't face her. I mean, you know, she got me in a heap of trouble. I mean she blew things way out of proportion on me. She made it out like I'd raped Serena or something. Like I was to blame, not that this broad had led me on or anything. Made me out to be some sort of campus rapist. I mean, you know, she should be apologizing to me, see." Abruptly he jumped up and swung around at us, that bottle in his hand making a wide arc.

I know I flinched, but Elwyn didn't budge. Joker went to lean against a porch post. Swigging from the bottle, he gazed up at the house.

There was a long silence. And the black flies were arriving. I longed to run inside and get the repellent. I'd never been stuck on my front step like this with sweat running down my neck, unable to move.

"I mean, she just makes me see red. Red. Then I can't think straight. All this shit because of her—four years down the tubes, like I can't even graduate with my class this weekend. Now that really makes me feel sore. Law school on hold. So I'm wondering why I should apologize to her." He swatted his neck.

"So you can join your brothers at the fraternity again." Elwyn reminded him.

"Yeah." Now the bitterness rang out. "I just want to graduate with my class on time, be where I'm supposed to be."

Elwyn slapped his knees as he stood up too. "How can we help?"

"How can you help?" Joker scoffed. "She can take back everything, I mean *everything*. How about that for a start? Though how that'll help me graduate on Sunday, you tell me. She could help get the charges dropped, that's what. Tell them how it was all just a prank. I just want to fucking graduate on time. Can't go to any of the parties. Can't even say good-bye to people. No one wants me around like I got AIDS or something…down the tubes, man. I want to be let off the hook now, you know. So yeah, she got me squirming enough, didn't she? Everyone on my case, my parents, the police, the college." His hands flew out in cutting motions. "I just want it to be over. Over. And this is where it stops, right here. I get off, right here."

Elwyn pondered the words, finger circling the lip of his seltzer bottle. "Say, Ida, does Viv have a lawyer?"

I jumped. "Yes."

"Say then. We can go up with you, Mr. Atwell, Ida and I can, and we'll all visit Viv together. You can apologize to Viv. She can apologize to you. We can discuss the issue over the phone with her lawyer, with the school, with your lawyer, get it sorted out. We send you back to your fraternity, put all this behind you."

Joker shrugged warily. "Okay."

"Why don't you help me unload those bales of hay, and then we can go up to the house together?" Elwyn started to walk out to the truck, drinking his seltzer as he went. Ever so easy. Like a good doctor, he was sporting one fine bedside manner.

I hadn't even opened my bottle of seltzer yet. It was very firmly clasped between my feet on the step.

Joker set down his unfinished drink by the post and followed Elwyn. It didn't take long to hoist the three bales onto the pallet I had laid out on the porch.

"Well then," Elwyn brushed his hands back and forth together twice. "Are we ready?"

"Just a sec," I said, "I want to get my repellent—"

"No!" Joker stopped me in my tracks. "Don't move!"

Now I swear I put my hands up though to this day Elwyn swears I didn't. But I do remember him raising a warning finger at me and I recalled his earlier words, 'I'm going to treat him as if the house is his.'

"Fine, I won't get the repellent. I just thought you might—"

"Maybe you just shouldn't think," Joker snapped.

Why the sudden belligerence? Jeezee peezee.

"Take it easy, son." Elwyn's voice hadn't changed a bit, calm and steady on.

It was then that I noticed Joker had been careful not to let Elwyn get behind him. Not once. He looked sideways at Elwyn suspiciously. "How do I know she's up at the house? How do I know you aren't just setting me up?"

"Sorry you feel that way. We have no reason to set you up. We just want to help," said Elwyn.

"Yeah? Well, I've changed my mind. I'm not going up there. You have to bring her here."

I chafed while Elwyn remained agreeable. "We can bring her down here, but if we all go together I think we can take the tension out of this. And that's where the phone is. That's something to consider. No phone down here." Clearly, he wasn't volunteering his own.

That really seemed to set the boy on edge. I could see his jaw tightening.

Elwyn just went on talking, "Once you've talked to her—and you won't have to face her alone—and we've made our calls and got everything in order, then we could, say, go over to the diner in town, if you want. You and me. Best roast beef, mashed potatoes and gravy. Get a meal into you before you go back and graduate. How's that?"

Man to man. Yep, this was definitely a man to man thing. I

began to regret I had come along. I was sure I was going to blow it. I was dying to ask him to hand over that rock in his pocket.

"Look," Joker shouted. "You just want to get rid of me—I can tell. Yeah, think I'm stupid. Think I'm gonna fall for that? Getting rid of me—I'm tired of being treated like garbage. No way. No way are charges gonna be dropped in time. Like hell. No way, I'm not gonna apologize to her. See here, see here!" And he reeled with a sudden motion. "I'm warning you, I'm warning you, man! And you'll do as I say."

Oh goddess, at last. Out with the rock then.

There he was, waving it. Brandishing it, is the term, I think. I looked on, transfixed. Not quite certain where he was pointing it. At me. At Elwyn. At his own head. I had never seen a handgun. It was not within my experience of reality. Simple as that. And I didn't believe it now. There are people left in this world who actually don't see guns on a day to day basis. This is true. This is absolutely true, I kid you not. I know it must sound strange. Doesn't mean guns don't have a way of invading our consciousness all the time, they do. But somehow, I really just don't have a vocabulary for—

"Oh honestly, put down that silly rock," I commanded, still in denial.

At that moment there was an earsplitting crack from beyond the barn. I jumped in response just as Fortissima shrieked in terror, rearing up before she wheeled and came careening down the pasture straight towards us.

In that instant, with Fortissima bearing down on us and with the last few feet separated only by a single strand of electrical wire, Joker's hand dropped—just a fraction—his head turned away from me, his body off-balance. I saw my moment to get my rock back. Leaping towards him ever so lightly in those purple sneakers, as though I could go ten steps in one, I hooked his closest ankle with my right foot and sent him sprawling directly in the path of Fortissima's thundering hooves!

Joker screamed in anticipation and rolled to one side, my foot then coming down on his wrist as his arm hit the ground. With all my weight I stood there as he screamed. And I screamed. Before he could struggle Elwyn had him pinned, pried the gun from his hand and with a gentle tap on my leg, "Why don't you see to your horse there—I can take care of him from here."

Fortissima, of course, pulled up on her side within inches of the hot tape—and us—swerving to lope into the paddock next to my hunting camp. Hey, she knew her boundaries. I left Joker to Elwyn and went to soothe Fortissima, opening the paddock gate for her to come in. She was compliant and sweet as could be, accepting the piece of apple I still had in my pocket. But still snorting fire from her wide nostrils! I busied myself putting a wallet of hay next to the out-door trough. Here she would stay until Lorraine came to her in the evening.

When I turned back to Elwyn, he had Joker with his hands behind his back, handcuffed, and sitting in the passenger seat of the truck while he talked on his cellular to the troopers. Apparently Viv had already called in, the minute she saw the gun waving, and they were on their way.

"Really glad you didn't get a chance to use that weapon, son," I heard Elwyn say to the drooping figure in the cab. "You're damn lucky you frightened that horse to bolting. She damn well saved your hide."

Wait a minute—didn't she save ours?

It was at that moment we saw Pepper emerge from behind the winter Solstice calender stone there by the woods, dressed in once clean jeans that were now mud splattered below the knees and a blue Lewiston High Girls Track t-shirt.

Elwyn doffed his hat, not looking anywhere as surprised as I was. He called, "So Pep-pah, you think this is the wild west here or something?"

She grinned that wide toothy way of hers. "Just passing through. It was a blank. Only thing I had handy was the pistol I use for track meets down at the high school...Hey, there Ida. Your eyes are like saucers." And she laughed deep and husky.

I gulped, "How did you—? What did you—?"

She shrugged, "Picked up the cellular call on my scanner. So I come over the back way and I see this fancy red number at Taylor's sugarhouse. Then I get to thinking, wait a minute, that's a hell of a place to walk—up the power line? No views and it sure ain't black-berry picking time. Some good mud in there still. Black flies." She brushed her thick hair back. "So I got out and took a stroll around. I see a box of bullets on the front seat. And if I know anything, I know they aren't for no *bird* hunting. Also, an empty vodka bottle—a fifth. So I get my pistol and follow the tracks I see and come right on up here, just as you were unloading the hay." She shuffled her feet, looking at me apologetically. "I kinda had a listen. Fortissima did too—so, you might say, I just gave her a bit of encouragement. Saw a chance and took it. Thought it would give Elwyn his chance to draw. Nice move there, Ida. So, well, gotta get down the hill for the girls' track practice or they'll be wondering. We have a meet later on. Think I'll be heading out before the law gets here." And the wink was for Elwyn.

* * *

At least the state troopers didn't arrive with blazing blue lights. Everything was handled quietly. Statements taken. Charges pressed: unlawful trespassing with malicious intent, concealing a deadly weapon—oh yeah, it was loaded all right—drunk and disorderly conduct—oh yeah, he was loaded all right. Something about crossing state lines, breaking bail conditions.

Thank god Lorraine wasn't there, because for the first time I had a real glimpse of what being invaded is like. Not just someone friendly invading your space, hey, I knew all about that from living in a collective.

This was far more complicated, because I understood that this wasn't over yet, that Viv and I had been pulled even further into a vortex. Already I was dreading the police reports, the newspaper, maybe going to court months later. Then I thought, what was that compared to what the real victims went through in their silence—Serena, Rune and Shari. Sill, I knew it would be a long, long time before I stopped expecting an intruder from the woods surprising me in my cabin. A summer of lots of people around would surely help, but maybe I'd have to get a dog before winter.

"His Dad will just fly up in his helicopter and bail him out again," Viv said glumly where we stood on the front lawn watching the troopers drive away with their prisoner.

"That right?" Elwyn said, leaning on the hood of his truck, having just hung up on making arrangements for a tow truck to take the impounded Mustang over to the state troopers' barracks. An initial search of the car had revealed a gun-cleaning kit on the front seat and indeed, a box of bullets for his .38. Also found, a sealed, stamped letter with his father's name and address on it. It was going to be a while before we knew what the contents of that would reveal. The troopers didn't tell us anything of their finds—they were most efficient and silent except for all the routine—or we might have been in the dark until the court date. But Elwyn must have thought we had a right to know that much, confirming Pepper's account.

"I'm sorry about wanting to go after my repellent, Elwyn. You had everything going so smoothly," I sighed with a shake of my head.

"No, no," he put up his hands to shush me, those stubby fingers waving in unison twice. "You were just acting natural. Makes me think those black flies were getting to him too. They were getting pretty fierce—could've been what made our four-footed friend there ornery too. A bit of repellent might have helped him feel more comfortable. I was watching to see just what moment would make him crack."

"So you expected it."

"Wahl, I was hoping with him not bein' alone, having allies, he could keep his cool. Didn't know just how brittle he might be or how far we'd get. Say, I'd better be over to the sugarhouse and meet that wrecker there." He began his motions to climb into the truck. Just before he ducked into his seat, he called across the cab with a grin, "Now see here, Ida, I was actually thinkin' about makin' you my deputy."

"You just send me the star, Elwyn. One for Pepper too! Then I'll know you're serious." I laughed and waved to his wave. "See ya."

"Don't know 'bout that," he said stroking his chin. "She's more like the Lone Ranger. She's got her own style. More like an outlaw who has more sense about what law means than the rest of us."

"Who *was* that woman?" Viv broke in, her eyes bugging.

"Your eyes are like saucers!" I said, imitating Pepper's husky voice. "Just a friend on her way to a track meet."

"Take care there, sis-tah," He pointed to Viv as he made his move to leave. "I'll be seein' you."

I called after him, "Elwyn, tell me honestly. Did you think he was going to shoot at us?"

"Wahl, you can never tell, there's always the risk," he replied slowly, scratching under his hat. "I'm used to dogs. They can be fierce, hackles up, but mostly they're just plain scared and insecure. Want help. Now you don't want to corner them. Mostly they're more than happy to hop in the truck for a good chew on a bone. Once in awhile you come across one that's rabid though."

"But did you have a gun handy?"

"For them rabid curs I do."

We let it go at that. I have a healthy respect for professional secrets.

As he drove away my knees buckled; I gave way to gravity and flopped on the grass, gazed up at a sky of mares tails. "I don't know about you, Viv, but I'm declaring most of the rest of the day off. And I mean Off. Clean house or no clean house for Lorraine."

She sat down on her knees beside me, having changed into her green plaid shorts sometime during the fracas.

"Nice pockets on those," I said.

"I didn't get to work anything out though," she said soberly. "He still won't graduate this weekend, so he'll still be sore."

"You seriously thought you could swing that? Don't you think it had gotten way out of hand for that to happen?"

She gave me a long, uncertain look, and changed the subject. What a dodge. "By the way, I punched down the bread dough."

I'd forgotten all about it, and raised my eyebrows, "Ah."

She leaned forward, elbows on the grass. I was amazed at how limber she was to look comfortable like that. She sighed, "I still don't want to go home."

"Ah."

"Say...Ida, Thanks, you know, for everything." She sat up with a slight shrug and a silly smile, girlish, reminding me of Kelsey. "I mean it. Why don't you keep the shoes. They suit you."

"Think so?" I wiggled my big toe out its hole at her, then rolled onto my side, propped on an elbow. "Just don't scare the shit out of me out anymore. Besides, I think we're even in the thank you department, don't you? "

"Then do you think I could stay on? Think you could ask Lorraine?"

I laughed lazily. "Now why didn't I think you were up to something? I don't know, Viv, you're pretty intense. You exhaust me."

"Me? I thought it was you. Give it a chance? I mean, Gem's not coming and all."

"Not till you tidy the living room!" Besides, I didn't have to ask Lorraine. I had a feeling Lorraine would be doing the asking. Why was it like that with Viv, I wondered. Hm?

Just then who should arrive like a blessing but Kite and Kelsey. A very excited Kelsey waving, jumping up and down the best she could in her car seat. Kite stuck her head out as she opened her truck door. "Ida! You haven't thrown your back out, have you?"

"Eeda, eeda big mosqueeda—" Kelsey cried out the window.

"No worse than usual," I called, not even trying to sit up.

She climbed out; Kelsey who had unbuckled herself, leapt across the driver's seat and threw herself out onto Kite, their faces scrunched together. "Turns out Kelsey got to stay on with me until this evening. Mel had lawyer appointments. So, I asked what did she want to do. She said yes she wanted to come here. We tried and tried to call, then we wondered if your phone was off the hook. Was it?"

"Yeah, I guess it was."

Using Kite as a pole to slide down, Kelsey came running around the front of the truck, arms wide. "Vivvy!"

With a big smile Viv jumped up to catch her and holding hands, they went dancing sideways across the front lawn. They were a pair, all right.

"We're off to see the horses!" They announced as they tore across the lawn.

"Hm, looks like a budding romance," I said, moving to brace myself up with my elbows.

"I guess!" Kite gazed after them fondly. "Hey, why you wearing Rune's shoes?"

"Viv's…I think she's given them to me."

"That's it—I knew there was something! Listen, Ida, I kinda had a hidden agenda coming here today. I wanted to know if it was all right with you if I asked Viv to come stay with me. I could use the help with Kelsey, especially since I like to take her out of day care at least for some of the summer. And they seem to hit it off. And frankly, it would be good company."

"Sounds like you're asking me for her hand in marriage," I kidded her. I couldn't resist; I'd be able to demand a dowry at this rate.

A smile came to those lovely bow lips. "Not quite."

"Do you think we look alike?"

"What?"

"If you did, then you might not notice if it were me instead."

"Sorry. You have no resemblance to each other at all. I'd know the difference. Not fair to tease. It's just I knew Gem was coming up soon, so I thought Viv might be in the way."

"Uh, wait a minute, she isn't actually. When did I talk to you last? Have I really not even told you that? It feels like years to catch up on. Pretty simple really. I've called it off with Gem. She took up with Natalie and I said I couldn't deal with it. I mean Nat is right there, you know, and I'm not. And haven't been for quite awhile, as it turns out. How can I deal with that? I think Gem really liked the idea of having me here in the country to come to and Nat there. Like, why would it matter to me up here, out of the way? It's too complicated to get my little brain around, let me tell you."

"What? I don't believe it. This is just so fortuitous! Maybe...see...I thought you'd be too...*busy*. But I've been talking with some friends in the restaurant business who are interested in setting up a CSA with me." Her words tumbled breathlessly.

By that she meant Community Supported Agriculture in which the farmer is fronted the money to grow produce rather than having to go into debt. Shares are bought and a certain amount of produce allotted per share in return. I turned to her with immediate interest, "Go on."

"My uncle down-sized his herd of Jerseys last week because of his health and agreed yesterday to lease me what I need. So it's all been happening *fast* and I've got to get the gardens going. But I'd need help. I thought Viv might like some work. I thought maybe you and Lorraine might be interested in handling some of the crops up here. Fall crops at this point—carrots, turnips, potato, kale, beets. Soup stock. And you know, I really want to build a greenhouse, get greens going for winter-time."

"I think that's an excellent proposition."

"You think?" And she reached out to grip my hand. We didn't let go.

"Yeah, marriage for Viv and work for me." I fell back. "Kite, Kite—I'm such a mess. Such a mess!"

She gave me a one-eyed squint. "You? I thought I was writing the book on that."

"What was it you said—about finally being able to take a step

202

for yourself? Well, I guess that inspired me to take mine too."

She looked down at me, a slight smile to the corners of her mouth, "No kidding? Both of us doing that right now?And both of us being sweet on each other for years and years?"

That made me sit up straight. "Kite? Are you saying what I think you're saying and which I never thought you'd bring out into the light of day?"

She shrugged. "Well, it's true isn't it? About time it got aired out."

"Yeah, mighty musty."

She squeezed my hand tighter. "Nothing a bit of sunshine can't cure."

"Ah well…but…you know…well, aren't we both on the *rebound* here."

"Rebound? Could be. Could be. On the other hand it could be that this is the very moment our planets are in conjunction." She hung her head then. "What if it was my only chance? I couldn't let it just slip by. What was it Spence used to say?—'If you're moving away from someone, it's usually towards someone else.'"

I laughed up at her and pulled her on top of me as we rolled in the grass. "In broad daylight!?"

We lay there gasping as Hecate came up, climbing all over us, shoving her nose between our faces, demanding her due. What a purr.

"Oh my," Kite said, rallying. "Summer is too rich a thing. Does make you crazy, don't it?"

"These last days have been a roller-coaster."

"Time to slow down then. We aren't in a hurry, are we?"

At that moment I couldn't really tell whether we were just kidding around or had begun something we'd hold to. All I could think about was how I needed to get down to my cabin and throw away a certain seltzer bottle still sitting there, before I could get to anything else.

So that's what we did. That's where we started.

By the way, Elwyn did send me one of those tin sheriff stars right from the kiddie shelf down at Hatch's, and I pinned it on my blue denim farm jacket.

Epilogue

Seems like I must have floated on Kite's arm as we strolled, or she on mine. Surely we were dressed in linens and cottons, in shades of white and tan. Eh, surely we looked like farmers, no matter what. She wore her chinos, of course. And I wore a creamy white, silk necktie, loosely with an open-necked shirt. (When she first gave it to me she whispered as she adjusted it, "This is how I've always wanted you," pulling me to her lips. Ah, those lips, just the right give, just the right take, her tongue asking me one simple question and only accepting yes.)

The crowd's conversation was light, pleasant, to a background of tinkling glasses—no, we weren't really walking around sipping from those *plastic* sort, were we?

Spence was there, you bet. In a grey tuxedo and cummerbund, inviting anyone to dance on her synthesized floor with her.

Willa had made it too. They even danced together laughing so much they almost fell off the platform. But mostly Willa stood near her display of clay altar goddesses, her small son clinging to her thigh, the laughter in him brimming in spite of his shyness. Her well curved figures were a cross between female Buddhas and voodoo queens what with their stylized, serene smiles, the dark glazes, incense sticks and feathers for hair, or holding votive candles. Kite and I eventually chose one—the chubby one with large breasts and tummy, one big gold hoop in her left ear.

Kristy actually came too, bringing her matted and framed costume designs, also some fabric examples on mannequins—like gossamer cloud cover. Her project was to clothe an alien race which sported wings on their backs for some *Deep Take on Space* episode or other, to be aired sometime in the winter.

Kristy stood tall and slimmer in a long blue gown. As enigmatic as when she used to be nude. Really glowing—after all, she was up there in the painting. Limelight was what she liked. She said, "People actually want this stuff—I'm designing angel-wear! My agent has lined up a whole greeting card set which is going to hit a market way beyond just Trekkies. You two must come see me in San Francisco." (Kite and I looked at each other, actually nodded at that idea.)

I wondered, as I strolled on, just how Dee Daniels would look in one of those get-ups. Or Pepper. Or Elwyn.

Now Mel didn't come, but she did send a sculpture made out of shellacked bread dough. A woman reclining on a massage table, one third life-size. Beautiful braid down her back, and her buns!—well, they were buns. Kinda goofy but it worked, as in 'Wow Ma, look at that Modern Art!' I thought Mel had a sense of humor after all. But Kite drawled slowly, "I don't think so."

And by this time Kelsey Maude was a free bird between her moms and so of course, she was there along with Viv. Both of them the life of the party.

We had three of Rune's screens framed and fitted in the windows above my own quiet corner. Kite had helped me with my piece a great deal, the white, gleaming temple fragment in subdued light, a neatly printed placard nearby explaining it. She had provided the carefully potted and shaped rosemary bushes for either side of the top step. Now and again she'd go brush by them so the air was filled with their scent. A great, subtle touch.

And of course Elsa's paintings were on the walls around us in surround color. Sheesh, you would have thought we were back at the farmer's market with our produce. Blue Corn Organic.

I turned at one moment to see Gem enter the gallery, dressed in lemon and pale greens which always looked good on her. Don't think I was past lurching at the sight of her. I was still very much getting un-used to her while working at being on good terms with her as well as Natalie, who was Viv's lawyer after all. Besides, Kite was still going through the same sort of thing as we both made sure we got used to each other big time. I already knew that not much more would transpire between Gem and myself, not really—much as I loved her. If I had an enduring friendship, oddly enough, it would be with Viv.

Natalie stood behind her and said, "Gerry, why don't I go get us something to drink?" Bowing away.

"Hey, Gem, so how's it going?" I stumbled.

"Fine, fine. Worked hard all summer on a paper for publication," she spoke with an affected wince. "Yeah, uh, it's about women in the agrarian movement west, nineteenth century. You know, basically about the lot of pioneer women on their homesteads. Culled plenty of rich information right here from the archives. I'm hoping it'll be the springboard for a whole book which would eventually include twentieth century too, and cite Viv's work, of course, since she did such a spectacular job. And you, how are the crops doing?"

"Good, " I mumbled, thinking my head was doing a Viv turkey-wobble. "Uh…harvesting now. Busy…Lorraine too, when she can, Kite and myself, and Flo too…uh…especially since we lost Viv back to school, you know. Uh, come over here and meet everyone."

Kite swept up at that moment to take my arm in one bold, spectacular motion— "Come and dance with me. Spence knows how to keep the base line going and we can embellish. Excuse us, will you?"—just as Natalie returned with two plastic glasses of white wine.

I was pretty oblivious, really. Heady to be among old companions. Viv was flitting about, easy with everyone. The kid who found the missing pieces of us, glued the shell back together, kissed us and broke the spell. Even brought us to the fairy feast. Took it all in stride with a shrug, "Whatever." And there we were still reeling, especially when she started on this jag of us tracking down Shari Hoyle's address, wanting us to communicate with her, maybe even go visit. Like we were to find out something? Us—that meant Spence and me. No rest for the weary if she has her way.

Spence, for one, is totally enamored of Viv these days, invites her to New York, takes her around. It's like she can't get enough of the girl. Beyond that, don't ask me. Viv did send me the newest Armatrading, but I think she did that just to get to me. Works.

And how can I forget when Spence took me for a slow dance on her creaky floor, hand stroking suggestively up and down my thigh, nodding over her shoulder at Kite. "So how's it with you two? After all this time. Is she the one?"

I laughed. "Yeah, Spence, I'd have to say she is the one for me."

Under her breath. "So, how's the sex?"

"God, Spence, you sound just like Viv."

"No, serious. I mean, you know, after waiting so long?"

I blushed hot as I rubbed my cheek against hers and whispered in her ear, "Total purrrrr."

She chuckled low in her throat. Heh heh heh.

After all, don't I get to ride around the fields on the tractor with Kite? Well, don't I?—You bet, my hand on her tanned thigh, the muscles tensing there as her foot presses the clutch.

Rune, baby—you think I've found the Torrid Zone?

More books from NEW VICTORIA PUBLISHERS
PO BOX 27 NORWICH, VERMONT 05055
CALL 1-800 326 5297   EMAIL newvic@aol.com

HERS WAS THE SKY by ReBecca Béguin —Pilot Hazel Preston and her lover Jo have become fierce rivals in a cross-country flying derby. This blend of historical fiction and mystery is based on the first women's flying Derby of 1929. $8.95

IN UNLIKELY PLACES by ReBecca Béguin —Chosen Best of the Small Presses by New American Writing. While following her dream of exploring Africa, Lily Bascombe finds herself searching for the elusive Miss Margery Poole. $8.95

RUNWAY AT ELAND SPRINGS by ReBecca Béguin —Anna, a bush pilot hired to track game for a white hunter, and Jilu, the proprietor of the safari camp at Eland Springs are forging their own paths in colonial East Africa of the 1930s. $7.95

CEMETERY MURDERS A Mystery by Jean Marcy —Conflict and competition dominate their erotic entanglement as Meg Darcy, dyke PI and Police Detective Sarah Lindstrom strive to be the first to find a killer. $10.95

NO DAUGHTER OF THE SOUTH A mystery by Cynthia Webb – Brash and humorous—Laurie returns to her Florida hometown and the white southern roots she has soundly rejected to look into the death her black lover, Samantha's, father. $10.95

TAKES ONE TO KNOW ONE An Alison Kaine Mystery by Kate Allen —In this third in the series, the Denver cop discovers the dead body of a lesbian "shaman" in the sweat lodge of a women's spirituality retreat in New Mexico. $10.95

I NEVER READ THOREAU A mystery novel by Karen Saum — From the author of the Brigid Donovan mystery series comes a quirky murder mystery set on a remote Maine island, involving ex-nuns, political refugees, drifters, and eccentric locals. $10.95

OFF THE RAG: Lesbians Writing on Menopause. Edited by Lee Lynch and Akia Woods —An exciting collection of writing, unique to the experiences of lesbians at this landmark change of life. $12.95

OUTSIDE IN A Cameron Andrews Mystery by Nanisi Barrett D'Arnuk —A dramatic, suspenseful prison thriller exploring power and the moral compromises of life undercover. $10.95

TALES FROM THE DYKE SIDE Humorous Essays by Jorjet Harper —Side-splitting spoofs, reports from the front, and real-life stories that demonstrate what it's like to be a lesbian in our changing times. $10.95

MYSTERIES BY SARAH DREHER

STONER McTAVISH —Introducing travel agent turned sleuth Stoner McTavish. On a trip to the Tetons, Stoner meets and falls in love with her dream lover, Gwen. $9.95

SOMETHING SHADY —Stoner investigates the mysterious disappearance of a nurse at a suspicious rest home on the coast of Maine. $8.95

GRAY MAGIC —A vacation turns frightening when Stoner finds herself an unwitting combatant in a struggle between the Hopi spirits of Good and Evil. $9.95

A CAPTIVE IN TIME—transported to a town in Colorado Territory, time 1871,Stoner encounters Dot, Blue Mary, and an enigmatic runaway named Billy. $10.95

BAD COMPANY —Stoner and Gwen investigate mysterious accidents, sabotage and menacing notes that threaten members of a feminist theater company. $10.95